‘Gi ux, wake up!’

I ponse, his fingers awed into his upper t , the sinews in his hand rigid, straining. S ing the muscular bulk of his shoulders b een her hands, she tried to shake him, tried t ift his upper body from the ground. But to n avail: he was too heavy. In desperation her e s searched the cottage interior, the uneven w lls, for something that might help, before a s den bizarre idea touched her.

B ood hurtled through her veins, blossoming in t skin of her face.

H nds on his shoulders, she dipped her head. K ssed him.

H r soft lips touched his firm mouth in a last a tempt to hush the demons of the night that c med him. A dangerous warmth stole over h r, melting her limbs, turning the muscles i her knees to useless mush; she shuddered, s ing to hold her body away from him. I s only a kiss, she told herself. A simple d ce to alleviate his distress. Yet the touch of h mouth spiralled each nerve in her body to a s ging desire, a yearning for more.

Meriel Fuller lives in a quiet corner of rural Devon with her husband and two children. Her early career was in advertising, with a bit of creative writing on the side. Now she has a family to look after, writing has become her passion. A keen interest in literature, the arts and history—particularly the early medieval period—makes writing historical novels a pleasure. The Devon countryside, a landscape rich in medieval sites, holds many clues to the past, and has made her research a special treat.

Novels by the same author:

CONQUEST BRIDE
THE DAMSEL'S DEFIANCE
THE WARRIOR'S PRINCESS BRIDE
CAPTURED BY THE WARRIOR

HER BATTLE-SCARRED KNIGHT

Meriel Fuller

MILLS & BOON

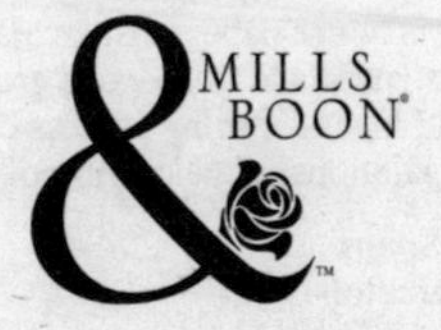

First published in Great Britain 2011
Paperback edition 2012
by Mills & Boon, an imprint of Harlequin (UK) Limited.
Harlequin (UK) Limited, Eton House, 18-24 Paradise Road,
Richmond, Surrey TW9 1SR

ISBN: 978 0 263 89220 8

Harlequin (UK) policy is to use papers that are natural, renewable and recyclable products and made from wood grown in sustainable forests. The logging and manufacturing process conform to the legal environmental regulations of the country of origin.

Printed and bound in Spain
by Blackprint CPI, Barcelona

HER BATTLE-SCARRED KNIGHT

Chapter One

Sefanoc, Wiltshire, England—January 1193

Brianna leaned her cheek against the cow's yielding flank, fingers reaching under the animal to squeeze blood-warm milk from the udder. In the early morning stillness of the byre, the liquid squirted noisily against the sides of the wooden pail, steaming in the chill air. She heard William, the farmer, talking softly to one of the cows at the other end of the byre, imagined him budging one animal out of the way, so he could start milking the next cow in line. He was much faster than her, milking two cows to her one. But his wife was ill this morning and Brianna had offered to help when he'd come knocking at the door of the manor house, blowing on his hands to warm them, his breath puff-ing white in the darkness. They couldn't afford to lose the milk; it was a vital source of income in these hard times. As with other estates, most of their money had been taken by King Richard to fund his crusade to the Holy Land. The manor was earning very little; she had enough coin to pay the farmer and his wife, who maintained the land and livestock, and Alys, who had served her family since Brianna was a child.

'Mistress! My lady!'

Brianna jumped at the shrill, tremulous warning, startled from the soporific rhythm of the milking. Her maidservant stood in the doorway, her face white, body quivering with fear.

'Alys, what is it?' Brianna twisted around on the milking stool, her auburn braids gleaming in the dim light of the byre.

Alys's eyes grew wide, the thin skin of her face stretched over her bony cheeks. 'They've come back. Count John's men; they're looking for you.'

Brianna grinned. 'Well, they won't find me at home, will they, Alys?' She patted the cow's flank, extricating the half-full bucket from beneath the pink udders. 'I'll put this in the churn, William. Butter sells quickly at the market.'

William stood, resting one hand on a cow's rump to lever himself up. 'Aye, you do that, mistress. Martha can churn, if she's feeling better. If not, I'll do it myself.' He tipped his head, topped with a mop of grizzled grey hair, in the direction of the manor. 'Do you want me to go and see what's happening?'

Brianna shook her head, clutching the pail of slopping milk to her middle as she rose to her feet.

'Oh, but, mistress, you're never going to go yourself?' Alys gabbled, her breath coming in short little pants. 'There's more of them this time, with torches, circling around, one of them banging on the door.' She shuddered. 'I slipped out the back of the kitchen…came to find you. What if they do something to our home? What if they…torch it?'

Brianna laid a hand on Alys's shoulder. 'Alys, you must calm down…they wouldn't do such a thing. It's the manor and lands that the Count wishes, remember. And they can't have it because I'm in their way.'

'They're stronger than you, mistress.'

'But I'm cleverer than most of their thick skulls put together.'

'Count John won't stop until he has what he wants, my lady.'

Brianna put one hand to her forehead, smiling. 'Please don't remind me, Alys. But I have no intention of being forcibly married off to one of those thugs, as I've made perfectly clear in several letters to Count John himself.'

Alys bit her lip. 'That Count is the devil himself, mistress, and he'll stop at nothing to give the manor of Sefanoc, and you, to one of his men.'

Brianna's light blue eyes blazed in the dimness of the byre. 'The manor of Sefanoc is not his to give away. It belongs to Hugh.'

Doubt flickered across the maidservant's face.

'Hugh will be back soon,' Brianna reassured her. 'Everything will be fine once he returns.'

'But…' The servant's voice faltered.

'Alys, I forbid you to look like that! Hugh will be

back. He's obviously been delayed on the journey in some way.'

'The Somervilles have returned, and the de Laceys,' Alys reminded her.

'And they remember seeing Hugh waiting for the boats on the beach in France,' Brianna replied, plucking at a loose thread on her girdle. 'My brother *will* be back soon. Now, come on, Alys, you can help us finish this milking.'

A crack of sunlight appeared across the eastern horizon as Brianna emerged from the warmth of the barn, drawing the hood of her short woollen cape securely over her head, covering the bright red-gold of her hair. She stepped lightly across the cobbles in the direction of her home. Her hands ached from the effort of milking so many cows; flexing her fingers, she tried to relieve the stiffness. Alys had stayed behind to churn the butter, the wan, exhausted face of the farmer's wife indicating to Brianna that she would be in no fit state to do anything today.

Rather than return home by the shorter route, through the forest, she decided to cut through the flat fields to the north—hopefully the open ground would enable her to spot Count John's men if they had decided to linger. It had been some time since Alys had raised the alarm, so it was entirely possibly that they had returned to Count John's castle at nearby Merleberge to break their fast. As her feet skipped across the frosted grass, she prayed they had become bored and hungry with the wait. Men like that, with no self-discipline, no stamina, couldn't last for long without food in their bellies.

Ducking through a gap in the stubby hawthorn hedge that divided two fields, she bit her lip. Despite her solid, confident smile in front of Alys and the farmer, she wondered how long she could hold out against the King's powerful younger brother. How long would it be before her own brother came home from the Crusades? A tight coil of fear began to unravel in her gut; she clamped it down fiercely before it gained momentum. She would hold out for as long as it took, she told herself sternly, she must protect and defend the manor of Sefanoc in Hugh's name. Instinctively her fingers moved towards the thick belt slung low around her neat waist, checking the knife in its scabbard that hung from it—the knife that would keep her safe.

Her feet broke through the thin layer of ice covering the standing water spread out in patches on the low-lying field, and squelched into the cold mud beneath, water seeping between the thick leather sole and uppers of her stout boots. The river, its course marked by an occasional stubby willow, the bright orange branches shining bright and straight in the rising sun, had flooded regularly this winter. The cattle had been restricted in the amount of grass they had to eat and the farmer had been forced to dig into their precious supplies of stored hay in order to supplement their diet. For a moment, she paused, sweeping her eye back over the field, assessing the amount of damage the most recent flood had wrought, and how much grass there was left for her dairy herd.

'Good morning, my lady Brianna.'

Her heart leapt in fright; the voice shocked through her, low and dangerous, a slick ripple of fear. She raised her eyes reluctantly to the man on the horse, a man, it seemed, who had appeared from nowhere. And behind him, two other soldiers on horseback, their surcoats bearing the colours of Count John.

'Lord Fulke.' She nodded with the briefest deference to the older man who had first addressed her. His buff-coloured tunic strained across his round belly as he adjusted his position in the saddle, the split sides revealing fleshy thighs stuffed into brown woollen braies. His iron-grey hair was thick, a greasy mat against his scalp.

'What an unexpected pleasure!' Lord Fulke exclaimed, his voice a sarcastic falsetto. He nudged his horse so that his booted foot in the stirrup moved on to a level with her chest. The other two soldiers, one darkly scowling, one a fresh-faced youth, manoeuvred their horses around to box her in at her back. She was surrounded. Her chest tightened, but she would not, nay, could not, panic. They would not harm her, they wouldn't dare! They had been sent to harass her, to force her to agree to Count John's ridiculous plan. They hoped to wear her down by their constant intimidation, but it wouldn't work!

'Let me pass, Lord Fulke.' Brianna fought to keep her voice level, calm. 'You have nothing to gain from this.'

Lord Fulke snorted with laughter, revealing a mouth

full of rotten teeth, some streaked with black, others a particularly nasty yellow hue. 'On the contrary, my dear lady, we have everything to gain. If only you would agree to the alliance with Hubert of Winterbourne, life would be so much easier for you.'

'And I've told you before—' Brianna tossed her head back '—Sefanoc is not mine to give away.' Crossing her arms over her middle to disguise her actions, Brianna clasped her fingers around the hilt of the knife.

Lord Fulke's heavy frame thumped down before her as he dismounted. Up close, he was about the same height as her, wide and thickset. His foul breath wafted over her as he spoke. 'I don't think you quite understand, my lady,' he continued silkily. 'Your brother is most certainly dead; he will not return now from the Crusades. All our men are home.' He tilted his head to one side. 'And the manor of Sefanoc needs a lord in charge.'

'Over my dead body.' Brianna expelled the words in a hiss of breath. 'You have no right to do this; you know I have the protection of King Richard…'

'But King Richard isn't here, is he?'

'He will return, just like my brother! Now let me pass!' In one swift, neat movement, she pulled the knife from its scabbard, holding the point to Lord Fulke's chest. Shock clogged the man's face; the two soldiers behind her moved in. One grabbed her shoulders to jerk her back sharply, the other knocked the knife away with a short, painful chopping motion, the side of his hand against her wrist.

Lord Fulke cleared his throat, adjusted his belt self-consciously on his padded hips. 'You've been without a man in charge for too long, it seems.' He licked his lips in a curious half-smile, eyes running lecherously over Brianna's diminutive figure, the perfect oval of her face. 'Your conduct is unseemly, wilful. Such behaviour cannot be tolerated in a lady; it seems we need to teach you a lesson. You will soon come to your senses, young lady. We will make sure of it.'

Count Giseux de St-Loup urged the muscled flanks of his stallion up the narrow sheep track to the brow of the ridge, leaning his tall frame forwards in the saddle to hasten the animal's ascent. His chainmail hauberk glinted dully in the morning sun, the bright orb partially obscured by wisps of white cloud. Halting the animal at the top of the escarpment, Giseux let the reins drop, lifting both hands to remove his iron conical helmet to reveal a lean, tanned face, bruises of exhaustion dabbed beneath grey eyes. Flapping open his leather saddlebag, he grabbed his water bottle, pulling the cork stopper to drink deep. The cool, sweet-tasting water poured down his throat like an elixir, driving back the waves of tiredness, reviving him. Wiping his mouth on the leather pad sewn against the palm of his chainmail mittens, he replaced the water bottle, then swept his gaze across the soft countryside below him, one hand unconsciously kneading at the dull ache in his upper thigh.

From this high vantage point, he could see the castle at Merleberge rising up out of the river mist as if it floated on air; a castle that Count John had made his own whilst his older brother, King Richard, was away on crusade. The valley fell away in gentle scoops of green, ridges rolling away into the distance, fading blue. Even the jagged nakedness of the deciduous trees in winter—the scrappy hawthorn, the majestic oak—all served to enhance, not detract, from the beauty of this winter landscape. His eye was unaccustomed to such sights and his mind baulked against it, resented it. Such exquisiteness made him restless, irritable, after the years he had spent on crusade: savage days spent marching endlessly through the scorching sand, pushing his men through inhospitable rocky valleys, a constant craving for water. But strangely, whilst all of his soldiers were relieved to be home, he wanted to be back there, back in those wretched conditions, pitting the strength of his mind and body against the elements, the sheer effort of keeping himself alive driving his mind from deeper, darker thoughts. He craved the harsh light of Jerusalem, needed it, deserved it.

But the crusade was finished, over; the agreement had been signed between King Richard and Saladin. Both sides, both Christians and Saracens, had won. In his heart, the victory seemed hollow, pointless, after so many lives had been lost in the process. The lives of his men in one of the last raids on Narsuf. And the life of… His hands tightened around the reins, seeking balance as the familiar rage, the guilt that haunted his days and nights, rose within him…nay, he would not think of that now. Soon enough he would find the traitor who had turned against them, avenge his soldiers' deaths…and hers. But now, he had to fulfil a promise to a fellow knight. He hoped it wouldn't take him too long.

'Will you agree?' Lord Fulke yanked Brianna's head from the water trough once more, podgy fingers snarled in her wet, dripping hair, twisting the strands tight, like a rope, pulling viciously against her scalp. She fought the urge to yelp with pain, gritting her teeth in determination; she wouldn't give them the satisfaction of seeing her suffer. Her short-lived marriage to Walter had taught her that, at least. Bracing her knees against the wooden trough, lined with puddled clay to provide drinking water for the cattle, she clutched at the rim with red-raw fingers, steeling herself for the next onslaught. Her wide blue eyes, lashes spiked darkly wet, blazed with fury.

'How dare you do this to me?' she managed to stutter out through lips purplish-blue with cold. 'The King will hear of this!'

'But nobody knows where he is, my lady,' Fulke reminded her. 'And until we know, we can do what we like.'

Her heart plummeted as he shoved her head beneath the water once more. They had broken the ice on the surface after they had manhandled her over to the corner of the field where the trough was situated. The water was freezing, instantly numbing the skin on her face, driving nails of ice into her ears, her eyes, her nose. Brianna held her breath for as long as she could, before allowing the air from her lungs to leak out slowly, hoping, praying that they would pull her out before…before she ran out. Desperation plucked at her chest, a scythe of panic. Surely they wouldn't kill her? Doubt crept into her mind, whispering, insidious, forcing her to acknowledge her vulnerability; she sagged momentarily as her chest began to burn. Then the cruel yank of Fulke's fist at the back of her head pulled her up again, and she gasped, sucked greedily, filling her lungs with fresh air.

'There is an easier way, my dear,' Lord Fulke commented smoothly, throwing a disparaging bloodshot glance over her dripping face, her sodden braids. 'You need to agree…agree to this marriage.'

'Never,' she vowed. 'You'll have to kill me first.' She crossed her arms over her chest, clutching at her arms in an effort to stop the incessant shivering. Threads of water trailed down her neck, beneath the collar of her cloak, wetting the rough fabric of her gown.

Lord Fulke mangled his thick lips into the semblance of a smile. 'Let's hope that it won't come to that.' The threat in his voice was unmistakable.

Fear coursed through her body, firing bolts of adrenalin straight to her heart. So they would kill her! She needed time, time to think, time to plan! But judging from the menacing look in Fulke's eyes, time was one thing she did not have. Closing her eyes, she pretended to faint, falling in a crumpled heap to the ground, up against the edge of the trough, her hand scrabbling about behind her in the mud for something, anything, that might be able to help her. A stone! Her fingers grazed against its roughness, cupped it swiftly into her palm. She hoped it would be enough.

Fulke cursed, eyes flicking moodily over the slumped figure.

'She's had enough, now, hasn't she, my lord?' one of the other soldiers remarked.

'Don't let the chit fool you, Stephen. She's a clever piece.'

Brianna smelled the wash of Fulke's noxious breath as he leaned down to her. Tightening her grip on the stone, she brought it round to smash it against his head with all the force she could muster. Only it wasn't enough. The gritty stone dropped from her fingers.

'Why, you little…!' Fulke roared, clutching at the gash on his forehead. The purpling cut oozed blood, startlingly red against the white slab of his forehead. 'You'll pay for this!' Before Brianna had time to anticipate his next move, the weight of his fist crashed into her jaw and her small frame crumpled to the ground, this time for real.

'We've got her now,' Fulke murmured, almost to himself. 'We've got her now.' He rose to his full height, jubilant, smug victory painted on his face, expecting to meet the smirking expressions of his younger henchmen.

But the soldiers' faces were turned away, fixed on the open gateway, slack-jawed, staring at something, someone. One of the men stumbled back, catching the back of his leg on the trough.

Alongside the scrubby hawthorn hedge, a huge black destrier flew across the marshy field, snorting impatiently, wildly, rearing its glossy head in a restless jangle of bit and bridle as it approached the three men, the fallen maid. Sprays of water flicked out from behind the horse's heavy hooves, loose droplets forming sparkling arcs in the weak sunlight.

A nervous laugh punched from Fulke's mouth; he licked his lips.

A black woollen tunic covered the horseman's chainmail; his shield was black, decorated with a raised silver lattice. No markings gave away his identity, no gilded family crest on the shield, no embroidery across his tunic; a bright steel helmet obscured his features. Hauling deftly on the reins, the unknown rider brought the animal slewing to a stop before the men, shuffled into a guilty line in front of Brianna, trying to hide the horrific extent of their intimidation with the bulk of their bodies. The warm air emerging from the horse's widening nostrils ghosted the air, steam rising from the very pit of hell.

'What the devil is happening here?' Through the slits of his helmet, the knight's voice was muffled, grim. He jumped off the horse in one easy, graceful movement, one hand on the hilt of his sword as he approached Fulke.

'Nothing to concern yourself about, I'm sure, my lord.' Fulke bowed obsequiously, spreading his hands flat before him, as if to physically reassure the newcomer there was no harm done. He cowered beneath the stranger's superior height, trying to step back before realising that the huddled form of Brianna lay behind his heels, checking him. 'This ignorant maid simply refuses to do as she's told. She needed to learn a lesson.'

'Then it looks like she's learned it,' the stranger remarked tautly, sweeping his gaze over Brianna's forlorn frame, tumbled against the trough. From her appearance, the maid was still unconscious; her face was pale, deathly pale, a livid bruise darkening rapidly across her jawline.

Fulke had the grace to look faintly embarrassed. 'Aye, well, we best be on our way.' He nodded significantly at his two soldiers, rubbing his gloved hands together in an industrious way. 'Lots to do, lots to do.' He paused, staring with curiosity at the plain, unadorned wool of the knight's tunic, trying to discern the man's features through the forbidding slits in his helmet. 'I…er…are you from hereabouts?'

'Nay. I am looking for someone.'

'Mayhap I could help you.' Fulke squeezed his hands together, kneading his fingers. He felt the need to make amends, to distract this stranger from the unconscious maid at his back. 'Whom do you seek?'

'Brianna of Sefanoc. Lady Brianna. I was told that she lives hereabouts.'

The colour washed from Fulke's face; he touched a hand to his chin, a self-conscious gesture. It was all he could do to stop himself looking over at the girl; he prayed fervently that his soldiers would keep their mouths shut. If certain parties heard a whisper of their actions, their treatment of a noblewoman, they would be punished severely. His name, Fulke, would be linked back to Count John, his lord and master, who would be highly displeased at the exposure, especially now. These were troubled times, the whole country jittery with the news that King Richard had been taken prisoner on his return from the Crusades. Only Count John, the King's younger brother, was rubbing his hands with glee, for if Richard failed to return, then he would surely be crowned King of England.

Fulke screwed the thicket of his eyebrows together in a semblance of thinking. 'No, I can't say I've ever heard of her,' he lied casually, carefully. 'It's not a name I know.' He began to sidle off towards the horses. 'I wish you luck in your venture, sire. Good day to you.' Fulke levered himself onto his animal, raising an arm in farewell as he kicked the animal into a fast canter, clods of frozen earth kicking up in his wake as he followed his men.

The maid appeared barely alive, Giseux thought, as he approached the spot where she lay. Crouching down beside her, he pulled off his chainmail mittens, pushing two fingers efficiently against the side of her neck, checking, reassuring himself. Her face was so white, devoid of any colour, with such a sickening blueness about her lips that he could have believed she were dead, yet to his relief her blood beat strongly beneath his fingers. He removed his helmet, then his shield, held against his chest with a worn leather strap, placing both on the grass, and pushed back the hood of the chainmail protecting his head. The metallic links, bound together to form a flexible material, fell in loose, snake-like folds at the nape of his neck; the light brown strands of his hair sprung free from their confinement, vigorous.

She lay flat on her back, sprawled across the ice-encrusted mud, one arm slung across her body, the other stretched out, her hand curled, small and white. Her unusual amber-coloured hair, darkened by the water, straggled across her bodice like ripples in the sand. A peasant girl, from the look of her clothes, he thought; her coarse woollen gown had been mended in several places with crudely cut patches. The garment hung like a sack about her frame, bunching in thick gathers at her waist; her creased leather boots, scuffed and caked in mud, stuck out from beneath the hem of her skirts. The shiny soles were almost worn through. He'd interrupted a domestic dispute, no doubt, a fight between servant and master.

The girl opened her eyes.

Chapter Two

Giseux's heart knocked against the wall of his chest. Sudden. Unexpected. Sounds diminished, fell away into the background: the incessant chirruping of a robin, diving under the blackthorn; his horse ripping up the frosted grass with massive teeth, chewing steadily. The maid's eyes were wide, bright blue, ice blue, luminescent as the sky at dawn. They snared him, sucked him into their amazing depths, a whirlpool so fast and strong that he had no time to think. His mind reeled within their power as he leaned forwards, amazed.

As he dropped to his knees, Brianna cried out—a long wavering wail of panic, the bundled-up fear bursting from her chest, fear that she had fought to keep under control throughout Fulke's mauling. And now he'd sent someone else to deal with her. Her vision hazed with fright as the huge soldier hulked over her, silver eyes sparkling with a predatory gleam; he would surely kill her! Broad shoulders blocked out the light, cast her in shadow, as her knuckles scraped desperately against the rough wooden trough, scrabbling for purchase, for some sort of stability as she screamed and screamed. Would no one come for her, would no one help her? Her shrieking rent the still air, piercing, pitching up a notch as firm hands curled about her shoulders, steadied her.

'Stop!' a low voice ordered, a rippling burr of sound close to her ear. 'Do you want to bring them back?' The warmth of the man's breath fanned her cheek, before he lowered his hands.

Her mouth shut abruptly. Pain in the left side of her jaw chewed into her, relentless, an ache beginning to spread up the side of her cheek. Blood tasted like rust against her tongue. Tears sprung from her eyes, her body trembling, as she hoisted herself up awkwardly, flinging her arms out to push the stranger away. Her fingers flailed outwards, skittering over the black wool across his immense chest; her pathetic attempts failed to shift him. Exhausted by unravelling fear, she let her arms fall limply to her sides.

'I can't take much more of this,' Brianna stuttered out, her voice a weak thread; her lips were dry, bruised. Energy seeped from her body, her small frame slumping back against the trough, her breathing rapid, truncated, puffing clouds of white in the cold air. The leather lace securing her braid had loosened; now the curling end was beginning to unravel, the magnificent amber hair shining against the sagging weave of her brown bodice. 'But I'd rather be locked up, or dead, than do what you want me to do.' The man's intimidating grey eyes glittered over her, incisive, piercing, as if they drilled down into her very soul. Another wave of panic lurched up, pushing out the sides of her chest, and she dug her heels into the mud, intending to scrabble backwards if he came for her.

Sitting back on his heels, Giseux watched the trails of sparkling liquid track down her puffy, mottled cheek, heard the great, gasping sobs seize at her chest. The girl obviously believed him to be in league with the thugs who had just roughed her up. A tiny pulse beat frantically at her neck, beneath the white, fragile skin in the hollow of her throat; her fear of him was palpable, radiating from her body in waves of tension. The sight of her tears bit into him, tugged cruelly at his memory, but he clamped down firmly on the encroaching vision. He had no wish to remember.

'Easy, maid,' he said in his deep, rumbling voice. The words of comfort felt untested, awkward, like dusty rocks in his mouth. The battle for Jerusalem had been long and relentless; there had been little opportunity or time to offer solace to others—had he forgotten how? Or had the ugliness, the cruelty of fighting driven it from his soul? The hard frozen earth jagged into his knees; as he shifted, trying to ease his cramped calf muscles, she reared backwards, abruptly, like a wild, cornered animal. A rueful smile twisted his mouth as he shook his head, shook out the gold-tipped fronds of his hair: a lion's mane, the blunt ends like spun gold around the rugged angles of his face. 'Nay, nay, I will not hurt you.'

Brianna eyed him blankly, disbelieving, driving the flats of her hands and feet into the hard mud to hitch away from him. Where was her knife? She had to protect herself! As she raised herself up from the ground, every muscle in her body aching, protesting, the voluminous gown that she wore pressed against her body, revealing her high, rounded bosom, the golden-red weave of her hair falling like spun net across her chest. She managed to make a small space between them, heart racing beneath his steely perusal before the heel of her boot snared in the trailing hem of her gown, preventing any further escape.

'Let me help you up. Can you stand?' Impatient not to prolong the episode, Giseux stretched out one hand, tanned and sinewy, to help her up.

She slapped at his fingers, catching the side of his palm. The sharp smack reverberated in the confined corner of the field, bouncing between the thorny hedgerows, studded with bright berries. 'Get away from me! Go! Leave me alone!' The shrillness of her voice screeched into his ear, scraping at the limits of his patience. 'You need to go away!'

'And you need to mind your manners!' Deep within him, the short rope of his temper began to fray; the girl's behaviour was ridiculous, unnecessary. It wasn't the physical blow—that had been nothing, a mere moth's touch from her slim fingers—but the girl's complete failure to comprehend that he was not her enemy. His initial intention to offer her comfort, to help her in some way, as any passing stranger would do, had gone seriously awry. He didn't have the time to squander on such foolish conduct, and at this rate, his act of mercy was threatening to take all day. It would be so much easier to walk away. But he couldn't leave her here, hunched, pathetic, like a half-drowned kitten that spat and snarled at him whenever he approached. It went against every code he had been brought up to believe.

'I am not going to leave you here, sitting on the frozen ground. I am not going to hurt you.'

'How do I know?' she threw back at him, her body rigid and hostile, cerulean eyes narrowing suspiciously. 'How do I know that this isn't another trick? The words emerged in jerky fashion, her voice wobbling with the cold. She wrapped her arms firmly about her chest, trying to stop the violent shudders that racked her body.

He set his lips in a firm forbidding line, a ripple of irritation lacing his big frame. 'I'm not one of them. You have to trust me.'

'Trust?' Laughter burst from her lips, a spray of jangled sound couched with a bubble of hysteria. 'Surely you jest? It's obvious you are one of Count John's men, sent to pick up the pieces.' Brianna wriggled her feet, attempting to move her frozen toes. She needed to find the strength, the determination, to stand up, to walk away. A cloying weakness dragged at her legs; this last attack had surely been the worst. And it appeared that it wasn't over yet.

Gathering the last scraps of courage from her body, she tipped her head defiantly, meeting his pewter gaze. 'I'll not go back with you. I'll not go back to Merleberge.'

'I have no intention of *making* you go anywhere,' he replied, his tone brimming with contempt. Sunburn dusted his high cheekbones, a reddish-brown colour that spoke of distant lands. His mouth was generous, top lip narrow, well defined, in stark, shocking comparison to the sensual fullness of his bottom lip. Brown hair, gilded, fell forwards in thick strands over his brow, ruffled by the breeze. 'But it would help if I could take you somewhere, to a place of safety. Sooner, rather than later.'

He propelled himself up in one sinuous, graceful movement; she instinctively raised her hands, as if to ward off further attack, but to her surprise he ignored her, heading towards his horse. Her heart eased as she watched him, noting that he limped—the slightest hesitation, a fraction of a pause, as his right foot moved forwards. His chainmail, glinting like fish scales, fitted his tall frame like a second skin, revealing the impressive breadth of his shoulders, the powerful strength of his long legs. The fine cloth of his surcoat held a dull sheen in the fragile sunshine, secured to his slim hips with a wide leather sword belt.

'Here, have this, you're freezing.'

She cast a cursory glance at the bundle of cloth between his hands: a cloak, of midnight blue, the collar edged in fur.

'I've told you, leave me. I want nothing from you.' She tried to inject some strength into her voice. Clutching valiantly at the trough with clenched, icy fingers, she pushed her body weight upwards. A raft of dizziness swept through her head as she stood up straight and she swayed, nausea boiling in her stomach. 'Go away,' she whispered. 'For the love of God, go away.' Her lids, blue-veined and pale, fluttered down, spiky black lashes fanning her cheeks. She wanted to recover from her humiliating ordeal in her own time, at her own pace, without this man, this stranger, witnessing her every move.

He assessed her wilting figure critically, the hint of a mocking smile playing across his lips; a large bear-like hand curled around her shoulder. 'Mayhap you should stay sitting for a while?'

Brianna wrested her shoulder furiously from his grasp, from the unwanted contact, eyes caged, fiery breath caught in the trap of her throat. 'Don't you dare,' she lashed at him, 'don't you dare touch me!' She turned, stumbling a little over the tussocky grass, spotting the gleam of her knife in the rough vegetation. Her head swam as she crouched to pick it up, to secure the blade once more in its scabbard at her waist. Then, without a backward glance, the blurry horizon line teetering before her, she took one step tentatively back towards the farm. Somehow, the thought of returning to her own cold, empty home failed to fill her with confidence.

'Where do you think you're going?' The stranger's voice boomed out over her, a snare of exasperation.

Maybe if she ignored him, he would go away. Brianna focused on the gateway, forcing her wooden, unwilling legs to move forwards, aware that her gait was unbalanced, wobbling even. If she could just stretch her fingers out to reach the gatepost…

A hand grasped her upraised forearm, strong tapered fingers snaring the point where the wide cuff of her rough sleeve had fallen back, exposing the limpid marble of her skin. Beneath the loose hold of his fingers, her pulse scurried along, too fast. Legs buckling, Brianna staggered against the oak gatepost, the wood split and grey, speckled with a frothing mat of sage-green lichen.

He was at her back, the rounded bulk of his shoulder curving into hers, the heat from his body burning her spine. The silken strands of her hair stirred with his breath…no, too close! Vexed, she squeezed her eyes shut, blinking away the hot threat of tears at his continued, unwanted presence.

'I swear you are the rudest, most ungrateful chit I have ever met.' His voice curled into her, hardened by iron-clad threads of irritation. 'Now, tell me where you live and I will take you there.' From his lofty vantage point, he traced the elegant arch of her dark copper brow, the creamy curve of her cheek. Her skin was fine, polished: the rich, sleek lustre of a pearl. Up close, the purpling bruise on her jawline looked savage; it must hurt like hell, he thought, suddenly.

'Nay,' she responded quickly. Her frozen skin tingled beneath the pads of his fingers. She tried to jerk away, to take one more tottering step, but he held firm. 'I don't want your help.'

'Oh, but I think you do,' Giseux responded calmly. He hadn't realised how small she was; if he leaned forward a notch, the top of her head would brush his chin. 'You can scarce take a step without nearly falling down.

However near your home might be, it would take you all day to reach it.'

'But I would reach it…eventually,' Brianna threw back, tilting her chin up with determination, 'without your help.' A rising anxiety fluttered in her chest at his proximity, clawing at her innards. He was like a solid, immovable wall, glittering, formidable. His hand fell from her arm and she clung to the post for support. She bit her lip, humiliated, furious at her own pathetic weakness, beset with a flooding sense of her own vulnerability.

Giseux sighed, folding his arms high across his chest. 'I don't understand you. For all you know, those men could be waiting for you in the next field over. Are you really that stupid?'

Lips set in a mutinous line, Brianna glared dully at the horizon, defeat clogging her heart. The man gave her no choice; she suspected he would dog her steps until he saw her to a place of safety. Then, and only then, would she be rid of him.

'I live over there.' She gestured vaguely towards the low roofs of the farm on the horizon, not trusting him with the truth. 'It's not far.'

'Then let's go.' Giseux gathered up his shield from the spot where she had fallen, slinging the glossy black armour across his body, securing his helmet and cloak to the rump of his horse, before catching up the reins.

A shout from the field beyond forced Brianna to lift her head. Spotting the round, familiar figure of the farmer trotting alongside the hedge, hefting a heavy iron mace between his thick hands, she almost collapsed with relief. The sides of William's leather jerkin flapped out from his hips as he jogged along, his normally jovial face red with exertion, his eyes wide with concern.

'William!' she called over to him. 'Over here!' Whirling around, she noted that the knight tracked the farmer's advance with interest. 'No need to escort me now.' She expelled her pent-up breath in a long gasp, her relief evident in the sag of her body, the brightness of her features. 'William can take me home.'

Granite eyes narrowed. 'You know this man?'

She nodded. 'He's my father.' The lie tripped easily from her tongue; she felt the need for some protection, however fictitious.

'He needs to keep a closer eye on you.' Swinging up into the saddle, a surprisingly lithe, efficient movement for such a big man, the stranger pulled up the reins, his stance relaxed, easy as the horse sidled beneath him.

'Tell me, do you know where I can find Brianna of Sefanoc?'

Breath punched from her lungs at the astonishing question, toes curling in her boots as she glared blankly at the broad expanse of blue sky, patched by fluffy white clouds coasting along in the breeze. She edged her gaze around, unsure whether she had heard him correctly. 'I beg your pardon?'

'Do you know where I can find Brianna of Sefanoc?' he repeated, slowly, witheringly, as if she were a half-wit.

Brianna's mouth set in an open jeer. 'You had better ask your friend, Count John. I've never heard of her.'

Moving towards William, she sucked in her breath at the painful stiffness developing in her body, keeping her frame rigid, stalking off in the opposite direction to Sefanoc, back to the farm. She didn't look back.

'Oh, mother of God, child, what in Heaven's name happened to you?' Alys emerged from the kitchen area that led off the entrance hall, wiping her hands on a linen cloth, as Brianna burst through the main door, shutting it firmly behind her, leaning her back against the solid oak panels, as if in confirmation of her actions.

'They were waiting for me, Alys, Count John's men! On the way back from the farm.' The explanation emerged in a rush; reaching up, rising on the balls of her feet, she shot the top bolt into its hasp, then repeated the action with the middle and bottom bolts.

'There.' She turned triumphantly to Alys. 'That should keep them out.' And *him*, if he ever found her, she added silently. Loosening the leather laces that closed the slash neck of her cape, she pulled it off, over her head. Her shimmering plaits, half-unravelled, swung down to her waist, the top of her head still damp from her dunking.

The linen towel dropped to the stone floor, drifting noiselessly to the flagstones. 'Your face, Brianna.' Alys raised her palms to her own cheeks. 'Your face.' She moved forwards in the gloom of the entrance hall, backlit by the torchlight flaming from the kitchen, her arms outstretched in horror.

'It's not as bad as it looks.' Her jaw throbbed persistently with a bruised heat as Brianna hung her cape on a wooden peg near the door. A slick of fear coated her veins. What would have happened today, if that man, that stranger in black and silver, hadn't come along? Did those men have orders from Count John to finish her off, to remove her, believing Hugh would never return? With no other living relative, with no one to ask questions as to her whereabouts, Count John would be able to grab the rich pastures of Sefanoc for his own.

'Sit down, let me put something on it. Come, I've lit the fire in the hall.' Alys pushed aside the small door set in the wooden panelling that screened the great hall from the front entrance.

'Nay, there's no time. I must fetch my bow and check the windows are secure in the solar.'

'Are they coming after you?' Alys questioned, a note of rising panic in her voice.

'They might...' Brianna paused, as a pair of silver eyes shone in her memory '...and possibly with reinforcements.' Had she misjudged the man who had tried to help her? With her mind befuddled from the attack, she had been so convinced he was an ally of Count John, sent to try a different tack to convince her to marry. And yet...he had asked for her by name. Her face warmed at the memory of his protective bulk at her side; she placed flat palms to her cheeks, seeking to cool the twin flags of heat.

'Oh, God save us.' Alys clutched at her chest. 'I wish the Lord Hugh had returned, or...or that we had a man about the house to defend us.'

'We can defend ourselves, Alys!' Brianna's eyes

flashed determination. 'I will not let these men bully us…bully me.' She yanked open the door into the great hall, heading for the solar at the opposite end of the house, and her bedchamber. She sighed; how tempting it would be to curl up beneath the bed furs at this very moment and sleep, sleep a deep dreamless sleep. But she strode on, her lips set in a tight line; she had to make certain the manor house was secure.

Alys touched her arm, halting her stride. 'Brianna… my lady…you can't keep going on like this… It's too hard for you to do alone.'

'I prefer to be alone, Alys, you know that.'

Brianna dropped her eyes, a silky curl of burnished hair looping over her cheek. Why did Alys constantly allude to her solitary life, her single status? Surely she, of all people, knew that Brianna could never be with a man, never trust a man, ever again? She drew in a deep breath, willing the faint tightness of panic in her chest to leave, to dissolve. This attack had frightened her, reminding her of that past she craved to forget. Clasping her hands together, she turned around, pulling her features into an expression, she hoped, of supreme confidence. 'Alys, if there's one good thing that came out of that ill-fated marriage, it was the ability to defend myself!' She picked her skirts up to continue striding in the direction of the solar.

Alys nodded dubiously, her face stricken. Brianna never talked about her short marriage to Walter of Brinslow; all she knew was that the kind, happy girl who had left Sefanoc to wed had returned just six months later as a broken woman. Five winters on and

Brianna had sprung back to her old self, although the scars of whatever that man had done to her still lingered, in the shadows behind her eyes, in certain mannerisms. It was why she had insisted that Hugh, before he left on the crusade, had taught her how to defend herself. Her gaze touched on Brianna, now hefting her unwieldy crossbow from the solar, her brows drawn together in concentration, trying to remember how to use the weapon. Both women deluded themselves, both knew that Hugh's tuition was not enough. It could never be enough against Count John's men.

The fine silver arc of a new moon hung low in the sky as Giseux approached Sefanoc. At least he hoped it was Sefanoc. The directions from the local people in the nearby town of Merleberge had been hazy, reluctant to divulge too much information to a stranger. It was only when he told them the purpose of his visit that they opened up, nodding and smiling at Lady Brianna's name. It seemed that Hugh of Sefanoc's sister was something of a heroine in these parts.

Over to his right, amidst the rustlings and twitterings of a forest, a vixen shrieked. Trees threw jerky angles up against the reddish streaks of the western sky, daylight fading rapidly. Under the trees, the light grew so dim that he dismounted, leading his horse along the barely visible track. As the cold mud seeped through the chainmail covering his feet, he regretted the haste with which he'd travelled to Merleberge. He hadn't given himself time to change into civilian clothes; his full armour was designed for riding, not for walking any great distance. The smell of smoke mingled with the chill evening air, the fresh scent of burning apple wood wafting over him; he could see lights in the windows up ahead, an encouraging sign, flooding down to reveal the stone steps leading up to the wide front door on the first floor.

Something whistled past his ear, barely an inch away from the steel helmet protecting his head. In an instant he had drawn his sword and ducked behind a tree, all his instincts poised, alert. Near to the spot where he had been walking, a crossbow bolt, quiver still vibrating with the force of the shot, stuck into the mud where his feet had been.

A woman's voice shouted down from the manor, across the darkness, 'Go away!' The clear, bell-like voice was delivered in an imperious high-handed tone.

Grimacing, he rested his back against the tree, stretching out the muscles in his long legs, easing out the tight spot on his upper thigh. He hadn't anticipated any antagonism and, after the shenanigans with that peasant woman today, this hostile behaviour was unexpected and annoying. Pulling up the visor of his helmet, he inched his head round the ridged trunk to project his response towards the house. 'My name is Giseux de St-Loup. I was told that Lady Brianna lives here. I need to see her, about her brother, Hugh.' His powerful voice reverberated around the stillness of the forest, echoed up into the trees. Through the branches above his head, against the velvet nap of the sky, the evening star glowed, a diamond pinprick.

Silence.

Irritation rose in his gullet—what in the devil's name was happening now? Sneaking another look round, he could see the silhouette of a woman at the upper window; to his surprise, he realised it was she that held the crossbow. He smiled to himself. She wouldn't be so lucky with her shot the next time; ladies were not known for their prowess with weapons. Leaving his horse by the tree, he moved out into the open ground, covering the space between the manor and the forest with long-legged strides.

Another bolt flew through the air, thudded next to him, surprisingly close.

'I told you to go away.' The modulated tones assailed him from the window, cutting briskly through the night air.

Caught halfway in the open grassy area between the edge of the trees and the house, Giseux tilted his head towards the window. All he could see was the woman's dark outline and the glint of metal from the crossbow cradled in her arms. 'And I told you,' he delivered the words slowly, patiently, 'that I have come about Hugh of Sefanoc. He is very ill and needs to see his sister. So I suggest you stop playing games and let me in. You're wasting precious time with this nonsense.'

At his back, an owl hooted, eerie, piercing.

'I don't believe you. It's another trick.'

'I have no idea to what you are referring.' Giseux narrowed his eyes, trying to discern the lady's face. 'Hugh said you'd be like this; he said you'd ask for proof.'

'Do you have any?'

Gisuex cleared his throat. 'He said, "Remember Big Belly Oak".'

He heard a gasp and what sounded like a rising sob. The figure retreated from the window, crying out an urgent command, before the iron bolts on the main door were drawn back. By the time the last one grated from its metal hasp, Giseux had sprinted to the top of the steps, was waiting when the door nudged slowly inwards.

'Take me to Lady Brianna,' he rapped out at the maidservant behind the door, giving her no more than a cursory glance. Yanking off his helmet, he pushed back his chainmail hood and shoved the unwieldy metal headgear into the servant's hands. His shield slid to the floor in the process. 'Here, take this.'

His gaze snagged.

He looked again, closer, scrutinising the pale oval face in the dimness of the entrance hall. Bright hair in plaits, translucent blue eyes, shoddy woollen dress. 'You! It's you!' Big hands reached out, tapered fingers snaring her shoulders. 'You little wretch! Why didn't you tell me you worked for Lady Brianna? You've done her no favours by protecting her!' In the corner of the entrance hall, another, older servant trembled, twisting her hands nervously, ineffectually, lined face taut with fright.

'I don't work for Lady Brianna…' the girl replied softly. Her small hands clutched around his helmet, as if in support. The bruise at her jaw seemed to have spread, darkening to a frightening array of reddish-purple blotches.

'You could have saved me a whole day of pointless riding about!' he blazed at her. 'Do you realise how much time I've wasted? Hugh, your lord, could be dead by now.' The harsh words felt good on his tongue; he said them deliberately to frighten her, to make her pay for his whole tiresome, wasted day.

A deathly white washed her face. He wondered whether she might faint, the hold he maintained on her shoulders changing to one of support. 'Tell me where he is,' she whispered, raising her beautiful blue eyes to his. 'I am Hugh's sister. I am Brianna of Sefanoc.'

. His wolfish look plundered her, dark brows drawing into a frown, eyes hardening to chips of granite. 'You…are…Brianna?' he pronounced slowly, incredulous, drawing his gaze at a leisurely pace from the top of her flame-coloured hair, over the tented and patched sack of her gown, to the tips of her toes. Her face grew hot beneath the deliberateness of his examination; she twisted away, all but throwing his helmet on to an oak bench in the entrance hall.

'I realise I'm not quite as you would expect,' Brianna explained briskly. In the confined space of the entrance hall, a restless energy rolled from him in waves, vital, pulsating, resonating through her body, making her shiver. The diamond chips of his eyes glittered in the sepulchral gloom.

'You can say that again,' he murmured. The luminous quality of her skin gleamed from the shadows. His fingers tingled, itched to touch, to test the alluring softness, and he frowned.

'I had to help out with the milking this morning, hence the clothes.'

'Help with the milking? Surely you have servants to do such work?' Giseux threw a penetrating glance over at Alys, who quailed visibly into the corner.

Brianna shook her head faintly, dismissing the subject; she had no wish to discuss her domestic arrangements with a complete stranger. She reached out her hand to touch Giseux's arm, then obviously thought better of it, withdrawing her hand quickly. 'Tell me about Hugh, please. I have spent so many days waiting, wondering. I can't believe he's still alive.'

Giseux sincerely hoped that he was. The loose sleeve of her gown had slipped back when she reached up as if to touch him; the skin of her wrist was limpid, fragile as parchment, covered with a network of blue veins; her fingernails were pale pink, delicate shells, against the raw skin of her work-roughened fingers. He swallowed, a sudden dryness catching his throat.

'Are you going to let me in?' He glanced archly at the sheathed knife in her belt. 'Or am I still considered a danger?'

He saw her take a deep, shuddering breath, saw the sheer exhaustion in her eyes. The tip of her tongue licked nervously at the rose-bud fullness of her bottom lip.

'Am I a danger?' he repeated. The low, husky tones enveloped her. An odd, teetering sensation spiralled in her belly, coiling slowly, blossoming.

'No,' she croaked. Indecision swamped her. She knew he had been sent by Hugh; how else would he have known of the 'Big Belly Oak' of their childhood, their secret hiding place? She looped her arms defensively across her stomach. There was something else about this man that caused every last nerve ending in her body to dance with… Was it fear? She couldn't be certain, at a loss to identify the feeling.

'Follow me.' Her lips compressed as she grasped the spitting torch proffered by Alys, holding the guttering flame aloft, showing the way.

He followed the rigid line of Brianna's back into the great hall, enjoying the tempting sway of her hips as they brushed against the inside of her gown. Who would have thought that she could be Hugh's sister, dressed in those torn, work-stained garments, her rippling coppery hair, like beech leaves in autumn, falling down past her waist in simple braids? Hugh of Sefanoc never wasted the slightest opportunity to boast about the substantial income he gained from his estates, from the farming as well as the forest. So why was his sister dressed in rags, working her fingers to the bone, courting the violent attentions of Count John's men?

Slinging the torch into an iron ring alongside the imposing stone fireplace, Brianna gestured abruptly to a high-backed armchair. Giseux folded his large frame gratefully into the hard wooden seat; after a day in the saddle it felt good, despite the inflexibility of his armour. He glanced at the fire, a pathetic business made up of a few damp sticks, spitting and smouldering in the enormous grate. The tiny heat thrown out by the feeble flames made little impact on the cavernous space; against the skin of his face, Giseux could feel the penetrating cold radiating out from the grey-stone walls. Up above him, the high ceiling was constructed of thick oak trusses, huge arches that spanned the length of the hall. The high windows had been shuttered against the winter weather, although he doubted it made much difference to the inside temperature.

'Tell me! Tell me how Hugh is, please!' Brianna rested one hand on the stone mantel to steady herself. She wanted to lay her head against the carved stone and weep tears of sheer gratitude, but she would be damned if she showed any further weakness before this dark stranger. Why, oh, why did it have to be him to bring the news? The man who had witnessed her humiliation by Count John's men, who had moved too close in his efforts to help her; even now, she could feel the burning imprint of his fingers from this morning. Her heart skittered.

Giseux sprawled back in the chair, stretching out his legs, his toes almost touching Brianna's hem. The dancing flames from the torchlight turned the brilliant colour of her hair to burnished gold. A wry smile crooked his lips as she twitched her skirts away from his encroaching feet, her nose crinkling a little in distaste at his nearness.

'Hugh is at my parents' castle, near Winchester,' Giseux explained. 'His sickness began as we waited for the ships to bring us back to England. He is very ill, sometimes delirious with fever, but always, always, asking for you.'

Brianna placed her palms flat over her face, physically trying to stop the tears from running down, emotion clawing in her belly. If only she'd known this morning, she would be with Hugh by now. 'Then why didn't you tell me?' she blurted out, her voice holding the sting of accusation, 'Why didn't you tell me who you were this morning, why you were here?' She flung herself into the chair opposite him, perching on the edge, scuffed leather boots poking out from beneath her sagging hemline.

'If I remember rightly, it was you who denied all knowledge of Brianna of Sefanoc,' he replied scornfully. 'If you hadn't, we would be with him now.'

'Then let's go!' She sprang out of the seat, headed towards the solar. 'All I need is my cloak.'

Giseux's deep voice halted her nimble stride. 'Lady, if you think I'm travelling anywhere tonight, then think again. I need food and I need some sleep before I climb into that saddle once more.'

'But Hugh…?'

'…is in safe hands,' he finished the sentence for her. He was reluctant to point out that if Hugh were dead now, then one night would make no difference. 'We'll ride on the morrow, in daylight. It'll be safer and we'll be able to see our way, which will make the journey quicker.'

Brianna frowned, spinning back on the ball of one foot to face him, bridling beneath his authoritative manner, his swift decision-making. 'That may be so, my lord, but I wish to see my brother now.' Who did he think he was, to give her orders so? She was used to making up her own mind, forging her own decisions; after her marriage to Walter, she had promised herself that, at least. 'I thank you, my lord, for bringing the message about my brother; you are welcome to some food and to spend the night here.' Her tone was formal, dismissive. 'I will fetch you something to eat right now.'

'Hold.' As she passed his chair, he snagged her hand in one large chainmail glove. The creased leather on the underside pressed into her palm.

'Let me go.' Brianna made an effort to deliver the words calmly, waiting for the familiar crawl of fear in her chest, bracing her body against the inevitable sickening panic she experienced when any man came too close. Her pulse skipped, her heart rate accelerating, but not in any way she remembered. She frowned; something was not right.

'What are you going to do?' he asked. His voice had a lilting, liquid quality.

'I told you, to fetch some food.' She tugged at her hand; his strong fingers tightened. Annoyed, she pressed her lips together, staring steadfastly away from his penetrating gaze.

'You feed me lies, my lady, I can see it in your face,' his silky tones accused her. 'You're planning to go to him, aren't you? Whether I agree to accompany you or not.'

'It's none of your business.'

'It is my business to deliver you safely. Do you think Hugh would ever forgive me if some harm came to you on the journey? He asked me to escort you and escort you I will.' He dropped her hand.

'Then go with me now.' She cradled her released

fingers, missing the warmth of his touch. What was the matter with her?

'It's not possible,' Giseux replied firmly, steel threading his voice. Since when had women become so outspoken? He could travel if he wanted to; he could ride for days on an empty stomach with little sleep, but something in her manner made him want to resist, to squash her a little.

'All right, we'll leave tomorrow,' she replied huffily, flouncing off to the kitchen. Leaning back in the chair, Giseux smiled. He suspected that he would have a battle on his hands, a battle that he would inevitably win. Oddly, he relished the thought.

Chapter Three

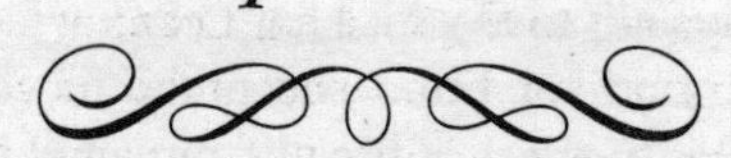

'Oh, my lady, what in Heaven's name are we going to feed him?' Alys knotted her fingers together endlessly, running helpless eyes along the wide empty shelves lining the kitchen.

'Nothing, if I had my way.' Brianna braced her hands flat against the well-scrubbed planks of the kitchen table, trying to assemble her angry, scattered thoughts. Her eyes snapped over to Alys, fiery blue. 'The man's a complete oaf! Did you hear what he said to me? Hugh's alive and he refuses to take me to him! He wants to wait… wait until tomorrow morning. Can you believe it?'

Alys hurried over to her, plucked at Brianna's sleeve. 'Keep your voice down, he'll hear you!' The thin skin of her face stretched over high cheekbones, mottled pink. She darted a nervous glance towards the open kitchen door.

'What do I care?' Brianna pushed her body upright,

whipping around to face the door, wanting Giseux to burst through, wanting to challenge him. 'He knows what I think.'

'My lady, calm down,' Alys pleaded, patting feebly at Brianna's arm. 'Come, let's fetch him some food—what about the stew?'

Alys's question forced her mind to concentrate. She considered the stew that she and her maidservant had been eking out for the last week: tough chicken legs occasionally enlivened with a few chewy winter greens. 'Nay, too good for him,' she pronounced, instead extracting a dry heel of bread from an earthenware pot, plonking it on a pewter plate. 'There, that should do.'

'He's a lord, Brianna,' Alys whispered, 'a nobleman. We can't feed him on stale bread.'

'I suppose he could have some cheese,' Brianna conceded, grudgingly. She unwrapped a long piece of damp muslin from a round of soft cheese, fresh and crumbly.

'And some mead.' Alys dipped a pewter tankard into an iron-girded cask of the amber liquid, setting it down on the tray next to the plate.

'Shall I take it?' the maidservant offered reluctantly.

Brianna smiled. 'Nay, let me. And he'd better appreciate it.'

Alys raised her eyes to Heaven.

Shouldering her way awkwardly back through the door to the great hall, carrying the tray, Brianna decided her main aim was to encourage Giseux, after he had eaten, to retire for the night. Alys had already prepared the guest chamber, accessed by a spiral flight of stairs from the entrance hall. Once he was asleep, it would leave the way clear for her to saddle up her horse and ride to Winchester.

Giseux's legs gleamed in their metallic skin, his bulging calf muscles clearly visible beneath the chain-mail as Brianna advanced towards the chair. He'd removed his chainmail gloves and they lay on the floor. She crashed the tray down ungratefully on the rickety, three-legged table at his elbow. 'Here you are, my lord.' Her bravado quailed as his eyes, midnight-fringed, devoured her with a single sweep.

'What did those men want with you this morning?' he demanded, ignoring the pewter plate at his side.

'I…er…' She hesitated, sweeping over to the shutters, checking the latches were secure, away from his heated perusal.

'What did they want with you?' Her spine shivered beneath the low rumble of his voice.

The metal hasp of the shutters felt cool beneath her fingers; she yearned to press her flaming face against the solid wood, to regain some solidity, some stability in her current situation.

'Count John's men?' Brianna tried to keep her voice light, even. She couldn't allow this man to know how much their beating had affected her. Taking a deep, shaky breath, she moved back to the fireside, perched tentatively in the seat opposite Giseux.

He bit into a hunk of bread, chewing slowly, silent.

Brianna shifted uncomfortably, stared at the floor, knowing he was waiting for an answer. 'Count John wants me to marry one of his noblemen, so that Sefanoc comes within his jurisdiction. He sent his soldiers to persuade me.'

'Their methods of persuasion leave a lot to be desired,' he murmured, taking a swig of mead, running the tip of his tongue along the generous curve of his bottom lip to catch a wayward drip.

Brianna touched one finger to her throbbing jaw. 'That's why bringing Hugh home to Sefanoc is so important,' she offered, tentatively. 'When Count John sees he's alive, well, then they'll stop tormenting me.'

'Then it's fortunate he is home.' Giseux steepled his fingers in front of his chest. 'Otherwise you might have ended up in a marriage against your will.'

Her expression was bleak. 'It would never happen; I told you before, I would rather die than have that happen again.'

His eyes flicked up at her final word; she clapped her hands to her mouth, startled, dismayed at her stupid mistake. *Again.* The word that gave away her past.

'Again?' Giseux queried, adjusting his position to lean forwards, elbows resting on his knees.

She sprang from her seat, mouth trembling, flustered, sweat clagging her palms. 'You need to finish your meal,' she announced briskly, 'and I must change out of these clothes. Please excuse me.'

So that was it, Giseux mused idly, as he watched the flick of her skirt, the shining coin of her hair disappear through a door at the end of the great hall. She had been married before, and not happily, judging from her reaction to his question. Where was her husband now? Had she finished him off with her crossbow, with a swipe from the knife at her belt? His lips twitched at the thought—she was perfectly capable. In fact, he doubted he had met another woman who fought with such drive, such ferocity, to hold on to the things she held most dear. It appeared she was paying a high price.

Seizing the mud-encrusted hem of her loose peasant gown, Brianna struggled with the coarse material to pull it over her head. Why, why on earth had she said such a stupid thing? And to him, of all people: a complete stranger! Blood bolted through her veins, rattling her; she forced herself to breathe more slowly, to calm down. The sooner she was away from him, the better. Leaving her chemise and woollen stockings on, and still wearing her stout leather boots, Brianna moved to the oak coffer at the foot of the bed. The carved lid opened with a protesting creak as she riffled inside. She only had two suitable gowns and one, she knew, had a long rip along a seam that she had been meaning to repair. The green wool gown was presentable, if a little threadbare. She settled the material over her head, smelling the dried lavender that Alys placed in the oak coffers every year to keep the clothes sweet. As the folds fell down about her shoulders, the wool prickled a little against her linen chemise, damp from her earlier dunking.

Pushing her head through the round slash neck, her fingers brushed against the silver embroidery that decorated the collar, the design raised, intricate. Her mother had done this, her beautiful mother who had spent many hours working her fine needlework on all the family's clothes. Brianna could see her now, sitting by the south window in the solar, the bright sunlight picking up the shining thread on her lap, the gold filaments in her burnished hair. Her breath emerged in a long, stuttering sigh. How she wished her parents could be here now, instead of succumbing to that horrendous, debilitating illness. They would be proud of her, she hoped, proud of the way she had kept the estate going in Hugh's absence, proud of the way she had scrimped and saved, so that there was something of worth, something of value for him to come home to. How could that man be so insensitive as to keep her from her brother, when she had waited for so long for him to return?

She smoothed the skirts of the gown down over her thighs, shaking out the creases and bringing in the waist with a woven girdle that settled over her slim hips. The woodenness of her fingers vexed her as she fumbled with the intricate ties of the belt. She placed her knife-belt and cloak across the bed, not wanting to alert Giseux's suspicions if she carried them out to the great hall now. Soon enough she and Alys would have him settled in the guest chamber and she would be able to slip away. Knotting her long braids together to form a loose bun, she jabbed the vibrant mass with several long hairpins in an effort to secure it, before covering her head with a gauzy veil. This she jammed into place with a golden circlet, the only one she hadn't sold, the metal cold and tight against her forehead.

She padded on silent feet towards the door, the hem of her gown a muffled whisper against the wide elm floorboards. Clicking the latch open, Brianna drew her spine up, preparing to face her rescuer once more.

Giseux's substantial frame spread out from the chair, his whole body polished in the light of the feeble fire. One arm hung out over the armrest, strong, tapered fingers suspended in mid-air.

He was asleep.

A curious flickering curled around her stomach, subtle, delicious, as she studied the man. For the first time she noticed the grey shadows beneath his eyes, hollows of smudged ash, crinkled lines fanning out from the corners. A hot, heavy sensation speared her feet to the floor; it was as if she were mesmerised. He looked uncomfortable, his big frame wedged into the narrow corner of the chair, and, with a rush of realisation, Brianna knew she should have offered him some of her brother's clothes. Hugh could never wait to dispense with his armour once he arrived home, always complaining how intolerable it was.

His chest rose and fell steadily, slowly, evidence of a deep sleep, the wool of his surcoat flattening taut over his chest and stomach, revealing the solid indentations of his muscles. He had loosened the leather laces that held together the slash neck of his hauberk; as the chainmail edges gaped, they revealed the strong, corded muscles of his neck, the tanned hollow of his throat. Brianna bit her lip; the temptation to touch, to test the honed perfection of his skin, was overwhelming. Her fingers burned with awareness.

She twisted her hands together, agitated, trying to dispel the tantalising craving, annoyed by her strange reaction to him. Was she in her right mind? Had the attack today left her so befuddled that she had forgotten her lonely path in life? Remember Walter, she told herself sternly, remember Walter controlling her to the point where she had wanted to scream in frustration, trapped in that bitter, loveless marriage. It had become his main amusement, deciding what she ate, what she wore, what she did all day, so that at some point in that hideous time, she truly believed she was losing the ability to think for herself. And she was not about to let that happen again.

Whisking back to her chamber, Brianna snatched up her cloak and knife-belt from the bed. Her mind rattled with details; she had to seize her chance to travel to Winchester now, whilst Giseux slept. As she tiptoed past him, a sudden nausea roiled in her belly at her daring and she trembled with the horrible notion of him leaping up suddenly, catching her red-handed. He could not, must not, catch her. She kept her gaze pinned to the door at the far end of the great hall, taking deliberate, considered steps, picking up her hem so she didn't trip. Every muscle in her body strained, held taut in the moment, alert to the slightest movement, the slightest sound from the chair. After what seemed like an eternity, her hand lifted the latch and she slipped into the entrance hall like a ghost, closing the door behind her. Her suppressed breath released; she sagged against the wall in relief.

Alys emerged from the stair that led to the guest chamber above the kitchens, eyes wide in her pale, wizened face. 'My lady? What's happening?' she whispered, frowning at Brianna's change of clothes, her cloak.

'Shh.' Brianna put a finger to her lips, seizing the maidservant by the hand and pulling her through the main entrance door, out, out into the frosty air, down the steps, down to the vaulted stables below the first floor. The smell of crushed straw, of faint, stale horse filled the air.

'Oh, mistress, nay, you cannot!' In the white slant of moonlight that poured through the archway into the stables, Alys brought her gnarled, arthritic hands to sunken cheeks when Brianna told her of her plans.

'It's the only way,' Brianna announced briskly, heart knocking against her chest, the image of the big man sprawled upstairs, asleep, tripping dangerously around the edges of her consciousness.

'At least let me come with you, mistress.'

In the startling brightness of the moon, Alys suddenly looked old, her gaunt frame bent over with exhaustion. Guilt surged through Brianna and she placed two hands on Alys's shoulders. 'Nay, Alys, I can't ask you to do that. You've put up with so much from me, you need to rest now. Go to bed, sleep. Lord Giseux can take care of himself.'

'But…?'

'Winchester is not above twenty miles from here…I know the way.' Well, most of it, Brianna added silently.

'But how will you travel?' Alys's gaze swept the empty stable. 'We have no horses left to ride.'

Brianna grinned, the metal bosses on her cloak glinting in the dim light. 'Aye, we don't,' she pointed out towards to fringes of the forest, where Giseux's large destrier was patiently cropping the grass, the reins conveniently looped around a low branch, 'but *he* does.'

It was the cold that finally woke him, digging into his bones like icy fingers, relentlessly, endlessly, so at last after a great deal of tossing and turning and trying to will his exhausted body back to sleep, Giseux reluctantly opened his eyes. The barest trickle of moonlight squeezed through the gaps in the long wooden shutters, enough to see by. The fire had burnt out, but not long ago, ashes smouldering dismally in the grate.

The chair cradled his body at a stiff, unyielding angle, compressing his bones. His right hand had gone numb; he gritted his teeth, flexing his fingers as the blood returned with a painful prickling. Shaking off the shrouds of sleep, his mind jumped into action, remembering, remembering the task that Hugh had set him. He recalled the spark of determination in Lady Brianna's eyes, the stubborn set of her mouth when he had informed her that they would not leave until morning.

Propelling himself from the chair, he strode over to the door of the solar, wrenching the door open. In normal circumstances, he probably would have knocked, but up to this point everything about Lady Brianna had been anything but normal. He knew, he just knew, before he'd even looked at the bed and saw that the furs lay flat, unused, that she had gone. Little witch! He had offered to come to Sefanoc as a favour to Hugh; in reality it was turning out to be an ordeal.

Stepping over to the bed, he hauled the covers back; the spotless, empty white sheet shone back at him, the slight indentation in the mattress where she would have slept mocking him. The scent of crushed lavender rose from the bedlinens, delicious, seductive, reminding him of those long, hot summers in Poitiers, and his heart jerked in memory. That all seemed so long ago now.

A small sound on the other side of the bed caught his attention.

'She's not here, my lord.' Alys sat up on low pallet bed, clutching the covers to her bony chest. Her frizzled hair stuck out from her head like grey lace. Her veins traced blue ridges on the backs of her hands.

'I can see that,' Giseux replied bluntly, his cheeks sculptured hollows in the sepulchral light. 'And against my better judgement I'm about to go after her.'

Big fat tears welled up in the maidservant's eyes. 'Oh, my lord, don't be too harsh on her.'

'Why on earth not?' he growled back. 'The woman's a prize fool, putting herself at risk.'

'She hasn't seen Hugh for such a long time. Once she has a plan in her head…' Alys trailed off miserably, her voice rising on a half-sob.

'She's difficult to rein in, I can see that,' Giseux replied, grimacing. 'When did she leave?'

'Not long after you fell asleep, my lord.'

'She hasn't had much of a head start.' He thought of the dying embers in the fireplace, calculating rapidly. 'What does she ride…a palfrey? She wouldn't go above a trot on one of those. I'll easily catch her up.'

The maidservant was silent, staring at him like a

ghost, her knotted fingers still clutching the coverlet against her. 'She…she took your horse, my lord.'

Through the dark tracery of bare branches, the moon appeared sporadically, shifting behind veils of cloud, dribbling a faint light down to the forest floor. A rising breeze sifted through the trees, a sibilant sound that spoke of the old stories surrounding the forest of Sefanoc, the drifting ghosts. The woods held little mystery for Brianna; she had grown up in this place, had laughed and played through the woodland with Hugh. She felt no fear as the giant skeletal shapes of the trees rose up before her, no fear as she glimpsed the deep pools silvered by the light of the moon and heard the twitterings and rustlings of the animals in the undergrowth. Nay, the forest did not scare her. But being caught by Lord Giseux de St-Loup did.

In despair, she kicked the rounded flanks of the horse beneath her once more. In her haste to leave for Winchester, she had failed to adjust the stirrups to the length of her leg and now they bumped uselessly against the horse's sides, polished metal hoops shining in the darkness. Even without the use of the stirrups, she considered herself to be an excellent horsewoman, but this animal simply refused to move at anything greater than a sporadic, half-hearted trot! Really, it was as if his master was controlling him from afar!

All of a sudden, the animal stopped, pointed ears moving round as if to locate a sound. And then she heard it—a shout on the wind. She failed to decipher the words, but she knew, knew it was him. Knuckles rounding tautly on the reins, her heart lodged in her throat—how had he managed to catch up with her so quickly? The horse begun to turn in response to his master's voice, Brianna yanking desperately on the reins to point his head back in the right direction, but to no avail. The horse turned abruptly in the narrow, muddy track, almost throwing her off in its excitement. In the last moment before the horse took off, Brianna managed to throw her leg over the horse's neck and slip in a flurry of skirts to the ground.

Head held high, she stalked forwards, marching purposefully, swiftly, along the lane towards Winchester, wrapping her woollen cloak firmly around her. She could have run to hide in the darkness of the forest, but what would that achieve? He would surely find her—his face held a lean, hunting expression, that of a predator. Moments later, the sound of galloping hooves thumped up behind her. Her heart plummeted, trickles of fear stinging her blood.

'Lady Brianna!' Giseux bellowed. The words rained down on her back as if they were physical blows and she hunched over, chest thudding painfully. *Don't cower like a guilty thief,* she told herself. *Face him!* Dragging herself up to her full height, spine straight and rigid, she spun around, the toe of her sturdy leather boot sinking into soft rotting leaves beneath her foot.

Giseux wore no helmet; his hair stuck up in rough spikes. His eyes, sparking anger, glimmered down over her. Despite her determined demeanour, she hoped that a great crevasse would open up beneath him and swallow him up.

'What do you think you are doing?' The roughness of his tone cut into her. His face glimmered with a sheen of sweat: he must have run to catch up with her before his horse turned back.

'You know what I am doing.' Not wanting to meet his eyes, to admit that she had defied his orders, Brianna stared mutinously at his mail-covered foot, stuck in the stirrup on a level with her chest, the gleaming armour dulled with spots of mud.

'I told you to wait until morning, then I would have escorted you.' His voice was low, level, but she detected a steely thread of exasperation winding through. The strengthening breeze stirred the wayward strands of his hair, making him appear more tousled…more devastating, she thought suddenly, a lump in her throat.

'I know the way,' she replied, truculently. Tilting her head to one side, she crossed her arms across her chest, a defiant gesture. In the shifting moonlight, her copper-coloured hair faded to a pale silk, loose strands drifting treacherously down from beneath her veil.

'It's not a question of whether you know the way or not,' he replied tersely, 'but the fact that you're a woman. No noblewoman goes out unescorted—it's utter madness.'

Brianna pushed the white froth of her veil back over her shoulder. 'Since Hugh went away, I have had little choice in the matter,' she replied practically, bending her gaze to his horse's flank. Beneath the animal's shining coat, a pulse throbbed near the surface, the beat regular and strong.

'Up to now, maybe not,' he agreed, 'but you knew

I would escort you to Winchester and you deliberately defied me.'

She jerked her chin up, eyes flashing fire at his chastisement. 'I wanted to get to Hugh—I haven't seen him for three years! Surely you can understand that?'

Aye, he could. He understood her need, her desire to be with her brother, especially after her harassment from Count John's men. He suspected the beating he had witnessed today was one of many.

'Besides,' she continued, 'who are you to order me about? You are not my lord, or my master. I can do what I want, go where I want. It's my choice.'

In the shadows of the forest, the silver embroidery along the hem of his tunic twinkled like starlight. 'So you do exactly as you please, without any consideration for others.'

Why, he made her sound like a spoiled brat! 'It's not like that!'

'How do you think Hugh would feel if something had happened to you?'

'I can take care of myself!'

'Hah! Like you took care of yourself this morning?' he growled down derisively. The moonlight turned the ruffled strands of his hair to gold. 'If I hadn't come along when I did…'

She shrugged her shoulders, trying to suppress the doubt that mired her chest. 'Those men are cowards… Lord Fulke is a coward! They would have left me alone soon enough. You, coming along like that, would have made no difference.'

'Fighting words, my lady! Yet I suspect even you

know that you lie to yourself. A woman alone is vulnerable, especially one who is stupid enough to believe she can best a man!' She reminded him of a wild animal, cornered and vulnerable, the display of viciousness masking its puny strength.

'I can—Hugh taught me how to use the crossbow… and the knife!' The pitch of her words notched upwards, emerging in a spiral of rising anger and, yes, fear as well. How dare he challenge her methods of self-preservation, her hard-won skill? Instinctively her fingers moved to the jewelled knife hilt on her belt.

Giseux's sparkling grey eyes honed in on her movement, his mouth twisting to a derogatory sneer. 'That knife is more a hindrance than a help; it can so easily be wrested from your hands and turned against you. You would be better off not having it at all.' The horse sidled beneath him; his big thigh muscles tensed as he maintained his upright position on the animal.

Hugh had given her the knife, before he went away. It was he who had taught her to use it properly, even though her brother could only guess at what she had experienced at the hands of her husband. She had told Hugh the barest details of her ordeal, not wanting to give voice to her time with Walter, not even with her brother. This knife, its heavy weight bumping against her hip, made her feel safe; now this man, this stranger, had the temerity to undermine its power!

'You have no idea of what you are talking about!' she flared up at him, long eyelashes fanning out around her blue eyes. 'You scarce know me, yet you criticise and condemn me! How dare you?'

In a single, graceful movement he slid down from the horse, from that treacherous animal that had refused to move faster than a snail for her, and stood before her, his angled face leaning down into hers. 'You're living in a dream world, thinking you can protect yourself with that blade.' He was so close that he stood within the folds of her skirts.

Instinctively, she backed away, throwing back the sides of her cloak as her fingers tightened around the hilt, sliding the knife from the leather scabbard. His arm flashed out, a lightning speed honed from years of fighting, muscular fingers upon hers, crushing, squeezing. An intense pain shot through her wrist, the knife slipping from her weakened grip. 'You're not being fair…' she gasped as it fell. Giseux's quicksilver reflex snared the blade as it flew downwards; in a trice, he turned the gleaming point, the blade a hairbreadth away from her frantically beating heart. For an endless moment they stood there, tense, taut, breathing rapidly, the moon highlighting the stillness of their bodies.

'See how easy it was?' His voice looped over her, dry, taunting. His hulking frame loomed so close that she caught the scent of him, a tantalising mix of spice and woodsmoke. A surge of adrenalin pulsed through her, exciting, wicked. She stepped backwards, appalled at the speed of the manoeuvre, appalled by his glittering proximity, then realised she could go no further, her heel kicking uncomfortably against the nubbled back of a trunk. Above them, an owl hooted, its call eerie within the confines of the trees.

'Give me my knife back!' Her voice, brittle, trembled

with confusion. Palms pressed against the immovable oak, her slender body felt exposed to him, vulnerable. 'I should have shot you when I had the chance!'

He laughed, a short bark of sound, teeth white in the shadowed tan of his face, flipping the knife back so that she could take the jewelled hilt. 'Death by crossbow might have been preferable to escorting you.'

Brianna glared at him, hostile, stabbing the blade back in its sheath. 'I'm not going back to Sefanoc with you,' she announced firmly. 'I'm carrying on to Winchester, whether you like it or not. You can't make me go back with you.'

Giseux's knee brushed against her leg; she flinched at the contact. His voice, when it came, was low, slipping velvet. 'I can make you do anything I want.' His eyes bored into hers, darkening gimlets of granite. 'Don't kid yourself that I, or any other man for that matter, could not…it's dangerous to think like that.'

'I've managed up to now,' she spat back weakly. 'And I'm still not going back with you.'

Giseux sighed. The woman was a complete fool. Of course he could make her return to Sefanoc—he could simply grab her spindly frame and dump her on his horse, kicking and screaming. Surely she realised that? He was twice the size of her, with muscle power to match. But he was awake now, and in no mood to wrangle any longer. Turning away, he walked over to his destrier, tightening the girth, before throwing himself up into the saddle. 'Mount up,' he ordered, kicking the shining stirrup free from his booted foot.

'Wh-what?' She stared up at him aghast. Vivid

images piled chaotically into her brain, images of herself tucked up comfortably in the arms of Giseux, her back against his chest, her arms cradled within his. No! She couldn't do it! 'I can't!'

'You seem to manage perfectly well when you stole my horse.' He stared down haughtily at her. Beneath him, his horse pawed the ground, dry leaves rustling against its hoof.

'I *borrowed* your horse,' she corrected him. 'Not that it helped much; he refused to move faster than an ambling walk.'

'He's trained only to respond to me,' he replied, disparagingly, holding out his hand towards her. 'Now, come on, mount up.'

This is wrong, she thought, as she grasped his hand and stuck her slender foot in the stirrup. A quivering coil of excitement licked along her veins as he hoisted her in front of him; she bounced up as if she weighed nothing. Her hips bumped back uncomfortably into the edge of the leather saddle; she scissored one leg over the horse's neck to ride astride. Leaning forwards, she grabbed a bunch of mane between her fists to maintain her balance.

'Lean back.' It was a command, not a request. His warm breath puffed over her veil; the material wafted against the nape of her neck making her shiver at the close contact. 'At the speed we'll be going, you'll fall off. Lean back.' His repeated order was terse, clipped.

I'm doing this for Hugh, she reminded herself over and over again as she moved gingerly against the solid wall of chest. Every nerve ending in her body sprang alive at the contact; beneath her layers of clothing, beneath the thick wool cloak, the gown of linen, she could feel his chest muscles ripple against her shoulder blades. The bunched muscle of his thighs pillowed her hips, rocking her intimately from side to side as the horse picked up speed. One arm snaked around her middle, the iron band yanking her more securely inwards as the horse kicked up clods of earth in its wake. She had never been this close to a man, this intimate, nay, not even with Walter; what she did now went against every promise she had made herself when she had left that horrible man. Against all inclination, she was thrown back into him, again and again. Brianna pressed her eyes together in shame, cheeks lit with flags of red.

The maid felt so fragile within his arms, her slim frame light against his chest, thought Giseux. Her appearance belied her inner strength, the innate courage that flowed within her. Like a delicate flower stem rocked by a fierce breeze, it would take a great deal to break her. He sensed she had come close that morning, that he had witnessed her teetering on the edge of total fear, of utter desolation. When those men had laid into her she had fought back like one possessed. Above the silken brush of her hair, his mouth tightened—no woman deserved such harsh treatment, whatever they had done, however they had behaved. Imperceptibly, his arms strengthened around her. Her shoulders rocked back into his chest; he grimaced as his body responded to the delicate press, the drifting lavender scent of her hair. He knew better than to become involved. Since that unspeakable time with Nadia, women, for him, had been reduced to a means of physical solace. He never asked their names in the darkness, never engaged in conversation. It suited him that way and, after what had happened, he preferred it. Without thinking, he rubbed at the aching muscle in his thigh, the single physical reminder of the woman he had loved in the East, the woman who had died trying to help him and his men. She had been on their side and had paid with her life for that loyalty. His wound was a small price in comparison, a continual ache eating into him, reminding him of his guilt, his culpability day after day. That, and the cavernous black void that was his heart.

Chapter Four

Once clear of the creaking depths of the forest and the maze of tracks within, the land rose in a series on undulating folds: gentle flat-topped plains, with pale tussocks of grass rippling violently in the wind, like hair under the water. The moon, its glowing orb travelling fast behind lacy wisps of cloud, bathed the landscape in a spectral light, accentuating the deep shadows, the brittle branches of a solitary hawthorn, contorted and bent over like an old man.

Giseux knew his location now, recognised the wide, open spaces of his childhood, or at least, his childhood before he had gone to the court of Queen Eleanor in Poitiers to train as a knight. In the forest, in the confusing bundle of trees and trackways, he had been reliant on the maid's direction, silently following her outstretched pointing arm, until the trees grew thin on the outer boundaries.

Touching his heels to the horse's flanks, he urged the animal up the steep sheep trail to gain the plateau above, his body leaning forwards with the altered gait. With the movement, Brianna shifted her position, arching her spine to break any contact with him. Giseux's mouth twisted into a grimace. The stubborn little chit was doing her utmost to make this journey as awkward as possible, acting as if he were inflicted with some horrible disease, not doing her a favour.

Gaining the top of the plateau, saddle creaking under the combined weight of both riders, Giseux kicked the horse swiftly to a gallop. Now she had no choice, she had to lean back into him or risk falling off. Winding one arm tight in front of her, he winched her into his chest, sensing every muscle in her body protesting with rigid, outraged hostility. Even through the layers of her clothes, the fragile bones of her rib cage pressed against his forearm, her heart fluttering chaotically against his wrist, a moth's wing of sensation. Despite her wilfulness towards him, she was afraid. The thought made him uncomfortable; she had no reason to be fearful of him.

The wind whipped around them as they rode, snaring Brianna's skirts, flattening them over Giseux's legs. It tore at her veil, sending the flimsy cloth flying across his face, in front of his eyes, blinding him. Hauling sharply on the reins, he clawed at the silk that filled his nose and covered his eyes, finally pulling it from his face and, in the same movement, tearing it from Brianna's head. The gold circlet spun out into the darkness, landing with a soft rustle in one of the tussocks of grass.

'My circlet!' she gasped in surprise. Before he had time to anticipate her movement, she slid haphazardly, chaotically, from the horse as it slowed to a trot, stumbling down on to the uneven ground, tipping forwards on her hands and knees. Momentarily winded, she sat back on her heels on the damp grass, casting her eyes about for the sparkle of circlet. A raft of weariness flooded over her, sapping her strength.

'Why didn't you wait?' Giseux shouted down at her, the fierce wind tugging at his words. 'I would have fetched your circlet.'

Brianna smoothed one hand over the wrinkled puddle of her skirts, pins and needles beginning to prickle in her foot as she remained in the kneeling position, sitting back on her calves. She felt safer on the ground. The prolonged nearness of his body, the strong warmth of his chest at her back, had made her leap from the saddle at the slightest excuse. She chewed at her lip, frowning; already she missed the close contact of his hard frame. The cold wind whipped at her cloak, flipping back the dark edges to reveal the shimmer of lining.

'We're wasting time.' Against the faded backdrop of the moon-soaked land, Giseux swung down from the horse, black surcoat glimmering with traces of silver flattened against his tall frame.

'You're the one who threw my veil away,' she chided, clambering to her feet, grimacing as the blood rushed back into her toes. She wiggled her foot, trying to reassemble her scattered thoughts. When was the last time she had *wanted* to be this close to a man?

'Only to prevent a more serious accident,' Giseux reminded her. He scooped up the white scrap of silk, the loop of gold, tucking them against his chest, behind the surcoat. 'I have them.'

Her mouth dropped open in surprise at his action and she held out her hand, skirts blowing out wildly behind her. The wind dragged at her hair, threatening to dislodge the silken bundle at the nape of her neck; hastily she lifted her fingers to push the pins back in. 'I'll have my veil now,' she demanded, attempting to retain a modicum of control in the situation.

Giseux shook his head as he paced back to the horse. 'Nay, it's too windy; the same thing could happen again.'

She opened her mouth to disagree once more, but her words were abruptly cut off as he seized her waist and threw her easily up into the saddle. 'You're delaying things by arguing,' he murmured, moving in behind her on the saddle. 'I thought you were desperate to see your brother!'

'I am,' she squeaked back, trying to wriggle her hips forwards, away from him.

'Then stop arguing with me, stop fighting me and let me take you there!' he rumbled back at her. 'And for God's sake, stop wriggling!'

The castle at Sambourne loomed impressively out of the wide river valley, old stones draped in a drifting mist. Holding a flaming torch aloft, a soldier stepped forwards from the archway of the gatehouse, taking hold of Giseux's bridle. He nodded, smiled, as he recognised the knight, standing aside to let them pass. After the flaring brightness of the torch, Brianna blinked rapidly in the darkness of the gatehouse, the horse's hooves clattering loudly in the confined space.

'My lady?' Giseux was already standing on the greasy cobbles of the inner bailey, holding one hand out to her. Her natural instinct, the *safer* instinct, was to refuse his help, to slide to the ground unaided. 'I…' She hesitated.

'Oh, come on,' he berated her impatiently, diamond eyes challenging. 'Accept my help for once; it would make your life much easier.'

She placed her hand in his, allowing her smaller fingers to be swallowed up by his burly grip as she swung her leg over. His other hand came around her waist, and, unbalanced, she fell against him, her cheek brushing fleetingly against his. A rush of awareness pulsed through her at the scrape of day-old beard against the soft swell of her cheek, the potent smell of him.

'Here.' Giseux dug her veil and circlet out from the depths of his surcoat and handed them to her.

Fingers trembling from the unexpected contact, she jammed the circlet on her head, securing the veil. 'Take me to Hugh, please.'

The gold band gleamed lopsidedly at him. His fingers propelled towards her head, rustling against the silk as he adjusted the circlet, setting it straight. Unprepared for his gesture, Brianna flinched backwards, eyes wild with alarm.

Giseux frowned. 'What's the matter with you?' Brianna's reaction had been exactly as if he had been going to hit her. 'You need not to be frightened of me.'

Oh, but I am, thought Brianna dully, as she dogged the substantial breadth of his back up the stone steps to the main doorway. *I am afraid...afraid of all men, and the things of which they are capable. That's why I hide myself away from them, shun all acts of kindness, recoil against any tenderness. What happened in the past could not, would not happen again.*

Giseux led her to Hugh's chamber, high in the north turret of the castle, up three steep flights of a spiral staircase. He pushed against a heavily planked wooden door, stepping aside to allow her to precede him. As she crossed the threshold, a solid wall of heat hit her in the face. At first, she could see nothing, only the glow of coals from a charcoal brazier in the corner, throwing their reddish light along the oak-panelled wall. She searched the gloom, saw the bed, found her brother.

His head was cushioned on an enormous linen pillow, his hair matted, stuck to his scalp. His face was chalk-white, apart from two spots of vivid colour on his cheekbones, the skin grown thin and gaunt. Blood-encrusted scabs flecked his dry, cracked lips; beads of shiny perspiration peppered his forehead. A linen nightshirt covered his frame, his forearms and wrists protruding from the too-short sleeves, stretched on the fur coverlet, palms facing upwards. Every now and again, a spate of shivering seemed to take hold of him, like some unknown presence shaking his body like one possessed.

'Oh, my God!' Shocked, Brianna's hands flew to her face. She spun around to Giseux, seeking some comfort, some reassurance from this man who she had known but a day. But his profile was grim, his bleak expression trained on Hugh. With a supreme effort, she forced her wooden limbs to walk over to the bed, to take her brother's hand. The slack muscles in his fingers curled loosely inwards. Panic threatened to bubble up within her—he could not die! She leaned closer to him, bending over his familiar face, hearing the faint trickle of breath emerge from his lips. Heat poured from him in rolling waves. Touching one hand to his forehead, her fingers sprang away, wet with sweat.

'It's far too hot in here!' Her hand jerked back from his scorching skin. 'No wonder he's burning up.' She sped to the window, hands fumbling with the iron latch that secured the wooden shutters, desperate to fill the room with fresh, cooling air. Giseux's hand came over hers, stilling her fingers, pressing her palm into the angular contours of the latch.

'Nay, the room needs to be hot. It sweats the fever out.'

Her jaw brushed inadvertently against his upper arm as it stretched over her shoulder, and for one brief, insane moment she longed to rest her head against that strong rope of muscle, to gain some comfort from it. The metallic scales of his armour had been cool against her flushed skin.

She pulled away, pulled her hand from beneath his, resentful of his nearness, of his intrusion into this reunion with her brother. 'How do you know?' she demanded, her voice churlish.

'It's a fever common to Crusaders, common to the Orient,' Giseux replied patiently, moving over to Hugh. 'I've seen it many times. Keep him warm, pile the covers high. He'll try to throw them off, but you must keep putting them back.' He poured a cup of amber liquid from an earthenware jug sitting on a three-legged table beside the bed. Perching alongside Hugh on the side of the bed, he slipped one arm gently behind his neck, lifting his lolling head. Brianna watched in relief as Hugh, his eyes firmly closed, swallowed some of the liquid, before Giseux laid him back down again. The simple act of kindness was so unexpected, so unusual in this arrogant man of war, that she caught herself staring in surprise.

'What are you giving him?' An enticing, unusual smell filled the room.

Sparkling grey eyes moved over her. 'Spices from the Orient mixed in with hot water and honey,' he explained. 'The Turkish people use it to quell their fevers.'

Brianna moved to stand before him, the front panel of her skirt almost touching his knees. 'I can look after him now,' she said. One loop of golden-red hair had come adrift, curling down over her shoulder, softly gleaming in the ambient light.

'Good,' Giseux replied. He ran an impatient finger around the inside of the neck of his chainmail tunic. He'd worn his armour for so long that the metal was beginning to irritate his skin. 'For I intend to sleep now, and sleep for a long time. There's a bed made up for you, there, if you wish to sleep.' He indicated a low pallet against one wall of the room, made up with fresh linens.

'Thank you.' She stared at the floor, unsure, or unwilling, to say the words that must be said. 'And thank you for coming to fetch me. I'm sorry…' She wanted to apologise for delaying them, for attacking him when she thought he was another of Count John's men, coming to persecute her once more.

He shook his head, his mouth set in a taut line. 'Forget it,' he replied tersely. 'It's in the past.' He stood up suddenly from the bed, running one hand through his hair, tousling the pale brown strands. 'It's enough that you are here and caring for Hugh.'

'Have you seen him yet?' Jocelin, Earl of Sambourne, bounded up the steps to the high dais to join his wife for breakfast. Leaning down over the bright, golden head, he planted a light kiss on his wife's cheek before throwing himself into the carved oak chair next to her. At nearly fifty winters, his lean, fit body seemed to contain an abundance of energy, evidenced in the graceful, athletic way that he moved, the keen sparkle in his dove-grey eyes.

'He was asleep when I looked in on him earlier,' Lady Mary replied. Next to her husband, she appeared delicate, willowy, her pale skin forming a dramatic contrast to his ruddy cheeks. She nibbled daintily on a bread roll. 'He seemed completely exhausted.'

'I'm not surprised, riding through the night! Can't

understand why he didn't wait till daylight. Hugh wouldn't have deteriorated that quickly.' Jocelin speared a slice of roast chicken with his eating knife, placing it on his pewter plate with a freshly baked bread roll. The great hall was quiet at this time of the morning; the peasants who worked on the estate had eaten their food at a much earlier hour, whilst it was still dark. A few servants moved about in the lower part of the hall, collecting dirty dishes and sweeping the crumbs from the earlier breakfasts on to the floor.

'He thought Hugh was about to die, Jocelin.' Lady Mary laid a hand on her husband's arm, the gemstone in her ring sparkling in a shaft of light pouring down from the upper windows. 'It was vital that he brought the maid back as soon as possible. Oh, here he is now!' She patted her plaited, coiled hair and rose to greet her son.

Giseux stepped through the curtained doorway, pausing for a moment on the threshold before climbing the steps to the top table. He had only seen his parents' home on occasional visits since he'd left for the French court over ten years ago. Vast, elaborate tapestries hung over the grey-stone walls, their colours vivid, lending a warmth and brightness to the high-ceilinged chamber. Shields interspersed the tapestries, carrying various coats-of-arms, each one different for every man in the family, so they could be easily identified in battle.

'Oh, my son!' His mother forged a nimble path between the chairs that ranked along the top table, reaching up to clasp him. 'Now I can greet you properly!' She had barely seen him when he had returned with Hugh, carrying the barely conscious knight up to bed, before leaving for Sefanoc.

'Let me look at you.' Linking her hands into her son's, she took a step back, running her gaze from head to toe, noting the leanness of his jaw, the ranginess of his frame. There was something else that had changed, something she couldn't as yet identify. A certain look, a fleeting shadow about the eyes, maybe? 'You haven't been eating enough!' she chided him, flapping her hands, scolding lightly. 'Come and sit here! I'll move along.'

'I was going to check on Hugh.'

His mother shook her head. 'No need. I looked in on him as I came down this morning. He's sleeping peacefully; his breathing seems much easier.'

'And...his sister?'

Lady Mary arched one fair eyebrow at her son. 'Why, she's sleeping too! In her clothes, poor girl. I should have thought to put a nightgown out for her.'

'I doubt she would have minded,' Giseux murmured. Lady Brianna seemed eminently capable of dealing with the most demanding of situations; he doubted the lack of a nightgown would concern her one jot.

His mother indicated that he should sit in her seat and shifted her plate along as Giseux threw his bulky frame into the chair, turning to shake his father's hand.

'Good to see you, my son!' his father boomed, smiling. 'It's been a long time.'

'Aye, it has,' Giseux acknowledged. A servant struggled up to the table with a unwieldy cauldron of steaming porridge. His stomach growled as he watched his mother ladle a bowl out for him, pouring on rich cream and drizzling it with honey for sweetness. 'Thank you.' He took the bowl from his mother, digging his spoon into the cooked oats.

Jocelin leaned forwards, eyes ablaze with curiosity, placing his elbows on the smooth white tablecloth. 'You know I'm eager to hear all the details of this latest crusade—' he stopped suddenly as he caught his wife's frown, unseen by their son '—but of course it can wait until you are fully rested,' he finished. Lady Mary smiled at him.

Giseux swallowed a mouthful of porridge. Lord, but it tasted good. 'There's nothing to say, Father. Nothing that you don't already know, anyway. It was moderately successful; Saladin has granted Christians access to Jerusalem.' His words were dull, toneless.

'You know that King Richard was captured on his way back to England?'

Giseux nodded. 'The German Emperor has demanded a huge ransom for him; it will take months to raise the money.'

'Queen Eleanor is keen for you to travel out there immediately, to see if you can negotiate an earlier release.' Jocelin threw his son a tepid smile, a myriad of lines creasing up at the corner of each eye. 'I know it's a lot for her to ask, especially as you've only just returned…'

'That woman demands too much of our son!' Lady Mary blurted out.

'She can ask whatever she likes of her knights,'

Giseux replied evenly. 'She is the Queen of England and in charge whilst Richard is held captive.'

'You can't go away again…look at you, you're exhausted!'

Giseux looked into the jewelled green depths of his mother's eyes, bright with love for him. 'I already had the Queen's orders, but I won't go immediately; there's something else I must do first.'

'But your duty is to the King, Giseux.' Jocelin frowned, rubbing fractiously at an old wine stain on the linen tablecloth. And to Queen Eleanor, his mother. 'It has been since the day you left for Poitiers to train as one of his knights. What could possibly be more important than travelling out to Germany?'

'It shouldn't take too long,' Giseux murmured. 'I will be on the road to the Continent before you know it.'

'Just make sure it doesn't,' Jocelin replied tersely, 'otherwise I'll have the wrath of Queen Eleanor on my back.'

His mother touched Giseux's forearm where it rested on the table. 'We had a letter…from your brother, William. He's back in Poitiers now.' Her voice trailed off miserably; she picked at a loose thread on the front of her gown.

'What does he have to say for himself?' Giseux asked slowly, carefully. He knew what the letter was about.

'He told us about the ambush, my son,' Jocelin chipped in. 'How some of your men were killed. I'm so sorry.' His father's voice, though gruff, was sympathetic.

'Did he say how it happened?' A wave of guilt sluiced through Giseux; he drank from his cup of mead, trying to cleanse the sour taste in his mouth.

'Nay, he didn't go into details. He said that you were injured, that you were unlucky.

'Bad luck had nothing to do with it.' He scraped out the last of his porridge, flung the spoon back in the empty bowl with a clatter. 'I should have died with those men; it was all my fault.' He pushed his chair back jerkily, a blank, frozen look in his eyes. 'Excuse me. I must check on Hugh.'

Giseux stood outside Hugh's chamber door, hesitating. Unwanted memories lurched into his brain and he squeezed his eyes shut, willing them to vanish, to disappear. Why, oh, why had William written that letter, especially for his mother's eyes to see? It would make life easier if nobody knew, make it easier for him to forget. But as the chamber door clicked inwards into the fuggy heat of illness, the screams of his men echoed in his ears and the vivid images of Nadia, sprawled against him as he cradled her dying body, burnt into his brain.

Trickles of sunlight crept through the gaps in the wooden shutters. His eyes flew to the pallet in the corner. Empty, its linens crisp and pristine. Scarlet cloak bundled heavily around her, Brianna lay on the bed, sprawled alongside her brother, curled into him. Dark lashes spiked downwards, spread over her rosy, flushed cheeks, her lips parted slightly. At least she had taken off her muddy boots; the green wool of her gown had bunched up around her calves, revealing slender legs and fine ankles encased in white-silk stockings. Her feet were small, narrow, the insteps high and arched. Something clawed at him, tore at his very innards, primal, savage; he clenched his teeth at the unwanted surge of desire spiralling into his body.

He knew in that moment he should leave. But the intriguing curve of her slender frame, her unshod feet, the seductive tilt of her hip, lured him towards the bed. In sleep the stubborn expression had slipped from her face, her mouth tilted upwards in a sweet smile, enchanting. His heart knocked heavily in his chest; he frowned at the unfamiliar sensation. Surely he was stronger than this in the face of temptation? And the chit that lay below him was hardly tempting! Aye, she had a certain beauty, but she had lied to him, shot at him and openly defied his orders, riding off into the night without his protection. She was wilful, headstrong and a nightmare to deal with. What was his body thinking? He'd been too long without a whore, that was the problem, too damned long.

He needed to move her away from her brother, though. She lay too close to him, breathing the same air as him, breathing in his sickness. For a moment he considered shaking her awake, forcing her to walk the few steps to the pallet, but one look at the deep hollows beneath her eyes made him reassess his decision. Brianna was exhausted. Wedging his hands beneath her, beneath the bulk of clothes that she wore, he lifted her supple weight with ease, shifting one hand around to support her upper back and one hand around her hips as he braced her against his chest. She mumbled softly with the movement, her head lolling into his shoulder; his heart kicked up a beat. The pure, fresh scent of lavender lifted from her heated skin, the spun sunshine of her flaming hair. Turning to the low bed in the corner, he bent over, kneeling on the elm floorboards to place her carefully, but speedily, on the bed. The thin, straw-filled pillow rustled as she moved her head uneasily, strands of brilliant amber snagging on the fine linen pillowcase. Her cheeks were bright red; without waking, her fingers tugged fitfully at the neck of her cloak, the scarlet colour of her material vying with the colour of her face. She was far too hot.

His hands trembled as he fumbled with the cord securing her cloak; he cursed the unfamiliar fastening. Two metal bosses, shaped like flowers, were attached to either side of the cloak, a cord passing through metal rings at the back. But where was the knot? He was damned if he could see it! His fingers felt too big, too ungainly to be performing such a fiddling maidservant's task.

'What in Heaven's name do you think you're doing?' A pair of azure eyes pierced into him, outraged, annoyed. Brianna slapped his hand away, pushing herself upwards sharply, brain still fuddled with sleep. 'How dare you?' She brushed a wayward strand of hair away from her cheek.

Giseux sprang to his feet, moving away to the middle of the room, scowling. 'You fell asleep with your cloak on,' he explained gruffly. 'The chamber is boiling; I thought to remove it.'

'You had no right,' she flung at him, voice quavering at the violation. 'No right at all.' She swung her stocking-covered feet to the floor, hugging her arms about her body, defensive, wary.

Silver-grey eyes assessed her. 'I was only removing your cloak, Brianna, nothing else.' By God, the way she was reacting it was as if he had been about to remove all her clothes!

'And why am I here, on this bed? Did I move myself, or—' she glanced at him suspiciously '—did you move me?'

The little chit had the temerity to speak to him as if he were a stripling! 'Listen, my lady,' he growled down at her, 'I was doing you a favour. Your brother's burning up with a fever; lying next to him as you were, there's a good chance you could catch his illness.'

'That's for me to decide, not you.'

'You were asleep.'

'You should have woken me up. I don't like the thought of you carrying me when…when I'm asleep.' Brianna flushed, a vivid image of the two of them together hurtling into her mind. She hated the thought of being vulnerable, exposed to this man, to any man. Heat pulsed through her limbs; she tugged irritably at the fastening of her cloak, releasing the strings. The enveloping material fell back, folds gathering on the bed behind her.

Without his armour, he seemed bigger, she thought suddenly. His intimidating presence filled the room, vital, powerful, his arms crossed high over the blue wool of his tunic. Long, muscular legs were encased in fustian leggings, cross-gartered with leather over the calves, before they disappeared into his stout leather boots.

'Go away. I can take care of Hugh.' Her voice was curt, snappish. She concentrated on tracing the whorls of a huge knot in the polished wooden floorboards, willing him to go, wanting to hear the door click behind him.

'Do you speak to all men in this manner, or have you singled me out for special treatment?' Giseux drawled. If anything, he had moved closer.

'I speak to all men in the same manner, if I have to speak to them at all.'

The hard iron of his iridescent eyes trailed over her forlorn figure. 'What happened to you, Brianna? What happened to you to make you like this, shunning all masculine contact? You assume all men are the same, that we're all bad.'

A rush of tears filled her eyes at the unforeseen sympathy in his tone. She drew a deep, raggedy breath, fingers digging into the piled softness of her cloak at her side, winding the fastening cord around her middle finger.

'I don't…' But even as the words of protest emerged, she knew she lied. She tried again. 'Hugh is a man…I don't think he's bad.'

Giseux laughed drily. 'Hugh is your brother, Brianna. That's a totally different thing. Are you telling me that he's the only man you would trust? What about romance, love, a husband?

'I've already had a husband,' she explained, turning her huge, limpid eyes upon him. 'And believe me, it's an experience I have no wish to repeat.'

Chapter Five

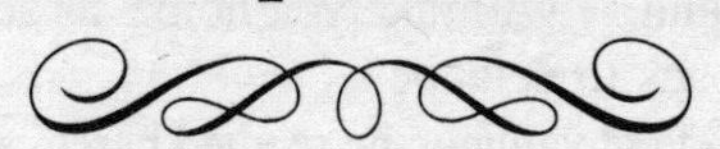

Brianna scowled at the door as it closed with a sharp click behind Giseux. Since when had she started blurting out her intimate secrets? Giseux's questioning had torn a strip away from her tough outer skin, revealing a piece of herself that she had no wish to show. But he had seen it all, seen into the very being of her with the incisive intelligence of his gunmetal eyes. Being so close to a man was a singular experience for her, especially one as physically attractive as Giseux. His powerful presence unnerved her, dominated her, sending her thoughts along muddled, unexpected routes, making every nerve ending in her body dance with… Was it pleasure?

'Brianna?' A husk of a whisper penetrated the silence.

Heart lifting, she whipped around. 'Hugh?' She flew to the bed, to her brother's side. Hugh's eyes were open, red-rimmed, bloodshot, but, aye, he was awake.

'Hugh! Thank God!' Brianna gathered his hands in hers, grasping his hot, clammy fingers. She smoothed back his tousled auburn hair, damp with sweat, leaning down to hug him.

'I knew Giseux would find you,' Hugh spoke slowly, as if having difficulty finding the words. 'I told him it was important.'

'I came as fast as I could,' she murmured, thinking of Giseux's stubborn horse refusing to budge beneath her command. 'I will take you home, as soon as you feel able, back to Sefanoc.'

Hugh nodded vaguely; he seemed barely able to hear her words. His fingers fretted at her sleeve, clutching at the threadbare material. 'Brianna, there's something you must do for me. I don't know how much longer I have…' His blue eyes, a perfect match to her own, constantly shifted, roved about the chamber, as if unable to focus on any one thing.

'Shh!' Brianna interrupted him, placing a finger to his lips. 'I forbid you to talk like this. You will recover.'

Hugh shook his head against the pillow, the pulse in his throat beating rapidly, too fast. 'I might not.'

'What do you want me to do?'

'It's a lot to ask, Brianna. I was going to ask Lord Giseux for his help once more—'

'No!' she replied a little too vehemently. 'Whatever it is, Hugh, I am sure I can perform the task quite adequately on my own.'

'He's a good man, Brianna. He brought me back to England, but we only knew each other by sight from the crusade. I scarcely know him. While we waited on the beach for the ships, he offered to bring me home when he realised how close his parents' estates were to Sefanoc.'

'It was good of him to come and fetch me then.' A wave of guilt passed over Brianna as she recalled her churlish behaviour towards Giseux. 'Even so, I am used to doing things on my own now… You've been away a long time.'

Hugh squeezed her hand; she winced at the tightness of his fingers. 'You always were so independent. Still the same Brianna.' A faint smile stretched painfully at his chapped lips.

She caught the criticism in his tone and tried to pull her hand out of his sweaty grasp. In his long absence, she had forgotten how Hugh could be—how he attempted, after the death of their parents, to wield his sibling power, expecting her to do his bidding, to follow his orders. He had often remonstrated with her over her wayward behaviour, but gently, so she had never paid much heed to his concerns, but now, now he seemed different.

Held fast within his grip, Hugh jogged her hand against the bedcovers, agitated, bringing her attention back to him.' Listen to me, Brianna, this is important. Before I left for the Crusades, there was a maid, her name was…is…Matilda. We were in love; unfortunately, her father did not approve of the liaison.' A derisive sneer pulled at Hugh's mouth. 'He had another richer, more powerful husband in mind. We had to meet in secret.' He closed his eyes for a moment, sapped by the amount of energy needed merely to speak.

Hugh had been in love? Surprise bolted through her—why had Hugh never told her of this? As children, they had been close, sharing everything, but, with the loss of their parents, with Hugh taking on the heavy responsibilities of Sefanoc, her brother had changed, becoming more distant, detached. Most of the time, he had paid little heed to her daily activities, and she missed the intimate closeness of their earlier days. Now, the character elements she disliked the most from that time after their parents had died seemed exacerbated in illness: the arrogance, the high-handedness. Reaching down, she retrieved a linen washcloth from a bowl of water on the floor. The sopping material trickled water over her wrists as she wrung it out, then placed it on her brother's burning forehead. He was so ill, it was bound to make him behave differently; soon he would be back to his old self.

'Ah!' He made a small sound of appreciation. 'I'm sorry, Brianna, I know you are shocked, but there's more. Matilda had a child, Brianna, a boy…my son.'

'Hugh…' Stunned by the revelation, Brianna stumbled to speak. 'Hugh…why did you never tell me?'

'The child was born just before I left on the crusade…he was barely a few weeks old. Brianna, I'm sorry, I believed that the fewer people who knew about Matilda, the less danger there would be…for them, and for you.' With supreme effort, he forced himself to lift off the pillow, one elbow supporting his weak, ravaged frame. A white crusty film covered his lips, his red-rimmed eyes running over her. 'Find them, Brianna, bring them to me so we can be married, so I can make the boy legally mine in the eyes of this country.'

'The boy will be your heir.'

Hugh sagged back against the pillow. 'Sefanoc is mine, Brianna. I want it to stay that way.'

His words stung her and she bit her lip, trying to ignore the pang of hurt that crawled in her chest. *Sefanoc is mine, too,* she thought. *And I have worked, and worked, and fought to keep it safe for you.*

Hugh's eyelids, thin and papery, fluttered down over his eyes. 'I am so tired, Brianna, so tired. I want you to promise me, promise me now, that you will fetch Matilda, and the boy. Before I die.'

Her hands shook slightly as she bent to place the washcloth back in the bowl, folding it carefully over the earthenware lip. 'You're not going to die, Hugh. I'll make sure of it.'

His eyes sprung open, intent on her face. 'Promise me, Brianna.'

'I promise.' She chewed her lip doubtfully at the wildness in his eyes, the sweat beading on his forehead. 'But I don't want to leave you like this. I'll take you back to Sefanoc—Alys and I will take care of you.' Her brain forged ahead, making plans; her brother was home, and alive, and that was all that mattered. She sprang from the bed, catching up her cloak from where it lay at the foot of the pallet. 'I must find Giseux's parents, talk to them about a litter to carry you home.'

He shook his head violently against the pillow. 'Nay, Brianna, 'tis imperative that you fetch Matilda. I am in good hands here. You must go.'

A pair of silver eyes flashed through her mind. They couldn't stay here, she couldn't bear to beholden to anyone; this family had already done enough for both of them. Hugh was simply not thinking straight. She would take him back to Sefanoc, first, and then continue on her journey to find Matilda.

'Brianna, there's one thing you must know. And although it's been a long time since your marriage ended, you may still be affected by what I have to tell you. Matilda's father is Walter of Brinslow.'

The cloak to the floor in a heap.

A bitter north-east wind stung Brianna's skin as she flew down the steps, out of the castle. She walked quickly, purposefully, as if she knew her direction, but in reality her mind filled again and again with the details of what her brother had told her, her eyes unseeing, oblivious to her surroundings. A door in the thick stone wall that circled the inner bailey presented itself; she twisted the heavy round handle and pushed through into some gardens. A blackbird, startled by her sudden entrance, squawked away in panic, flying low under a holly hedge, sharp leaves glossy. She pressed the door shut, leaning for a moment against the wooden planks, heart racing. How could this be happening to her? Hugh had placed her in an impossible situation, asking her to find his love, the daughter of the man who had made her own life a living hell.

Voices rose up from the inner bailey; she spun her gaze sharply around her surroundings for the first time—she wanted to be alone. The gardens had been set out formally, a row of clipped holly trees lining the uneven flagstone path that ran down the centre of two enormous rose beds. At the far end, the shining curve of a river was bounded by drooping willows, their naked branches sweeping the smooth surface of the water, trailing like hair. Brianna spied a bank of snowdrops alongside the river, white heads nodding in the light shade of a spindly hawthorn hedge. She headed for the drift of white, seeking sanctuary, some time to think.

'She looks like she has the weight of the world on her shoulders,' Lady Mary remarked as she followed the girl's progress from the vantage point of her solar, three floors up in the west tower. Giseux moved to stand behind his mother, pinning his eyes on the solitary figure.

'No doubt,' he responded drily. 'She certainly goes out of her way to attract trouble.'

'She didn't ask for her brother to become ill, Giseux.' His mother's green eyes flashed a reprimand. 'That was pure bad luck.'

Giseux rested one hip on the high stone windowsill, crossing his arms over his chest, the blue wool of his tunic pulling taut across his shoulders. 'Aye, you're right. But she's so stubborn, insisting that she does everything, and I mean everything, for herself.'

'She has such a sweet face.' Lady Mary smiled at her son. 'I'm sure she has her reasons for behaving as she does.'

Giseux raised his eyebrows, idly tracking Brianna's progress, her determined gait across the gardens.

'You're too forgiving, Mother. I've only known the chit one day and that has been long enough.'

'What has she ever done to you?' Lady Mary moved away from the chilly draught sneaking through the window and resumed her seat in the chair by the crackling fire. Picking up her needle, she selected a length of blue tapestry wool from the willow basket at her side, scrunching up her eyes to thread one end through the tiny eye of the white-bone needle.

Giseux watched his mother perform the delicate manoeuvre with practised skill before she leaned over the large tapestry frame set up before her and began to sew. 'She stole my horse.'

His mother's needle paused halfway into the tiny-holed canvas. 'I beg your pardon?' Her fair head turned back to Giseux, eyebrows raised in question.

'She stole my horse, and that was after she shot at me.'

Lady Mary's merry laughter rang out across the solar. 'Oh, Giseux, that is so funny! When I think of your reputation, your prowess on the battlefield, your years of training. She dared to shoot at you! She certainly has courage, that maid.' His mother's voice contained a note of admiration.

'Maybe, or stupidity.' Giseux scanned the gardens once more, searching for the diminutive figure in the thin green gown. Where had she vanished to?

'I noticed she wasn't wearing a cloak and it's freezing out there. Would you take her one of mine?' Lady Mary asked softly as she took one careful stitch, then another. Was it wishful thinking, or did she imagine the hard, intractable lines on her son's face softening when he spoke of the girl, despite his derogatory words?

Shoving one big shoulder against the stone wall, Giseux propelled himself away from the window. 'If I didn't know you better, Mother, I'd say you were trying to send me after Lady Brianna on false pretences.'

'Would I do such a thing?' Lady Mary drove her needle in and out of the canvas to secure the thread, a teasing smile tilting her lips.

Giseux grinned. In truth, he found himself wondering what had sent Brianna speeding off in the direction of the river. Hefting the weighty velvet of his mother's cloak from the oak coffer beside the fireplace, he left.

Lady Mary's fingers touched her needle as if to start work once more, but seemed to change her mind, moving across to the window to watch her son stride out into the cool morning. A small smile played about her lips.

A narrow path led up the bank through a gap in the hawthorn hedge; Brianna pushed through, twigs snagging at her veil, catching at the fragile white silk. The sound of the river was louder here, closer, the repetitive burbling soothing her frayed nerves, her troubled thoughts. Lifting her head, she gasped. A glade of trees spread out before her on a flat piece of river bank, and, beneath the light shade of the trees, vast tracts of snowdrops. Their inverted heart-shaped heads trembled in the breeze, a dab of brilliant green centred between each snow-white set of petals. A lopsided bench, constructed from rough-hewn pieces of timber on to which the bark still clung, nestled beneath a vigorous ash, brilliant orange fungus sprouting out from one of the rotting supports. She would pick a bunch of these beautiful flowers for Hugh and carry them back to his festering sickroom, but now she headed for the bench and sat down, turning her pale, tear-streaked face up towards the faint sunlight filtering through the fretwork of bare branches.

Brianna relaxed, her spine slumping against the ridged trunk behind, the air in her lungs expelling in one long, tight breath. The muscles in her body ached, her head felt sore, braids pulling too tightly against her temples. She yearned to release them, to savour the cold pulse of air against her scalp. Her eyes popped open. She was alone, definitely; all she could hear was the incessant gurgling of shallow water looping, plashing over the stones in the river and the melodic, liquid trills of a solitary blackbird. Casting aside her circlet and veil, placing them on the moss-covered bench, she reached up the back of her head, releasing the pins that secured her hair. She caught the curling ends as they fell forwards over her shoulders, unwrapping the leather lace that tied each red-gold braid. Splaying her fingers through the dark amber tendrils, the soft air sifted against her head, touched her scalp with a sweet, blissful sensation. Again and again she raised the tresses upwards, savouring the wonderful free sensation of her hair released. The waterfall of bright copper fell forwards over her shoulders, tumbling into a chaotic puddle on her lap. Leaning back against the supporting trunk of the ash once more, she closed her eyes, the weight of her worries slipping away as she relished the sheer, intense pleasure of the moment.

At the entrance to the glade, Giseux stopped, senses knocked to heightened consciousness as he caught sight of her, sitting alone in the forest glade like an angel. Pale, exquisite face tipped up to the light. Eyes closed, the corners of her shell-pink lips pitched upwards, the briefest hint of a smile. And her hair! A magnificent river of liquid amber spilling forwards over her shoulders, loose and lush, shimmering down to her lap. Fire burst in his belly, an incessant, ravening need to touch, to plunge his calloused hands into that bundle of shining beauty, to hold that silken abundance against his skin. Fighting to damp down the slow, coiling build in his loins, he cursed his unwanted desire.

He had read the bleakness in her eyes, the hollowness of her soul. Like a fragile flower underfoot, her spirit had been crushed, her character altered in such a way as to make her fear all men. She had hinted that her marriage had not been a pleasant experience; no doubt the reason why she pushed him away at every single opportunity, spurned all his efforts to help, believing in her own independence, her own puny strength. An overriding sense of protection swept over him, forceful, clamorous, knocking beneath his ribs, but who was he to offer help, shield her from harm, when his own men had fallen under his command? And Nadia, the woman he had loved, had died in his arms.

He watched her for a long time, until the clouds shifted above, obscuring the sun, and he saw her shiver in the cooling breeze. Fallen leaves, brittle, scuttled along the ground in rustling flurries, obscuring the sound of his footsteps. His leather boots trampled over the nodding snowdrops as he made his way towards her. 'My mother thought you might be cold,' he announced, a hoarse edge to his voice.

Brianna jolted upright, eyes flying open, the cerulean blue of her eyes searching out the source of his voice in confusion. A look of sheer horror spread across her face as she clawed at her hair, trying to hide it with her hands, embarrassed by her unbound locks. A delicate flush spread across her cheeks.

'Oh, I…' Baffled by his appearance, she jumped up, agitated, struggling to find the words to explain her existence in the glade.

Up close, her small, tip-tilted nose, her cheeks, held a smattering of light brown freckles across the pearly sheen of her skin, evidence of much time spent outdoors. Giseux cleared his throat, the bright banner of her hair drawing his velvet gaze. 'Here, my mother asked me to bring you this.' He lifted the cloak by way of explanation.

'How did she…you…know I was here?' The breeze picked up the trailing ends of her hair, made them dance around her, bronze threads glittering in the drifting sunlight.

'We watched you from my mother's chambers.' His straight hair kicked up at the front, feathery strands ruffled by the breeze, lending his face a less harsh, boyish air. Shafts of sunlight daubed the strands of light brown with patches of gold.

The red blotches deepened on her cheeks; she shifted

uneasily. 'I thought I was alone.' She tugged down at the drifting locks of hair, trying to control its wanton mass.

'I can see that.' Fledgling desire pulsed through his heart.

She turned away from the jagged intensity of his eyes, confused by what she saw within those granite depths. 'I… We can't stay here. I want to go home, I want to take Hugh home. Today, if possible.'

Her hair fell past the gentle curve of her hips, he noted, tracing the curling ends. 'It's not possible.' The flint edge of his voice cut into her.

Filling her lungs with the fresh morning air, she battled for composure, for balance. 'Why ever not?' she challenged. 'Hugh seemed much better this morning, certainly recovered enough to travel in a litter back to Sefanoc.' Off to her left, tips of willow fronds danced on the surface of the river, causing the water to eddy and swirl.

'I've seen this illness before, many times. It's quite common to experience periods of complete lucidity in between the fevers, the delirium.'

Her shoulders sagged. For one single, insane moment, Giseux wanted to wrap his arms about her, this wild, ferocious creature, and pull her into him, comfort her.

'Why must you continually thwart me?' Her voice rose in a half-sob.

'Believe me, I don't do it deliberately.' He caught the glint of tears in her eyes and grimaced. 'I'm telling you the truth, Brianna. Your brother is not well enough to travel anywhere, least of all Sefanoc.'

'What do you mean, 'least of all, Sefanoc'?

He raised brown eyebrows, a shade darker than his hair. 'With the greatest respect, my lady, Sefanoc is hardly the place for an invalid to recover...'

'For what reason?' she demanded. Her hands balled into fists at her sides.

Giseux recalled the pitiful fire in the great hall at Sefanoc, the platter of stale bread, the rancid cheese. 'Forgive me, but your home is damp and cold, you have hardly any food—how in Heaven's name can you care for an invalid? How would you cope?'

Her eyes darkened, an intense, vivid blue. He thought he would drown in those fathomless pools of light. 'I'll cope as I've always done, my lord, even if I have to go without.' Her voice rose, a treacherous wobble.

'Seems as though you have gone without for a long time,' he replied quietly.

Her eyes widened, startled by the tenderness of his speech. Tears threatened to bubble up; she blinked rapidly to clear her blurring vision.

'I have to go,' Brianna said, aghast at her reaction to him, to the kindness in his voice. Surging forwards, blinded by unshed tears, she knocked inadvertantly against Giseux's side as she headed for the gap in the hedge. Tanned, square-cut fingers tangled in the flying ends of her hair, stopping her in her tracks, wrapping the wayward length around his hand, again and again, drawing her back slowly.

'Stay,' he murmured.

About to protest, her mouth snapped shut, bewildered, her whole body reverberating under the seductive note of his voice, the throaty tones pulsing shudders of delight down her spine. His breath fanned the top of her head; in a quicksilver shiver of shock, she realised she was very, very close to him. 'Stay.' Giseux's voice was low, deep, laced with iron-clad arousal.

His fingers buried into the silky strands of her hair, cradling the back of her head as she tilted her face up to him, searching his expression for some meaning to his actions. The tips of his fingers were warm against her scalp, creating a heady, unstable feeling fluttering straight to her heart.

He dipped his head, the unworn cloak pooling at his feet.

She had a fleeting impression of silvery eyes, burning with dangerous passion, looming close. 'I…?' Brianna breathed, unsure, unknowing, her hands fluttering up, hesitantly, instinctively beginning the movement to push him away. The lean planes of his face angled near, his mouth seeking hers. As her tentative fingers sketched over his chest, his shoulders, her own heart leapt in joy, bumping against her ribs in exhilaration, with the sudden realisation that within the circle of his arms, she was not afraid.

The cool, firm curve of his mouth brushed hers, lightly. At the butterfly touch, she wanted to scream with joy at the sheer, unadulterated pleasure of it. Hunger exploded within her, a relentless craving, insistent, relentless, a yearning she had never before experienced, an aching need…for what? She didn't want to ask, to question these strange fires that consumed her body, the breath punching from her lungs in sharp little bursts, the fiery, melting chaos: all was so new to her.

And then it was over.

Giseux broke away, expression glowering, eyes shimmering with unresolved desire. Breathing heavily, he raked one hand through his hair, sending the blond-tipped strands awry. Above them, a pair of buzzards began to circle upwards in the rising warm air; their plaintive calls rent the stiff breeze.

'I'm sorry,' he muttered. 'That was unforgivable.'

No, she wanted to scream at him and shout, pound her fists against his chest and beg him to continue. Giseux had come closer to her than any man had ever done; how could she tell him that the feel of his lips against her own had been one of the most exquisite sensations her body had ever experienced?

Brianna threw him a tremulous smile, wrapping her arms self-consciously across her chest, trembling, burning from the fire of his kiss. She began to walk towards the castle, the overlong hem dragging through the snowdrops. Stepping up to the gap in the hedge, she paused. Giseux stood in the centre of the glade, the brooding haunt of his eyes tracking her movement, his face a dark scowl.

'I forgive you,' she said. But she wondered if he had heard her.

Chapter Six

'Come, child, come and sit by me. I'm so sorry I haven't had a chance to meet you yet.' Lady Mary rose elegantly from the top table as Brianna stepped into the great hall. Giseux's mother was a beauty: tall, willowy figure encased in a sumptuous gown of crushed pale pink velvet, extravagant sleeves almost sweeping the ground. Her white-blond hair was arranged into numerous plaits, pinned in an elaborate style beneath the shimmer of a cream silk veil, topped with a silver circlet. In the strong light of the sun pouring through the south-facing windows she seemed to glisten with celestial light.

'You didn't expect me to arrive in the middle of the night.' Brianna smiled, the hem of her pale green gown dragging across the cold flagstones as she approached Lady Mary. After she had fled the wooded glade, lips burning with the imprint of Giseux's kiss, she had bolted to the relative safety of Hugh's chamber. Thankfully, he had been sleeping peacefully, and, perched on the low stool beside his bed, she had managed to bundle her hair into some semblance of order. She had sat beside him, unsure what to do. Her fingers fluttered to her bruised lips as her heart flipped in terror at the thought of meeting Walter again. When a servant appeared at the door carrying her circlet and veil, and informing her that Lady Mary wished Briannna to join her for the midday meal, she welcomed the distraction from her brooding, fearful thoughts.

'I'm not sure where the men are,' Lady Mary said brightly, the movement of her regal head poised and delicate, bird-like. 'Jocelin will join us soon, and Giseux… He was with you, wasn't he?'

Brianna blushed, chewing doubtfully on her bottom lip and reddening the tender skin as she took her place beside the older woman. 'Aye, he brought me your cloak. Thank you.'

'It's my pleasure.' Lady Mary dipped her head. 'When I saw you dashing out into the cold…in only a gown!' She gave her head a small shake in maternal concern. 'I hope it kept you warm out there.'

Brianna's flush deepened, her fingers worrying at the knot across her midriff that secured her girdle, as she recalled the cloak falling to the ground, her body bowed into Giseux's muscular frame.

'Aye, it did. Thank you,' Brianna managed to croak back. 'And thank you for your hospitality, everything you've done for Hugh.'

Lady Mary waved her hand in the air, the heavy

rings on her long white fingers sparkling richly. 'I'm pleased to see them both home, after what they've been through.' She sighed. 'Although if Jocelin is to have his way, Giseux is set to travel to Germany as soon as possible to secure Richard's release.'

Brianna nodded, relieved to be away from the subject of the cloak and the morning's activities. 'I heard the King had been captured.' It was one of the main reasons that Count John had made her life so difficult: Richard's younger brother fully expected to be King if his brother never returned. The lack of sibling love between the two royal brothers was renowned.

'Trust Queen Eleanor to pick her favourite nephew to perform the task!' A note of complaint entered Lady Mary's voice. 'When she has so many knights to chose from, she chooses him.'

'Nephew?'

Lady Mary smiled, indicating with a nod of her head that the servant, walking behind the row of high-backed chairs with a brimming jug of mead, should fill her pewter goblet. 'That's correct, my dear. Jocelin, my husband, is Eleanor's younger brother. Out of wedlock, of course.'

'Then Giseux is King Richard's cousin?' Brianna replied in a rush. 'I almost shot him yesterday!' The words blurted out; she clapped her hands over her mouth in consternation.

Lady Mary laughed out loud, her translucent features alive with merriment. 'Aye, he told me! Don't worry. I'm sure he deserved it.' She picked up Brianna's hands, her eyes sparkling with interest. 'You strike me as a very independent young woman. I admire you.'

Tears prickled at the back of Brianna's eyes as she caught the flare of admiration in Lady Mary's voice. It was a long time since anyone had praised her actions, her hard-won self-reliance.

'Look, here they are now.' The older woman released Brianna's fingers, signalling with practised efficiency to the waiting servants. Steaming platters of hot food appeared as Giseux and his father strode towards the high dais, deep in discussion. At a pause in the conversation, Jocelin glanced up, caught sight of Brianna and lifted one hand in greeting. His hair was a darker brown than his son's and streaked with grey, but other than that, his likeness to Giseux was uncanny: the wintry grey eyes, a firm chiselled jaw. But whereas the carved angles of Giseux's face were set in grim lines, Jocelin was smiling at her.

'So glad you could join us!' he boomed, throwing himself into the chair next to Brianna. 'I trust your brother is on the mend?'

'Aye, thank you, my lord. I must make some arrangements…to take him home.' Giseux had no right to decide what happened with Hugh's welfare; Alys and she could make Sefanoc comfortable for him, without a doubt. 'We have taken too much of your hospitality.' From the corner of her eye, she caught the flash of Giseux's blue tunic as he sprawled on the other side of his father; she pursed her lips, fixing her gaze steadfastly on the food before her.

'Nonsense.' Jocelin lifted an earthenware jug,

poured mead liberally into his goblet. 'Hugh must stay here, until he is better. I insist.'

'I told her the same thing.' Giseux's voice was harsh, disapproving.

Aware of the obvious annoyance in his voice, Brianna drew her spine up straight. 'Then I must ask you, my lord, if I could send a message to Sefanoc. My maidservant will be worried, anxious for news.'

'I can do better than that.' Jocelin patted her hand, a fatherly gesture. 'Giseux tells me that Sefanoc is vulnerable to Count John and his men. I have taken the liberty of dispatching soldiers to your home. They will protect it, and any servants you have, until you return.'

Brianna regarded him with relief. 'I am grateful, my lord. My home is everything to me…and my brother.' Her fingers shook as she selected a bread roll to put on her plate, mindful of the heat permeating her slender flank. Even with the muscled bulk of Jocelin between her and Giseux, her body tingled with jittery awareness, with hesitant anticipation. It was as if Jocelin had vanished and Giseux sat right next to her! Why hadn't she slapped him across the face when he kissed her, or run away? Why had she stayed and openly revelled in his embrace?

'Giseux was just asking me about one of Count John's men,' Jocelin addressed his wife as he loaded his plate with mounds of potato. Steam rose up from the heaped food. 'Curious…a man with a sickle-shaped scar on his cheek…have you ever come across anyone like that? You visit the market every week in Merleberge; it's possible you might have seen him.'

Brianna swallowed so fast that the lump of bread lodged in her throat, pappy and thick; she began to cough.

'My dear, are you quite well? Here, take some mead.' Concerned, Lady Mary pushed a pewter goblet into Brianna's hands, urging her to drink. As the amber liquid poured down her throat, releasing the clot of bread, Brianna threw her a wan smile, indicating that the crisis had passed.

Giseux leaned forwards, elbows resting on the table, dark brooding eyes pinned on Brianna. She forced her expression to remain neutral, cradling her goblet to her chest.

'Do you remember seeing such a person?' Jocelin prompted his wife once more.

Lady Mary frowned, faint vertical lines appearing in the fine skin of her forehead. 'No, I would have remembered. Is he a nobleman?'

'Aye, a knight, a Crusader.'

Giseux drained his goblet, stood up, abruptly, knocking his calves against the edge of the wooden chair. 'I think we should ask Lady Brianna.'

Vivid blue eyes collided with silver.

'Do you know him, Brianna? Have you seen such a man before?' In one long stride Giseux stood behind her, hands clasped around her chair-back. He glared down at her neat head, the rough coils of her pinned hair beneath the gossamer veil. His knuckles grazed the flimsy material, almost, almost touching the exquisite silk of her hair. His gut wrenched at his lack of control. He had allowed himself to become distracted by this delicate, vulnerable maid, with her stubborn, obtuse behaviour and her soft, pliable lips. She tested his patience, yet intrigued him in the same moment. How could he have allowed his rigid self-restraint, his iron-clad guard around women, to slip? His mind still held the taste of her lips, the perfumed scent of her mouth; even now, as the tight pale green wool of her gown embraced her slim arm where it rested on the table, his loins contracted. She made him forget his true purpose, his final promise to Nadia, the promise that he would track down the man who had betrayed them. That he would kill him.

'I…I'm not sure.' Crumpling her napkin on to the table, she rose, hesitating, wanting to extricate herself from Giseux's oppressive presence, his questions. If she admitted that she knew this man, who knew where it would lead.

Giseux's hand clamped around her shoulder as she twisted around, trying to free herself from the confines of the table. 'You know him.'

'I…I might do.' Brianna rolled her shoulder angrily beneath his grip, clenching her jaw. 'Let me out of here!' she hissed at the broadness of his chest, refusing to look up into the dark angles of his face. The weight of his fingers fell from her shoulder and she tilted her hip sideways, manoeuvring her way out from between the two chairs. Arms folded across his chest, legs astride, he blocked her way.

'Don't play games with me, Brianna. You know who he is. Tell me.'

'Giseux…I really think…' Lady Mary's protest died

on her lips at the raw, flinty expression on her son's face. Scrunching her napkin between pale fingers, she glanced at her husband, wanting him to alleviate the situation, to remonstrate with Giseux for his treatment of Brianna. A small shake of Jocelin's head, barely noticeable, warned her to keep quiet.

'His name is Almeric of Salis, he holds land to the north of Merleberge.' Brianna spoke quietly. 'Now let me pass.'

'How do you know him?'

Brianna shrugged her shoulders. 'He's well known in Merleberge, he's lived there all his life—one of Count John's cronies.'

'You know what he looks like.'

'Aye, he has the scar you talked of, here, on his cheek.' Brianna lifted one pink-tipped fingernail, traced a crescent shape on the side of her cheek.

'Take me to him.'

Aghast, her mouth sagged in horror. 'Wh-what?'

'You heard.'

'I've told you where he is, you can identify him yourself,' she muttered rudely, hurriedly, pursing her lips in a mutinous line, acutely conscious of Giseux's parents following their conversation with undisguised interest.

'I want to make sure I have the right man.' Giseux tilted his head down so she could hear the low, velvet throb of his voice, his lips inches from her face. Heat flooded her skin.

'That's an excellent idea!' Jocelin pushed back his chair and moved to stand beside his son, wiping his mouth with a linen napkin. 'You can't afford to waste any time, Giseux, not with Queen Eleanor on your back about travelling to Germany.'

'I can't!' she protested, cheeks bright. 'Hugh wants me to...' How could she even begin to reveal the enormity of the task her brother had set her? Her words failed as Giseux's blistering gaze devoured her. 'Hugh needs me,' she finished limply.

Lady Mary rose from her seat, her step graceful, fluid. 'You know he's well cared for, my child; in his present state, he will not miss you.' Giseux's mother laid a reassuring hand on her arm.

A wave of powerlessness swept over Brianna as she stared at the three people ranked around her, crowding her. Giseux's parents had been so kind, so generous with their home and their time; as she stared into their smiling faces, her brain failed to conjure up any other viable protest. They were right; they could look after Hugh, but, as her gaze swept over Giseux, over the sensuous curve of his top lip, the diamond glitter of his eyes, she wondered if she had lost the ability to look after herself.

'Have you any idea where this Almeric might be?' Hauling back on the reins, Giseux called across to Brianna as the pace of his destrier slackened. The golden-brown strands of his hair flattened upwards in the freshening north-east breeze, the taut skin of his high cheekbones chafing red. His semi-circular blue cloak billowed out from his broad back, revealing the glossy lining, as the stalled horse sidled beneath him.

A name...he finally had a name for the faceless

traitor who, along with the dying screams of his men, the image of Nadia sliding down to the ground, had haunted his nights and days. A traitor who deserved everything he had coming to him. His only clue to finding him had been Nadia's final words: *Find the man with the sickle-shaped scar, carrying the colours of King Richard*. Her tapered finger had traced the shape of the scar into his own tanned cheek as she lay slumped against the door at the end of the narrow alleyway, the door that had been purposely locked against him and his men. They had gone there, thinking they would gain access to the city of Narsuf, to infiltrate the city and break the long siege. Nadia believed she was helping him and his men by giving them the information; as she had rattled the handle of the locked door, she realised she had been tricked. They had been caught, like rats in a trap.

Giseux's mouth set in a grim, immutable line; the thought of revenge had been the only thing that had kept him going in the year after Nadia's death, the only thing that had made him feel barely alive as he went through the hollow motions of living. And now, now, revenge was so close he could taste its bitter sweetness on his tongue; justice would be done.

Brianna gasped with relief as Giseux drew his horse to a halt; it seemed as if they had been riding for hours, when in reality Merleberge was not above ten miles from Sambourne. At first she had welcomed Giseux's unceasing pace, wanting the journey to be over as soon as possible, but now her muscles ached from continually gripping the rounded flanks of the horse. She hated being away from Hugh. Guilt swamped her like a cloak; she should be travelling to fetch Matilda at this very moment, but instead she rode in the company of an uncommunicative knight of short acquaintance who ordered her about as if she were a foot soldier. A knight who had kissed her.

'He'll be at the castle.' Brianna's diminutive grey palfrey carefully picked its way over the parched grass, bleached pale yellow by the weak, wintry sunlight, before they began to descend into the wide river valley that held the town of Merleberge. A mist hung in the valley, suspended a few feet above the sinuous curve of water, a swathe of ghostly material.

The cold had stained Brianna's cheeks a deep rose, the vivid brilliance of her eyes dancing with exhilaration. The hood of her cloak had fallen back on the ride, the fine wool gathering around the nape of her neck, warming her. Lady Mary had leant her some gloves, fine stitched leather lined with squirrel fur, but even with their protection, Brianna's fingers felt stiff, numb around the reins. Against the backdrop of the washed-out blue sky, the hazy circle of the moon lying high out to the east, the gauzy silk of veil floated out about her head, framing her face. The fading bruise on her jawline did little to diminish the flawless perfection of her skin.

'I'm sorry…?' Snared in her beauty, Giseux failed to hear her next words.

'The castle—how are we going to get in?' she repeated the question, frowning at him, steering her horse towards the start of a narrow chalk path leading down the ridged side of the hill. The slope faced north, and even at this hour of the afternoon, when the sun had been on the land for hours, the white frost still clung to the grass, a pearl-like sheen.

Giseux nudged the flanks of his horse, following her, cursing his inability to focus on the task in hand. Where was the rage, the anger that had kept him awake night after night, the guilt that plagued him? In a moment, it seemed to have vanished. A picture of Nadia budged into his consciousness: the sleek darkness of hair, wide brown eyes, the sensual dusky curves of her body. *Remember,* he told himself, *remember who this is for.*

He laughed sourly at her back. 'They know who I am. Count John doesn't see me as a threat.'

The horses skittered down over the loose stones of the path, reaching the boggy ground along the river. Both riders kicked the horses to an easy canter, aiming for the main trackway that led to the town gate of Merleberge. The muscles in the animals' shoulders rippled as they powered up to the road.

'I hope this isn't going to take too long.' Brianna jogged forwards in the saddle, urging her palfrey up the steep slope to gain the road.

Giseux flicked his steely gaze over her. 'It will be faster with your help. But I do realise you have no wish to be here.'

'Merleberge is not my favourite place, for obvious reasons.' She fingered her bruised jawline self-consciously.

Leather-covered fingers touched her arm. 'Stay by my side, Brianna, and nothing will happen to you.'

Her heart warmed, blossomed under the note of protection in his voice. She told herself not to be foolish, to pay no heed to it. Giseux meant nothing by it; she was of use to him, that was all.

'And I have my knife,' she added, patting the embossed leather sheath on her hip.

He scowled at the jewelled hilt resting against her cloak. 'I should chuck that in the river, for all the use that will do us.' Squeezing his bulky thighs against the embossed saddle, he began to negotiate a passage across the stone bridge that crossed the ditch to the town gates. People scurried all around them, some visiting the town to sell their wares, others riding out on horseback. Ladies wearing colourful gowns huddled against the cold in their covered litters carried by puffing servants, their husbands riding patiently alongside. The crowds parted as Giseux and Brianna made their way through, side by side, then joined again at the rear of their horses, like a river running around an island. A couple of people recognised Brianna and waved at her, before they vanished beneath the shadow of the gates.

Lord Almeric was easy to find. Peering down from the high wooden gallery down into the great hall of Count John's castle, keeping behind the folds of a massive brocade curtain that hung from the ceiling, Brianna pointed down to the group of men at the top table.

'Look, there he is, to the right of Count John.' With Giseux at her back, a strange exhilaration flooded her limbs, giving her courage.

Looking over the top of Brianna's head, Giseux

tracked along the direction of her pointing finger, moving along the row of portly, and obviously drunk, noblemen. Count John was in the middle; he recognised the petulant pout of the youngest son of Queen Eleanor, his soft features containing little of the hard determination that marked King Richard's demeanour.

'Do you see him?' Brianna whispered. The warmth of Giseux's chest at her back radiated through her cloak, the thin weave of her dress.

'Aye.' Giseux narrowed his gaze on a shorter man, a big belly rounding out the contours of his tunic, a cruel-looking scar on the side of his face. 'I see him.'

'What do you want with him?' Brianna turned, her eyes alert with curiosity. Her shoulder nudged into the rigid muscle of his chest and she inched away, heat rushing through her, coiling precariously.

In the shadows, his eyes glimmered, dangerous. 'He owes me.'

'What? Coin? Is that it?' Her questions sounded falsely bright. Somehow, Giseux didn't strike her as the sort of man who would chase after money.

'Nay, Brianna.' A muscle jumped in the chiselled slash of Giseux's cheek. 'He owes me a life. More than one.'

'How?' she breathed.

Giseux's bleak expression raked her face. 'Do you really want to know?'

She nodded.

'Count John will stop at nothing to be King, even if that means killing his own brother. He sent Almeric to

Jerusalem to set up an ambush. And he killed the girl I loved to do it.'

Brianna's heart went cold, plunged steeply downwards at his revelation. Regret wrapped her chest; so, he had loved another. Still loved her, judging from the depth of his emotion, the bitter desolation in his eyes, the despair. 'What are you going to do?' Her voice faltered, aware of a curious jealousy crawling through her veins. Why, she was acting as if he belonged to her!

In reply, he drew a curved, lethal-looking blade from behind his back; he must have carried it in a leather sheath beneath his cloak. The silver steel glinted in the half-light, ominous, frightening.

'Nay! Giseux, you cannot! You cannot!' she hissed at him, clutching the fine wool of his tunic, as if by holding on to the material she could stop him and physically hold him back.

His free hand crushed around her fingers. 'I will avenge Nadia's death, Brianna.'

Nadia. The woman he loved had a name. She sucked in a deep, angry breath, scrabbling for balance, for logic. 'I would never have shown you who Almeric was if I'd known this was what you were about to do!' she blazed at him. 'Do you think murdering will make you feel better? The blood will stay on your hands for ever.' Furious, she wrestled her hand from his grasp.

'Nadia's death is on my hands.' Giseux's voice was so low, so devoid of emotion, that Brianna had to nudge closer to hear his words, catching the masculine smell of him: an intoxicating mixture of woodsmoke and spice mingling in the confined air of the gallery. 'If we hadn't been in love, then she would never have been compromised by that man…' he jabbed his finger down into the great hall '…and she would be alive now. As would several of my men.'

'If you do this, you will never be free of it. It will haunt you for ever.'

'Nay,' he disagreed, the shadowed cleft beneath his mouth emphasising the fullness of his bottom lip, 'it will be over, at last.' He glanced briefly down into the great hall, reassuring himself that Almeric still sat there. 'Go and wait with the horses, Brianna, I will meet you there.' His command was clipped, brutal.

She whipped around to the end of the gallery, blocking the only exit with her slender body, one hand on each side of the open archway. Against the thick grey stone, the knuckles on her clenched hands gleamed white. He couldn't do this, she couldn't let him do it! It was so wrong.

'Move out of the way, Brianna.' His voice was deep, a husky request. 'This doesn't concern you.'

'I brought you here, I will be culpable too.' She tipped her chin up to him, openly challenging. 'Once a soldier, always a soldier, I suppose. Killing must come naturally.' Her voice held the thread of mockery, her slim frame swaying with emotion as she held on, clinging tightly, to the curving stones. 'You condemn Almeric for being a murderer, yet you are about to do the same, in cold blood. You will be a murderer too. You're all the same.' Tilting her head to one side, her mouth twisted in derision. 'How can you live with yourself?'

In the shadowed light, her skin adopted the sheen of creamy alabaster, shining eyes, deep blue glass, imploring him to change his mind, to change the single action that had driven him on, had kept him in a semblance of life for the last few months. How could he tell her of his inability to live with himself now, in the present day? He already had blood on his hands; a little more would make no difference.

'Out of my way, Brianna.' His big arms roped around her, lifting her easily aside. 'Go to the horses, as I told you, and wait outside the town gates. This will not take long.' A roar of laughter lifted from the hall below, a sound of clinking glasses, of merriment.

Brianna planted her hands firmly on her hips, bracing herself, eyes spitting fire. 'I'll not take orders from a killer! I'll do what I want. I can't believe you brought me here, to help you…do this, do this terrible thing.' Her voice rose, shaky with outrage, with emotion.

Raw despair clagged his eyes. 'What would you have me do? It's the only way, Brianna, the only way I can avenge Nadia's death.'

'It won't bring her back, though, will it?' she replied bluntly. 'And you'll have that man's blood on your hands.'

He leaned into her, the silver soot of his eyes wild, dangerous. 'I want his blood on my hands, Brianna. Don't you understand? He deserves to die.'

'Nobody deserves to die, Giseux.'

But he had gone.

A bridle looped in each gloved hand, Brianna marched furiously through the fallen leaves, boots kicking up layers of golden yellow, russet, crimson-edged foliage. Blood pumped through her chest, burned in her ears, raging; she wanted to hit out at something, someone: *him*. An enormous sense of failure leached through her veins; she had failed to persuade Giseux, failed to change his mind against something she was certain he would regret for ever. Why had she even expected him to listen to her? He barely knew her, the younger sister of a Crusader knight, had met her only one day ago. She was nothing, a nobody to him. Yet, in the dim confines of that upper gallery, she had witnessed the look of anguish, of loss in his eyes, and knew that killing was not the answer; at least she had tried.

She had ridden the docile palfrey up to the fringes of the woodland, but her arm, angled awkwardly behind her, had begun to ache as she clutched on to the bridle of Giseux's destrier. She could have sworn that brutish stallion dragged its feet once more, it had literally bared its large oblong teeth at her when she had led the animal away from Merleberge. In a fit of pique, she had taken Giseux's horse, wanting to punish him—let him walk back, she thought angrily, if he escaped unscathed. But he would walk out of that castle in one piece, safe; he was that sort of man, invincible, relentless, utterly irresistible.

Irresistible? Had she completely lost her mind? Stalled in the swirling leaves, daylight gradually fading, she clutched on to the bridles like a lifeline, in horror. Since when had she started thinking of him as irresistible? He was a stranger, a rough, arrogant soldier, who'd broken through the tough, outer shell of her numb, cloistered life, and flipped it upside-down. He asked her questions she had no wish to answer, scrutinised her with a searching gaze she was unable to interpret and pulled her along with him into things she had no wish to be involved; she hated it, she welcomed it. She felt alive.

One big fat raindrop touched her face, startling her out of her reverie. Overhead, lumpish grey clouds amassed, signalling the onset of rain, and she started walking again, increasing her pace. Sambourne lay due east from here; she would reach it before the light went completely from the day. Rolling her arm in its socket, the ache in the back of her shoulder subsiding, she decided to ride once more. Hitching her skirts up, she stuck her foot into the gleaming stirrup, her other leg bouncing comically across the spongy mess of leaves as she attempted to lever herself into the saddle without the aid of a convenient mounting block.

'Allow me.' Firm hands either side of her hips boosted her upwards. Hastily scissoring her legs over the horse's back, Brianna narrowed her eyes through the slanting rain, refusing to acknowledge the flare of relief in her heart.

'Why didn't you wait for me?' Giseux bellowed up at her, raindrops sluicing down his face. Droplets hung, like brilliant jewels, from the tips of his hair.

'I don't wait for murderers!' she shouted back, contemptuously, yanking her hood over her rapidly flattening veil. Yellow, star-shaped leaves floated down diagonally between them, hastened by the squalls of rain; one landed on Giseux's shoulder, gold against the blue cloth of his cloak. 'What you did was despicable!'

In response he bunched the leather straps of her horse's bridle between his fist, pulling her horse into the lea of a stand of larch trees, out of the stinging rain. 'And let go of my horse!' she scolded him, childishly.

Beneath the shelter of the trees scarcely a raindrop fell; the air filled with an audible hush, an expectancy. Giseux's head was on a level with her midriff, his eyes bright, translucent in the dimming forest. Above his head, the bronze needles of the larch fanned out against the silvery sky, small rosettes of cones bunched like seeds at the end of each branch, swaying gently.

'I let him live, Brianna.' He released her bridle, throwing himself onto his destrier in one easy movement.

'You…?' Her mouth, opened to harangue him once more, snapped shut. The full impact of his words swept over her, her heart sung.

'Aye, that's right, Brianna,' he growled out, staring out at the slashing rain. 'I let him live. Against my better judgement, probably,' he muttered, swinging his brilliant eyes towards her.

'Does he still have his legs?' Brianna's question held the tint of apology. Her anger at him ebbed away, drained from her body like the receding tide.

Giseux laughed; there was no humour in the sound. 'He had no idea I was there.'

'But why?' Brianna asked, incredulous. 'What made you stop?'

You, Brianna, he thought. Her simple, powerful

words had seeped into his soul, reached into the far corners of his frozen heart, warming, nurturing. The fog, that cold, listless fog, had lifted from his brain; he could think clearly again. Her words had penetrated his dark thoughts, forced him to acknowledge the consequences of his actions. Brianna was right—killing would not bring Nadia back.

'He was not worth bloodying my sword for,' he replied, lightly, peering out into the gloomy drizzle.

'What was she like, Giseux?'

His leonine head whipped around, astonished by the temerity of her question, astounded by the way the words kicked him, hard, driving into the middle of his solar plexus. The destrier pawed the ground, nervous, sensing his rider's tension.

Reading the sadness in the diamond chips of his eyes, Brianna expelled a deep, shaky breath. She had gone too far. 'I'm sorry,' she whispered, her throat closed with remorse, 'it's none of my business.'

He tried to conjure up the image of Nadia, attempted to recall the details of her face, her hair, the smell of her. Unusually, he wanted to speak of her, describe her to Brianna, but all he could see was the sweet oval face of the maid before him, her lips sheened with the colour of the palest rose petal, the wayward tendril of coppery hair escaping from her hood.

'She was beautiful,' he said, finally. 'Like you.'

Chapter Seven

Giseux shoved a few clothes into a leather satchel, his movements quick, efficient. Glancing around the chamber, at the rich grain of the panelled walls, at the extravagant folds of the velvet bed curtains, he told himself he had no need of such wealth, such trappings. He was just as comfortable in a tent, with scant possessions and a horse to travel on, alone. Or he had been. The restlessness that had plagued him since he returned from Jerusalem seemed eased somehow, lifted, the frozen lump that chilled the marrow of his body shifting, melting slowly. But it was time to go, on the direct order of Queen Eleanor, to find her son, the King, and organise his release. A few days ago, he would have relished the chance to travel, to throw himself into the difficult task, now, curiously, he had no wish to leave Sambourne.

A pair of bright, periwinkle-blue eyes swung into his mind. Brianna had been so cross, so angry with him in Merleberge, when she realised his intentions; her furious little face turned up to him like a brilliant flower, cheeks flagged with fury. Her scornful speech had driven the rage, the anger that fuelled his revenge, from his body, now, he was amazed at the uncomplicated strength of her words, the effect they had wielded upon him. Shaggy brows furrowing over his glimmering eyes, his chest tightened as a dawning realisation flooded over him: he would miss her.

Someone tapped lightly at his door.

'Come in.' His deep voice was terse as he turned to sort out the muddle of his chainmail, piled in a heap in the corner of his room.

'Giseux?' His mother's light tone tripped across the chamber, her eyes drawn immediately towards the silver pile of armour, the shield, the sword. Her lips pressed together, a sign of regret.

He turned and smiled ruefully, pushing back a lock of sable hair that fell over his forehead with the movement. 'If I'm going to wear this, I'd better sort it out before I… What's the matter?' Lady Mary had moved swiftly across the room in a flurry of green silk, her delicate veil fanning out behind her, and now clutched at his arm.

'Hugh is asking for you…he wants to speak with you, urgently…and alone.' Her heavy emphasis on the final word forced Giseux to concentrate on her words.

'You mean…without his sister overhearing?'

'Precisely. I managed to persuade her to take some breakfast with your father; she was so tired from yesterday that she went straight to bed last night.' Mary threw her son a critical glance. 'Did you find who you were looking for…in Merleberge?'

'Aye, Brianna took me straight to him.'

'She's a plucky little thing, don't you think? Managing to cope for all those years with just a servant for company?'

'She's courageous, I'll give her that,' Giseux agreed, moving around his mother to stand in the open doorway, 'but she's vulnerable too.' He frowned. 'I can't imagine what Hugh wants to say to me without Brianna's presence. They seem so close.'

'You'd better go, now.'

'Could you go down to the great hall…maybe stall her a little?' Giseux walked alongside his mother out into the corridor.

Lady Mary's fair head bobbed with approval. 'It would be my pleasure.' She paused at the top of the steps, one hand clasped around the curving iron-forged banister that snaked downwards alongside the spiral staircase, and glanced back at her son, a small smile on her pale pink lips. 'I do enjoy talking with her.'

At the sight of Giseux, Hugh pushed himself up on one elbow. 'Thank God you came! I need to speak to you!'

'How are you feeling?' Approaching the bed, Giseux dipped his upper body to lay a hand on Hugh's forehead. His skin was cool and the disorientated, crazed look had disappeared from his eyes. 'Much better, obviously,' he pronounced his own verdict. He dragged a wooden chair over to the bed, and sat down, elbows resting on his knees as he leaned forward. 'What is it?'

'Giseux, I've done something...it's to do with Brianna...' Hugh hesitated, eyes shifting to the door, checking it was closed. The clear, periwinkle blue of his eyes matched those of his sister. 'She'll not like what I've done, but believe me, I have her best interests at heart.'

'Why not speak to her about it?' Giseux replied evenly, an uncomfortable feeling nagging at his innards. He glanced downwards, studying the scuffed toes of his leather half-boots.

Hugh plucked at the bedsheet. 'If she knew, she would refuse to go through with it.'

'Go on,' Giseux urged.

'I've asked Brianna to find my betrothed and my son.'

Giseux's eyes widened fractionally. Hugh had talked to him briefly about Matilda and the little boy on the journey back to England. Brianna had not mentioned such a task to him, but then, why would she? He was nothing more than a stranger to her.

'I don't know if I will survive this illness; I need to marry Matilda, to make sure the boy, my son, inherits Sefanoc.'

'And Brianna?'

'Matilda's father has agreed to give his daughter's hand in marriage on one condition.' Hugh rolled on to his back, stared at the ceiling, his eyes fluttering closed for a moment. 'Brianna will see the sense of it, once she becomes used to the idea.'

'What condition?' Giseux's question sounded hollow,

his tongue awkward within his mouth. For some unknown reason, the image of Brianna, sprawled and helpless against the frozen water trough, leapt into this mind. What was Hugh about to tell him?

Hugh rolled his red-rimmed eyes towards Giseux, a loose smile contorting his dry lips. 'On condition that Brianna marries him. Walter of Brinslow, Matilda's father, wants Brianna's hand in marriage…again. He wants her back, Giseux. She was married to him before…and she ran away before the year was up. By all accounts he was happy to let her go. But now, he wants her back.'

Giseux rose abruptly, stepped over to the window, his hands balled into fists on the stone ledge. The movement prevented him from going to the bed and violently shaking Hugh. So this was the marriage to which Brianna had referred in this very room, when he challenged her about her behaviour, her voice bitter and cold, her whole body quivering in the aftermath of her outburst. And Hugh was proposing that she go through the whole thing again.

He turned around, propped one hip up on the ledge, folding his big arms over his chest. His toe knocked against the pallet bed, skewing the light wooden frame across the glossy floorboards; the linen pillow still held the crushed imprint of Brianna's head. 'She would never agree to it, Hugh, surely you can see that?'

'She doesn't have to agree. Brianna has no idea of that part of the plan. If she did…well…'

'…she would run a mile.' A half-smile touched his lips: aye, the knife would come out, and the crossbow no doubt; the chit certainly had the wits and intention to defend herself, even if she didn't have the muscle power. A raft of admiration sifted through him. He remembered her sobbing speech after he had rescued her from Count John's soldiers, when she had believed him to be her enemy, that she would rather die than go with him.

'Precisely.' Hugh's lips tightened suddenly. 'That's why I want you to go with her.' He coughed, a wheezing rattle emerging from his lungs.

'It's not possible. I have orders to go to Germany.' Giseux's response emerged, clipped and tight. 'There's a boat leaving from Southay this evening.'

'It wouldn't take above a couple of days to deliver her,' Hugh wheedled, the faintest trace of spoilt grumpiness in his voice. 'You could take another boat in a couple of days.'

Deliver her? Was that what Brianna had been reduced to? An inanimate package to be hauled from one place to the next? 'Hugh, she's your sister, for God's sake!' Giseux bellowed at him, flint eyes snapping. 'How can you do this to her?' Hugh scrabbled back on to the pillows as Giseux hulked over the bed, his broad shoulders blocking out the light from the window, his demeanour threatening.

'Sit down,' Hugh croaked. 'I didn't know you cared so much.'

Giseux forced himself back into the chair beside the bed, squashing down smartly on the flare of disquiet he felt for the maid. 'She's been through so much,

Hugh, surely you can see that? Life has been hard for her whilst you've been away.'

But Hugh wasn't listening. 'I suppose I'll have to find someone else then. It'll be difficult; she's so stubborn, set in her ways. I blame our father; he allowed her to make decisions too early, gave her too much independence. Now she's a devil to handle, far too wilful. I assumed that's why her marriage was annulled so soon, because she was so difficult. Walter must be mad for wanting her back.'

'She's kept Sefanoc going for you, managing both the estate and lands, on her own.'

'She knows how important it is to me,' Hugh replied pompously.

Giseux glanced at him, surprised at the smug haughtiness in his tone. He had only known this man in sickness; now, with his return to health, Hugh's true character seemed to be emerging: Hugh the landowner, Hugh the arrogant lord. Without thinking, he rubbed at the cramping soreness in his right thigh. 'Brianna loves you, Hugh; she wouldn't expect you to do something like this.'

'Brianna needs to learn to do as she's told,' Hugh retorted, bending his arms upward behind his head.

A dangerous light entered Giseux's eyes; he sprang from the chair, prowling on noiseless feet about the chamber. 'Brianna has had enough. You need to leave her alone.'

Hugh twisted his thin, mottled face up to Giseux's, blue eyes narrowing. 'Brianna is my sister, Giseux, and she is my property; I decide what happens to her. She is nothing to do with you.'

Rage clouding his vision, Giseux wrenched the door open.

Brianna stood in the passageway, the light slanting down over her amber hair from the window in the stairwell, her hand suspended in mid-air, about to press her palm against the wooden slats to push the door inwards.

'Oh, it's you!' A faint colour bloomed immediately across her cheeks; she crossed her arms over her bosom, acutely conscious of the tighter fit of her borrowed dress. Lady Mary had insisted that her pale green gown, her only gown, was sent for laundering, lending her one of her own garments as a replacement, a slim-fitting gown of mauve silk velvet. The silver trellis of flowers decorating the curving neckline winked and sparkled in the half-light...

'What's the matter?' she breathed fearfully at the wild, precarious look in Giseux's eyes. He filled the doorway, his rumpled hair almost brushing the heavy oak lintel, broad shoulders encased in a brown fustian tunic. 'Is it Hugh?' The memory of Giseux's words sang through her, he had told her she was beautiful, like the girl he had loved in the Orient. For some inexplicable reason, the tiniest sliver of sorrow washed through her veins.

His body melted at the sight of her, as if all his muscles recognised her presence, and softly acquiesced, cleaving forwards. The form-fitting bodice of her dress smoothed over the rounded curve of her bosom, the slashed neckline gaping fractionally to reveal the shadowed gap between her breasts. 'Hugh is all right,' he bit out. *Apart from the fact that he is about to betray you, about to push you back into a marriage that you will do everything in your power to avoid, he is all right.*

'Brianna...is that you?' Hugh's querulous voice rose from the bed.

'I must go to him.' Brianna lowered her head, indicating that Giseux should move to one side.

'Wait,' he murmured huskily, lowering his lips to within an inch of her shell-like ear. A delicious perfume rose from the warmth of her neck; his breath stirred the dainty silk of her veil. 'Meet me in the stables, as soon as you can. It's important.' His eyes, smoking silver, bore into hers. 'And don't speak of this to Hugh.'

After the noon-day bell, after the peasants had stumbled in from their morning chores and eaten their fill at the scrubbed, rickety trestle tables in the great hall, under the watchful eye of Jocelin's bailiff, the castle slumbered. On this icy day, cold hands and feet warmed quickly with the heat blazing out from the huge fire; drowsy faces reddened and heads nodded, bodies somnolent, exhausted from the early morning start. Despite the time of year, there was plenty of work on the estate, from tending the livestock to hedging and ditching, and working in the forests to ensure enough timber to keep the fires burning.

Carrying her brother's empty tray, Brianna stepped lightly down the spiral staircase from Hugh's chamber, her embroidered hemline slipping behind her, the rich material lapping down each polished stone step.

Hugh seemed much recovered, with more colour in his cheeks; she had left him propped up against several feather pillows after he'd finished sipping the broth brought by one of the servants. He had talked and talked, speaking of his plans for Sefanoc, for his son. In the years that Hugh had been away, Brianna had forgotten what it was like to be bossed around by him; now, she found herself balking at his authoritative tones. All the time he had talked to her, mouth full of soup, or bread, Brianna's fingers fidgeted along the side of her chair, flickers of nervous anticipation coursing through her frame, resisting the urge to leap up, to chase down after Giseux. Her mind failed to concentrate on Hugh's words, her thoughts darting hither and thither like butterflies: what could Giseux possibly wish to say to her? Her heart thudded treacherously.

When Hugh had finally leaned back against the pillows, eyelids drooping, muttering about how important it was for her to travel to Walter's castle, about how he would ask Jocelin for a couple of soldiers to accompany her, she had leaped at the opportunity to carry his dirty dishes back downstairs. Reaching the main entrance hall, she handed the tray to a passing maidservant, the girl bobbing a quick curtsy before diving off behind a thick brocade curtain, no doubt in the direction of the kitchens. Twisting the chunky iron handle of the main door, wooden panels studded with iron rivets, Brianna stepped outside, wrapping her arms about her midriff to ward off the blast of the icy east wind. Her cloak lay upstairs in the chamber; to have worn it would have been to alert Hugh to her destination outside. Guilt swept over her; Hugh had always been her confidant, her only confidant, but something, something in his manner, made her hesitate. His illness was obviously affecting him. Striding across the cobbles of the inner bailey, the breeze chasing around her stocking-covered shins, she headed for the uneven row of open-fronted barns.

After the blasting whip of the wind outside, the air in the stables was hushed, muted, ripe with the smell of horse, of dry, rustling straw. The glossy, curving rumps of powerful horses stuck out from the wooden stalls, heads tethered near the mangers where they munched contentedly on hay. Brianna edged carefully past their hindquarters, mindful of the force in those back legs, keeping over to the wall on the right-hand side. Light filtered down from a narrow opening that ran the length of the wall; through the small gap she could see white froths of cloud scudding across the blue.

'Brianna?'

Her gaze jerked from the scintillating chink of sky. Giseux moved around the shining chestnut rump of his destrier to stand before her, the silver skin of his chain-mail glittering in the gloom. He had changed clothes; a black tunic, emblazoned with the golden lions of King Richard, fell to his knees, split up to his bulky thighs at the front revealing the buff-coloured lining. His leather belt hung low on his slim hips, the jewelled hilt of his sword winking in the sporadic light.

Dryness scraped her mouth at the sight of him. 'Are you leaving?' she blurted out, abruptly. Regret churned her stomach.

'I must, Brianna. I have my orders.' He took a step forwards, white teeth gleaming in his tanned skin.

Her hands fluttered upwards, momentarily, before she altered the involuntary movement to tuck a non-existent strand of hair behind her ear. 'Aye, of course,' she replied, briskly, her voice sounded a little too loud, too hoarse, in the hush of the stables. A betraying rush of colour stained her cheeks. Why had she expected him to stay here, at his home, with his family? He was a paid knight, in the employ of the Queen. Even so, the realisation that he was leaving pushed daggers of ice through her heart, pure fear. Her lips clamped together angrily at the unwanted, unnecessary feeling—since when had she come to rely on this man? She wriggled her toes in her boots, the cold seeping through her thin soles from the packed earth floor.

'Why did you not tell me what Hugh asked you to do?'

Her head jerked up, heart clamouring frantically against the wall of her chest. 'I…er…' Brianna hesitated. In truth, she hadn't wanted to think about the task herself. She shrugged her shoulders. 'Because it's family business. Why should I tell you?'

Because I want to know, he thought, with a rush of awareness. *I want to know everything about you.* 'I thought you might have mentioned the small fact that Hugh wants you, in his stead, to claim the daughter of the man to whom you were married.'

Her lashes flew up, dark spikes of black velvet, startled by his words. The gilded band securing her veil twinkled in the shadowed gloom of the stables, making her appear magical, ethereal, like a fairy sprite. Even though he stood a good few feet away, he sensed the agitation running through her lissom frame, every muscle tensed and ready to bolt, to escape, like a small deer on the edge of a forest. She wrapped her slim arms about her chest, tightly, her mouth hard and set.

'Hugh asks too much of you,' Giseux murmured, reading the haunted vulnerability in her eyes, the gap in her defences that she battled to hide, for no one to see. But he saw it, vivid and clear, as if pinned to her gown like a full-blown rose. What had her husband done to her, to make her shrink back into herself at the slightest reference to her marriage?

Brianna drew her sagging shoulders up. 'Nay, I will do it.' She shook her head, violently, trying to dispel the image of Walter's slobbering, cavernous mouth. He had never managed to kiss her, in that whole, horrible half-year of marriage. Every time his foul breath lurched near, she had ducked her head, so that his wet lips landed on her cheek, or in her hair. Even that had been too close. She shuddered. 'I'm stronger now…it's been a long time.'

'Not long enough, methinks,' Giseux observed wryly. She jerked back as his fingers stretched towards her, cupped the side of her face. The bruise on her jawline had faded to a mottled patchwork of blotches. 'See how you flinch every time I come near you?'

'That's because I don't want you near me!' she snapped. But her words belied her actions; she failed to pull away. Her breath caught in her throat, the sweet press of his lips nudging her memory. The warmth from his wide thumb seeped into her cold skin, brushing the sensitive side of her mouth, before it dropped away. How could she tell him that she didn't flinch from fear, but from the anticipation of what might happen?

'Brianna, I want you to stay here, with my parents. Don't go to fetch Matilda—we can easily send soldiers to bring her back.'

Her eyes flared over him, puzzled by the concern in his tone. 'But Hugh asked me; he wants me to go.' She knotted her fingers together, knuckles twisting. 'Apparently I'm the only person Matilda will travel with. She trusts me.'

'Hugh has another reason for wanting you to go, Brianna.' Giseux took a deep breath, fumbling around for the correct words, words that would keep her safe. 'He wants to see you settled, Brianna, married. I…'

Mouth gaping in horror, she rounded on him, expression wary, guarded. 'Has he been speaking with you about this?' Her fists curled into little balls at her sides, tension rattling through her body. He wanted to reach down, seize each hand in turn and untwist those rigid fingers, one by one. The light silk veil brushed delicately over her shoulders as she shook her head, pulse beating rapidly in the silken hollow of her throat. 'You have it wrong, anyway. Hugh wouldn't want me to marry…he knows I don't…that I have no intentions in that direction.' She lifted her liquid blue eyes to Giseux. 'Hugh will look after me—he is my brother, after all.'

Giseux turned away to his horse, pressing one shoulder against the animal's flank in order to tighten the girth strap on the saddle, mouth pressed into a grim line. Looking after Brianna seemed to be the last thing on Hugh's mind; he had traded her to achieve his own ends. But how could Giseux convince her?

'Hugh wants you to marry Walter, Brianna.' The smooth pelt of the horseflesh warmed his cheek as he hefted the leather strap, his horse snorting in protest. He turned back in time to see her face wash with grey, a deathly pallor.

'What are you saying?' she whispered, swaying a little. 'Why do you say such things?' Her fingers clutched at the end of the wooden stall.

'Because it's the truth, Brianna. Why do you think Hugh wants you, and only you, to fetch Matilda? My father has a whole raft of soldiers at his disposal who would perform the task—why ask you?' Shards of silver flecked the mineral darkness of his eyes.

Brianna edged backwards, trying to escape his cruel words. She hadn't wanted him to go, but now she couldn't wait for him to leave. 'It's not true, I don't believe you!' The hem of her skirt snagged on a rogue splinter in the wood-planked wall and she yanked at it, angrily.

'You need to watch your back, Brianna.' In two quick, rustling strides he was in front of her, preventing her exit. He read the rigid dismissal in her eyes, the shuttered hostility, and knew he had failed. Why should she trust him, a stranger she had known not above two days, above her own brother, someone she had known a lifetime?

'I always watch my back,' she replied bluntly, spinning smartly on her heel to stalk out of the stables. At the entrance, she paused, the flash of her wide blue eyes seeking him out in the gloom. 'Thank you for everything you have done for Hugh.' Her tone stung him, jerky, distant. 'This is the last time we will see each other…so, farewell.' The sinuous curve of her spine, encased in silk velvet, vanished into the howling wind.

Giseux folded his arms high across his broad chest, staring at the open doorway, the image of her slight figure imprinted in his mind long after she had gone. *Nay, my lady,* he thought, recalling the azure spark of her eyes, the sheer courage bound up in her small frame. *This will not be the last time.*

Chapter Eight

High on a ridge, the flat-bottomed valley below, Brianna pulled gradually on the reins, slowing her horse to a walk. She leaned back across the saddle, feeling the stretch in the muscles of her back, reaching out her arm to rummage in her leather saddlebag for a water bottle.

'Shall we stop for the night, my lady?' One of the two soldiers who travelled with her—she thought his name was John—reined in beside her, the strong wind whipping his horse's tail. The individual strands fanned out, feathers on a bird's wing.

Brianna squinted at the grey, lowering sky, the faintest blush of sun discernible on the western horizon. 'We'll ride until it's dark.' She resented the presence of the two soldiers, unwilling to give them orders, unwilling to think for them as well as herself, but Jocelin had insisted, especially with Lady Mary urging him on at her side. For Hugh, Brianna simply couldn't have left soon enough; his palpable eagerness to see her *en route* to Matilda left a faint bitter taste in her mouth. But now, wiping the drops of liquid from her lips, she dismissed his behaviour; her brother was scared, that was all, scared that he wouldn't survive his illness and that Matilda and his child wouldn't reach him in time.

And Giseux? She clapped the leather stopper back into the bottle, stuffed it back into the bag on the rear of the horse and kicked the palfrey into a trot, indicating that the soldiers should follow her down the narrow sheep path off the ridge. Giseux had left, soon after their stilted conversation in the stables. Brianna had watched, covertly, from Hugh's upstairs window, as his tall commanding frame had clasped his father in a huge hug and kissed his mother's tear-wet cheeks, before springing into the saddle with athletic grace. Her body hummed with the memory of him: the solid hulk of his muscular chest and legs, the swift appraisal of his intelligent grey eyes, his dynamic presence ripping holes in her hard-won confidence. And she would never see him again…or be kissed by him. She scraped her top teeth roughly against her bottom lip, chewing thoughtfully, canting her body back to counter the palfrey's downward path from the top of the hill. There it was again; that thrill through her body, a nebulous fluttering that welled up in her chest, her stomach. A latent excitement, a kindling.

'Mistress?' The soldier's voice knocked into her thoughts; she forced herself to concentrate. 'We can cut through here to Thornslait; it will be quicker.' Brianna followed the direction of his uplifted arm. They had reached the bottom of the valley; a definite trail led westwards, with the bulk of deciduous woodland before them. Brianna eyed the stark outlines of the trees doubtfully; she was vaguely familiar with the route westwards, but in fairness, their destination lay to the north. 'Are you sure?'

'Oh, aye, mistress, I was born in Thornslait, I know the way,' the younger soldier reassured her. The fierce breeze flattened his sparse blond hair to his protruding forehead.

'You had better lead the way, then.' An uneasy feeling scampered through her veins; she told herself to ignore it. Jocelin was paying these men to protect her; he had picked them out himself. Even so, she touched her knife-belt, moving her fingers along to the scabbard, checking the hilt was snug, secure.

The woods were dim and still. Moss covered the damp, spongy ground, bright green mounds against the grey-brown trunks, mottled with sage-green lichen. Crisp brown bracken lay folded over in forlorn heaps, curling fronds singed by frost, waiting for spring. Birdsong sprung out haphazardly, startling the quiet; at the end of the day most birds sought a safe haven for the night. The two soldiers rode up front, the metallic links of their chainmail rippling like fish skin beneath their tunics as their destriers followed the path that skittered this way and that through the looming trees. Neither wore a helmet, or carried a shield; presumably both considered the level of threat to be minimal on such a journey. A heaviness grew in Brianna's heart; as reluctant as she was to reach her destination, and face her husband of old, she wondered whether these two knew their direction. Thornslait was only the first stop on a long journey; after tonight, they had at least another day of travelling.

The trio reached a spot where the stark canopy of bare branches broke overhead and the grey forbidding light poured down, illuminating the sheen of a murky, stagnant pool. Clumps of bleached, exhausted grass flung over the water's edge, like brittle, sea-soaked hair.

'Let's stop here,' the older soldier announced abruptly, wheeling his horse around in front of her, jumping down from the saddle. Her palfrey's head jerked up, stopping just in time to avoid bumping into the rear of the younger soldier's horse, who also was dismounting.

'Nay, not here!' Brianna frowned at their presumption. 'We will stop in the village, as we said.'

The older soldier grinned at her, his leering smile gapped with missing teeth. 'We prefer it here, my lady,' he drawled, stepping over to hold the palfrey's bridle. Pinpricks of stubble shadowed his chin, his upper lip. 'It's much quieter.'

The younger soldier snorted, unable to conceal his glee.

'And I prefer to spend the night in the village.' Her voice climbed a notch; suddenly she felt very unsafe. 'And let go of my horse's bridle!' She yanked downwards on the leather, but the soldier held firm, sneering up at her. 'Let go!' she said again, more firmly.

'We take orders only from Lord Jocelin.' The older soldier swept insolent eyes over the curve of her bodice.

Overheard, bare branches rubbed together, creaking and shifting in the brooding stillness.

'And Lord Jocelin isn't here,' the younger soldier reminded her, moving in on the other side of her horse, effectively trapping her.

Dear God, so it had come to this. *Breathe, breathe deeply and concentrate,* she told herself. *Don't panic, don't lose your head.* The mens' position, below her, made it difficult to use her knife. Instead, very, very slowly, beneath the concealing fall of her skirts, she nudged her toes out of each stirrup.

'Lord Jocelin will hear of this.' She condemned them with her tone. 'Your behaviour is despicable.'

'We haven't done anything yet, little lady,' the older man chortled, 'and we've the whole sweet night ahead of us.' As he lurched towards her, no doubt intending to pull her from the horse, she kicked up smartly, catching the toe of her boot against his grizzled chin. With a yelp of pain, he stumbled backwards, cursing, releasing his hold on the reins. At the same time, she kicked up with her left foot, but the younger man was too quick for her, holding fast to her boot before it made any contact with his body, fingers clamped around the toe.

She jabbed her leg continually against his grip, but he clung on, his narrow, spiteful face split into a huge grin. 'You can't escape now, my lady. We'll soon sort out your high-and-mighty ways!' The boot had always been a loose fit on her; the leather moved slackly over her calf, her ankle. She stopped kicking, flattening her toes so that the boot slipped off easily and experienced the briefest moment of pleasure as the young soldier flew backwards into a patch of brambles, clutching her empty boot. Then she seized the reins once more, jabbing desperately with her heels at the palfrey's rounded sides, navigating skilfully around the older man who half-rose from the ground, clutching his bleeding chin.

'You'll pay for this!' His expression was one of wild fury, mouth twisted into an ugly snarl. He lifted a fat fist, the whites of his eyes, bloodshot, bulging from his flabby face. Great pockets of sagging flesh hung beneath his sockets. 'We know these forests—there's no way you'll escape us!'

Panic drummed in her veins, hot blood rushing to her ears as she urged the horse forwards, faster, faster, plunging once more into the trees. She screwed up her eyes to decipher the trail in the dimming light. It was narrow, indistinct, thick brambles, ferns and clinging ivy crowding in from each side. How could she ever hope to escape them? The thought emerged on a half-sob, a clawing pressure in her chest. Already she could hear the chink of a bridle behind her; the men were mounting up, would soon be in pursuit.

The path, restricted by so much vegetation, prevented the palfrey from moving faster than a trot; with a sinking heart, Brianna realised she must continue on foot. She could never outrun those men; her only option was to hide, hide deep in the forest of impenetrable brambles that tore at her skirts, plucked at her arms. Slipping from the docile, ambling mare, she patted her rump, encouraging the animal to move on, but the horse merely looked at her curiously, with one round, unblinking eye, before beginning to tear at the short grass alongside the bare earth of the track. Brianna began to run, forwards at first, grimacing as stones poked into her left foot, covered only by a silk stocking. She ran fast, swiftly, filling her lungs with great gulps of air to speed her on, adrenalin firing the muscles in her legs, her back, knife jolting on her upper thigh. She pushed on, and on, until she heard the shouts of the soldiers behind her; they had reached her horse. Then she slowed, searching the brambles for a gap, a space into which she could squeeze and crawl away from the main path. Crouching down, she levered herself under the big, arching sprays of vicious thorns, careful to not disturb the undergrowth at the point where she had entered. Falling on to her hands and knees, she began to crawl forwards, fingers sinking into the wet, spongy ground, releasing a pungent, sour smell of rotting leaves. She heard them slashing at the undergrowth with their swords and forced herself onwards, faster, a small voice telling her not to panic, to keep going, quelling the bubbling fear in her chest.

Giseux. The name burst into her brain, carrying with it the power of the man, the sheer visceral strength. The force of her feeling shocked her. She wanted him, here, now, longed for his formidable energy, his protection. But he was far away and her heart folded in on itself at the feeling of utter loss, of absolute loneliness. Before, she had prided herself on being able to look after herself; now, she hated it.

Brianna sprung from the thicket of brambles into a scoop of land, covered in a mess of fallen leaves, shrouded by huge, massive beech trees. It was almost dark, the silver crescent of a new moon peeping through the net of branches above. The land rose up into a small mound, one side covered by a fallen beech, cracked into two pieces, the trunk white and brittle. Working her way carefully up the slope, breath punching out in short, sharp bursts, she spotted a dark hole where the tree had split, the jagged entrance fringed with waving tendrils of ivy: a natural hiding place. Sobbing with relief, Brianna wriggled into the space, ripping the veil and circlet from her head, fearing their brightness would betray her. Here she would hide, gather her scattered thoughts and wait until the soldiers became bored, or tired. She was prepared to wait for a long time.

She must have dozed fitfully for a while, her head leaning awkwardly against the smooth, grey bark of the lower trunk. Her eyes felt sore, itchy. Her neck jarred as she lifted it and she was thirsty, swallowing a couple of times as she tried to relieve the scratching dryness in her throat. Her face and hands were icy, limbs cramped and stiff after sitting still for so long. Drawing her knees up, she clasped them with her hands, listening intently. Was it safe for her to leave? She could see very little through the thick curtain of ivy, only a glimmer of moonlight highlighting the shadows. Her best plan would be to retrace her steps to the trail, then follow that back to the main path from which they had deviated earlier. Then she could return to Sefanoc, before embarking on the trip to fetch Matilda. Maybe she would ask one of the farmhands to accompany her;

somehow, her courage to travel alone seemed to have deserted her.

Inching cautiously from her hiding place, shoulder catching on a jutting-out section of rotten wood as she crawled forwards, she pushed out into the open, head drooping a little with fatigue. The wet leaves on the ground soaked through her stockinged foot as she levered herself slowly to her feet. The bowl of land was almost quiet, the low-slung branches shifting, whispering in the slight breeze, the squeakings and rustlings of night creatures, birds, filling the silence. She stumbled forwards, limping, her progress lit by the faint light of the rising moon. In the shadows, she realised a path led to the left of the bramble thicket through which she had previously fought her way and her heart lifted. Would they have taken her horse, or would they still be waiting for her? An oak tree lunged out of the darkness at her; she started at the wide trunk, its bark twisted, warped, like the grotesque face of a wizened crone, a witch. In her tiredness, she could even make out the hollowed eyes, the gaping mouth. She wrenched her gaze away, marched past firmly, dragging her cloak around her. Exhaustion was making her stupid, foolish; mistakes were one thing she couldn't afford to make.

When she finally reached it, the trail was empty. She peered round a supportive trunk, hugging the rigid knots that pinched her chest, and scanned first north, then south, the bare earth of the track ash-grey in the moonlight. Nothing. Maybe, in finding itself abandoned, her horse had made its way back to the clearing, seeking water? Her feet made no sound as she walked carefully back to the scene of her attack, her eyes and ears vigilant for any sight, any sound of the two soldiers. Apart from the delicate silver embroidery around the low, curving neckline of her gown, which she made sure was covered up by the folds of her cloak, she felt sure no sparkle of silver, or flash of gold, would give her position away. Her veil and circlet lay buried in a hole beneath the fallen beech tree.

A soldier and his horse stood by the pool, his back turned towards her. She saw the glimmer of chainmail beneath the enveloping cloak, the bare head, and knew they had waited. Waited for her. Her breath seized in her lungs, parcelling up her energy, turning her limbs to wet rags. Tears, hot and itchy, flooded her eyes. Foolish girl! Why had she not struck out on to the other side of the forest, pitted her wits against the unknown territory? She had wanted to find her horse, to make the journey easier on herself, and now she was going to pay for it.

She twisted around and fled, filling her lungs with great gulps of air to speed the muscles in her legs. Had he seen her? She hoped, prayed, it was the older soldier who she had seen, for he had looked as if he couldn't run further than a few steps. Great pounding footsteps echoed about the forest behind her; her heart quailed and she almost stumbled with the panic coursing through her veins. Sharp stones ripped at the soft sole of her left foot, unprotected with no leather boot, but she gritted her teeth and ploughed on. But the heavy, thudding footsteps gained on her; he was so close now, she could hear his steady, even, breathing.

Frustration rose in her chest, mingled with the slick of fear: this could not be happening!

An arm snaked out, caught at her waist and brought her down to the hard-packed earth. Breath punched from her lungs with the impact, from the solid ground smacking into her body, from the heavy weight sprawled over her back, crushing her. She lay, lips pressed against the dry soil, tasting the dust in her mouth, and wanted to howl. The energy drained from her slim frame, seeping into the earth around her. She tried to tell herself to fight, tried to conjure up words of strength, of courage, but found, with dismal sadness, that she simply had no strength left.

'Are you hurt?' a voice demanded in a harsh whisper, strident, oddly familiar.

The pressure on top of her lifted and a hand on her arm rolled her over on to her back, gently.

'What?' Eyes shut firmly, she mumbled, raising tentative fingers to her forehead, wondering if she were dreaming.

'I said, 'Are you hurt?' Talk to me!'

Brianna opened her eyes. Giseux hunched over her, kneeling, concern etched into the taut angles of his face. His hair stuck out in all directions, pale sable wisps falling over his forehead.

'Is it really you?' she whispered, without thinking, her eyes tracing the sensuous curve of his bottom lip. His grey eyes roamed over her, possessive, territorial. She raised one arm, hesitant, fingers touching the rugged slash of his jaw. The soft prickle of his beard rasped against her palm.

'Aye, of course it's me,' he snapped, drawing his breath in sharply at her feathered touch. What in Heaven's name had happened to her? The pale, delicate skin of her face was marked, fragile skin scratched with thin trails of blood; her cloak was torn.

'But…I thought you were leaving,' she breathed out, perplexed. 'I saw you leave…saw you ride out from Sambourne.' Strands of rust-coloured hair, tempered by the ethereal light, floated out around her head, spilled over the cracked, rutted earth.

'I changed my mind.' He chewed the words out. After his failure to persuade Brianna to stay with his parents, he had ridden straight to the castle of Robert de Lacey, an old friend who had been willing to travel to Germany in Giseux's stead to take up the cause of King Richard. The need to protect this woman had rushed over him, inexplicable, confusing, powerful. Knowing what Hugh had told him, he couldn't leave Brianna alone, vulnerable: he told himself it was his knight's duty, at least, to protect her.

'You changed your mind,' she murmured, incredulous. What was he saying—that he had come back… for her? Her befuddled mind failed to make sense of his words. Fighting to contain the spinning in her head, Brianna levered herself into a sitting position. She sagged forwards, palms resting against her knees. 'I thought you were them,' she stuttered out. He caught the flash of half-dried tears on her cheek. 'I waited and waited…I *hid*—' her arm flailed out as if to indicate a vague hiding place '—and I thought they would be gone.' She shook her head, the chaotic bundle of hair at the nape of her neck threatening to dislodge. 'Why didn't you call out to me, why did you chase me like that? I thought I was finished.' A great gulping sob tore at her chest, but she bound her arms tightly about her bosom, suppressing it.

'I'm sorry,' he replied, cursing his actions. 'I had no intention of scaring you. But moving silently has its advantages. Those soldiers might still be about.'

Brianna shuddered.

'I found your boot.' He dangled the buff-coloured leather before her.

She took it from him, bent down to jam her toes back into the supple leather, ignoring the pain as the boot constricted the cuts, the lacerations on the sole of her foot. Her eyes pricked with tears. 'It came off in his hands,' she responded, her voice hitching with the memory. 'When I kicked at him.'

His calm eyes sparkled over her, grimly assessing. 'What happened?'

'They attacked me...they were going to...' She dropped her face into her hands, feeling the tears gush through her fingers. His arms wound around her shoulders, pulling her head into his chest, his heart lifting as he acknowledged the softening of her body against him, no resistance. The smell of sweet lavender rose from her hair, tantalising his nostrils. She had been through so much, this maid, he thought. He had chided her for eschewing any help, for fighting her own battles, and now, when protection was forced on her, this had happened. Who could she trust?

Him. She could trust him. If only he could persuade her of that fact.

Brianna rested her forehead against the finely spun wool of his surcoat, the steady, reassuring beat of his heart pulsating against her skin. His tunic smelled of washing soap, a mixture of rose water and lye, mingled with the musky scent of his skin, a hint of exotic spices. His warmth, his energy, percolated through her frazzled senses. Her head brushed against the curve of his upper arm where it joined into the muscled mass of his shoulder and she gritted her teeth, fighting the temptation to pull even closer to him. She wanted to stay there for ever.

'Brianna?' The smoky timbre of his voice echoed over the top of her head. 'We need to move.'

She lifted her head reluctantly, the skin beneath her eyes bruised, swollen with exhaustion. The lean cut of his jaw seemed very, very close, blond bristles hazing his chin.

'I suppose I need to keep going north.' Her voice was a dull monotone, lacklustre, her energy deflated by the recent events. She shook her head, once, a sharp, jerky movement, picking erratically at a loose thread on her girdle that hung over her knife-belt. 'Your father picked those soldiers out to protect me…and look what happened!'

'Those men will be found and punished for what they did.' Giseux studied her bent head. He should never have left her alone.

In the drifting moonlight, her skin shone like alabaster, her beautiful hair glinting like spun gold. The onset of night had brought a corresponding drop in temperature; a tremble seemed to seize her slight figure.

'We need to find somewhere to shelter for the night; it's too cold to sleep in the open.' He touched her arm, meaning to help her up, lead her to the horses, but she pulled back, hesitating, and his arm fell away.

'Why did you come?' Her brow creased in puzzlement. 'The last time I saw you, you were riding for Germany.'

That was before I realised I... He smothered the next word before it entered his brain, but it hung, teetering on the edge of his consciousness, taunting him. No, never that…had he gone completely mad? Thunderstruck at the wave of emotion that pulsed through him, he sprung upwards, lunging away from her hunched figure to fetch both horses, patiently cropping the short grass by the pool.

'Someone has to stop you rushing headlong into the trap your brother has set for you.' He towered over her, both sets of reins in one hand.

She scowled at the metal rivets on his boot lacings. 'Why do you persist in this false reasoning? I've told you before, Hugh would never do a thing like that to me.'

'Not even for the love of his life, the girl he has dreamed of returning home to after three long years away?'

'Nay.' She shook her head slowly, trying to ignore the creep of doubt inching through her chest. 'And I don't need you to come with me.' Her protest sounded feeble, even to her own ears. 'I don't need you.'

Giseux snared both sets of reins in one hand, covering the ground back to her seated figure in three great strides. He bent down, scooping her easily to her feet, bracing her into his side as she teetered. 'Nay, Brianna,' he murmured, warm breath fanning her pale cheek, 'you need me.'

And as his silver eyes glittered over her, she realised that it was true.

Chapter Nine

A huddle of cottages gathered around a small patch of green formed the village of Thornslait. The houses were simple, rectangular buildings, walls made up from a mixture of mud and straw plastered over a mesh of woven sticks. Smoke poured from holes in the thatch roofs, spilling into the night air like dark liquid.

Through gritty eyes, Brianna watched as Giseux dismounted, handing her his reins to hold, and walked towards the nearest house. An old man opened the door at Giseux's knock, his face shadowed by the overhang of thatch that protected the walls from rain and snow. She heard the brief exchange of speech, too far away to decipher the actual words. A perplexing detachment stole over her; it felt strange for someone else to organise her night's accommodation—normally she would have insisted on deciding for herself where she was to sleep. She couldn't quite believe that this man, this knight, had changed his plans for her, had come after her; she wanted to pinch herself, to make certain she wasn't dreaming. Giseux handed the man some money, a gleam of silver in the gloaming, then, wrapping himself into a threadbare cloak, the old man took up a long walking stick, moving off into the centre of the village.

'Giseux,' she hissed, glancing anxiously after the hobbling figure. 'What are you doing?'

'Securing us a bed for the night.' Before she could argue, he laced his hands around her narrow waist and swung her down from the palfrey.

'But…where is he going?'

Giseux tied both horses to a rickety wooden post near the cottage, releasing the girth straps to haul the heavy saddles from the horses. He dropped them onto the ground, in the lee of the roof. Taking her fingers, stiff with cold, he led her through the door. 'He will sleep on a pallet bed, at his daughter's cottage.'

'But to turn him out of his own home!' Her gaze fixed longingly on the dancing flames set in a circle of stones in the middle of the packed earth floor, a rustic hearth. The smoke curled upwards, slowly, filling the air with a slight haze, before sucking up through the hole in the roof.

Giseux turned to her, his sculptured profile lit by the orange glow from the fire. 'He was happy to go, Brianna. He and his family will not want for food for many months.'

'But…?' The heat from the fire seared through the front of her gown, her legs; an involuntary shudder passed through her, as her frozen limbs began to warm up.

'Stop fretting,' he countered firmly. 'You need to sleep.'

She searched the interior for some form of bed, a pallet, but found nothing.

'Up there.' Giseux pointed, the fine metallic scales of his chainmail glinting, rippling over his broad shoulders.

Brianna followed his outstretched arm, up a makeshift ladder cobbled together from wonky, ill-fitting pieces of wood, to a sleeping platform, set high up beneath the rafters. 'And where will you sleep?' she asked sternly. The fleeting memory of his kiss scalded her brain.

He grinned. 'I will sleep here, in front of the fire.' He quirked one eyebrow at her, challenging her to disagree, to wrangle with him.

But to his surprise, she nodded, then turned away, climbing the ladder with a graceful agility. He caught the tantalising glimpse of pale, stocking-covered calves above her short boots, before she threw herself down into the mound of straw that would be her bed for the night.

Easing her boots off, wincing, she wrapped herself in one of the many blankets that were folded neatly to one side of the sleeping area, then popped her head over the edge of the platform. Giseux was still standing, contemplating the dancing flames.

'Giseux?' she called out, her voice tentative. One loop of burnished hair hung down behind her ear.

He looked up, eyes burning with black fire, dangerous.

'Thank you.'

At first, Brianna wasn't sure of the identity of the sound. Reluctant to be drawn out of the comfortable, delicious sleep that had claimed her almost immediately after her head had touched the straw-stuffed pillow, she rolled over, away from the noise, hoping it would disappear, vanish. But no, there it was again, a low-pitched moan, then a shout. Her eyes popped open, heart racing. It was Giseux.

Lying on her back, her body supported by a deep mound of straw, she studied the rafters above her head. The layer of thatching reeds formed neat, vertical lines between the uneven cross-beams. Should she go to him? Very, very slowly, she crawled to the edge of the platform, dragging the blanket with her for warmth, and peeped down.

Her heart rolled, Giseux lay on his back, quiet now, limbs sprawled beside the dying embers of the fire. A blanket tangled around his chest and legs, the white linen of his shirt stark against the dull brown of the wool. He had kept on the braies he wore beneath his armour; his feet were bare. She jumped as he shouted again, one hand jolting downwards to clutch at his right thigh through the blanket. The movement galvanised her; all logic, all conscious thought drove from her mind at the sight of him. She had to help him.

The rungs of the ladder bit into her bare feet as she descended; she sucked in her breath sharply as the cuts on her foot throbbed. She had been so tired, she had forgotten to look at the injury. Kneeling at Giseux's side, Brianna perched back on her heels, unsure, hoping that he would wake up, would pull himself up out of this nightmare. But no, he continued to thrash from side to side, his eyes tight shut, deep in some other terrifying world. Sweat strung through his hair, turning the pale brown strands darker, more sable, the chiselled panels on each side of his face taut with some unseen agony. Sunburn touched his high cheekbones, lending him a wild, predatory appearance.

'Giseux,' she said loudly. 'Giseux, wake up!'

In response, his fingers clawed into his upper thigh, the sinews in his hand rigid, straining. Snaring the muscular bulk of his shoulders between her hands, she tried to shake him, tried to lift his upper body from the ground, but to no avail: he was too heavy. In desperation, her eyes searched the cottage interior, the uneven walls, for something that might help, before a sudden, bizarre idea touched her.

Blood hurtled through her veins, blossoming the skin of her face. Hands on his shoulders, she dipped her head. Kissed him.

Her soft lips touched his firm mouth in a last attempt to hush the demons of the night that claimed him. A dangerous warmth stole over her, melting her limbs, turning the muscles in her knees to useless mush; she shuddered, striving to hold her body away from him. It was only a kiss, she told herself, a simple device to alleviate his distress. The rigid frame of his body beneath her stilled, quietened.

His lips moved beneath hers; responded. She told herself to draw away, to sit back on her heels, but her heart told her otherwise. The touch of his mouth spiralled each nerve in her body to a singing desire, a yearning for more. The regular beat of her blood picked up speed, throbbing, driving logic from her brain, forcing her to feel, not think. His tongue played along the seam of her lip, teasing, testing, and she opened her lips above his like a flower unfurling in sun, wanting more. His mouth roamed, insistent, demanding, as his arms came around her, his hands moving along the graceful rope of her spine, pulling her into the broad expanse of his chest. Against the pliant curve of her breast, his heart thudded.

Giseux groaned, one big hand smoothing over the tempting flare of her hip, the top of her thigh, hitching the fabric of her gown with questing fingers. Brianna's eyes shot open at the intimacy of his touch. Lurching away from him, heart bumping erratically against her ribs, she knelt back into the pile of straw, cheeks flaming.

'You were dreaming!' Her voice was hard-edged, on the defensive. She tucked a wayward strand of hair carefully, behind one ear, smoothed shaking hands over the plush velvet skirts spread over her lap. Had she truly lost her wits? It would have been far safer to throw the contents of his water bottle over his head. Her mind crawled with embarrassment.

Giseux's eyes shone, pellucid, fathomless pools of grey flint as they roved over her kneeling figure, the taut curves packed temptingly into the lilac gown. 'You were kissing me.' Astonishment traced his voice. He sat up, the blanket falling in rough folds into his lap. The gauzy linen of his shirt stuck to his chest, the slash of the V-neck tugged to one side to reveal his strong, corded throat.

'You were having some sort of nightmare, Giseux,' she explained, trying to control the race of her breath. 'I… You wouldn't wake up. It was, well, the only thing I could think of doing.' The blush on her face deepened, a scarlet hue, as she continued, limply, staring at her hands. 'I could have thrown some water over you.'

His hand stretched out towards her, fingers beneath her chin gently lifting her drooping head. His gaze burned into her, mouth curved into a half-smile. 'I'm very glad you didn't.' His voice, wrenched from sleep, was husky.

She frowned, ignoring his sensual reference. 'You were shouting out. It must have been a bad nightmare.'

'It was.' Yet for some inexplicable reason, the details of this dream were hazy, subdued by the sweet taste of Brianna's lips, the featherlight touch of her fingers searing his shoulders. Absentmindedly, he rubbed at his leg, using his knuckles to try to knead away the burning ache. 'I'm sorry I woke you.'

'What happened to your leg?'

Seizing a couple of branches from a loose pile against the wall, Giseux threw them into the glowing embers, sending sparks shooting upwards. The sweet smell of burning apple wood filled the air. 'That time I told you about…with Nadia.' Brianna read the shadows in his eyes and tried to ignore the flip of regret in her heart as he spoke his lover's name, clasping her hands sensibly in her lap. 'An arrow went into my leg. It could have been worse.'

'It obviously gives you pain,' she chipped back, gently.

The lilting tones of her voice swept over him, tender, caring. In the glowing embers of the fire, she appeared like an angel, her magnificent hair, uncovered, like a halo of flame. *Not any more,* he thought. *Not with you.* What had happened out there, in the hot and dusty desert land, the memories that covered his every waking moment with a black suffocating film, seem to recede in her presence, her lightness of heart, her sympathy. Or was it empathy, for she had surely suffered too?

'Most of my men were killed in the attack, Brianna,' he said finally.

She shook her head. 'I am sorry.' The crushed silk velvet of her gown shone, glimmering damson-coloured in the light of the flames. Instinctively, her fingers reached for his, a simple gesture of comfort. His strong, sinewy hand engulfed hers.

'It was a long time ago,' he murmured, pupils widening, black pools of desire.

Without thinking, she tipped her upper body forwards, wrapping slim arms around his breadth, drawing him close. Beneath the pads of her fingers on his back, his muscles on his back were tense, inflexible, and, recklessly, she pulled him closer, touching her body to his.

The yielding contours of her figure butted up against

his chest, the swell of her bosom nudging the gauzy linen of his shirt. His innards liquefied, the flicker of desire that kindled steadily, constantly in his gut rupturing into a stark, uncontrollable craving. His arms came up, clasped her shoulders, squeezing her tight. His nostrils trapped the shifting perfume of her hair, loose strands floating silkily around her head, plucking at the light from the fire to turn each strand into a glowing, vibrant filament. Her eyes, large ovals of opulent blue, held empathy, not pity. And yet as Brianna held him, a small voice in his head jeered at him. He was using her, taking advantage of her kind nature to drive the demons from his head. He didn't deserve her comfort, or her sympathy; she didn't deserve to be dragged down by his dark soul. Breathing heavily, his body growing warm beneath her touch, he shoved her away, the movement so unexpected, so brusque that she blinked at him in surprise. 'Go!' he ordered her, his eyes bright with desire, burning into her startled face. 'Go to bed, now, before I do something that we both regret.'

Rolling herself back into the rough woollen blanket, the coarse weave grazing her cheek, Brianna told herself she should be grateful to Giseux, grateful that he had stopped, rejected her. She had made a mistake, for even in that simple act of comfort, those strange flames of excitement had leapt up again, stirring her belly. Her limbs tingled with the frustration of his rebuff, his abrupt rejection, every muscle quivering with the anticipation of what might have been, then shrivelling with the cold knowledge of desertion.

Angrily, she twisted on to her side, tucking her cloak fastidiously around her. How could she want anything at all from a man after her time with Walter? Surely that experience had taught her all she needed to know about men? Enough to realise that she was content to live a life without one. She was treading on dangerous, unstable ground, breaking her own rules; it was imperative that she kept her distance from him. Her life, her own sanity, depended upon it. Whether her heart agreed or not, was an entirely different matter.

Raising his arms to lever his hauberk over his head, the cold metallic scales sliding over his face before settling in their familiar positions over his shoulders, his chest and thighs, Giseux shouted up to Brianna. He had woken early, listening to her steady, even breathing above him, aware of a heady lightness, a weightlessness around his heart.

'Brianna!' he bellowed upwards once more. He had already saddled both horses in his shirt-sleeves, breath puffing out in the frosty morning air.

'I'm coming.'

He waited, impatiently, cocking his head to one side, expecting to see her appear at the top of the ladder. Nothing.

'Brianna? What are you doing?' He planted one foot at the bottom of the ladder, then climbed quickly to the top. His tousled head appeared on a level with the platform, his chest leaning against the wooden edge for support. Brianna sat in the mound of straw, wisps of dry grass clinging to her skirts. Her knees were drawn up, her feet were bare, pink toes flashing daintily against the dull yellow of the straw. Her pale stockings lay in a wrinkled pile beside her.

Giseux frowned. 'You're ready. Put your boots on.'

Brianna fixed him with a sapphire stare. 'I can't.' The skin on her face was taut, white, stretched across her fine, high cheekbones.

'Why not?' he barked.

'Because I've done… Because I ran barefoot through the forest, after I lost my boot. It's all swollen.' She stuck out her foot to show him. Bloodied cuts and deep grazes in the underside of her foot marked the tender skin. Bruises bloomed in the puffy flesh, blue and purple, marred by black specks of grit and dirt.

'You little fool.' His gaze pounced on her, immediately condemning. 'Why didn't you say anything last night?'

Because you were kissing me, she thought, erratically. *I was kissing you.* 'It wasn't hurting last night.' Her shoulders sagged.

'It needs to be cleaned.' The svelte contours of his face loomed closer. 'Come over here, let me help you.'

She stared at his outstretched fingers, heart bumping treacherously as she remembered his hand clamped fiercely to her hip, his heated breath at her throat. 'I can probably make it down…alone.' She chewed at her lip doubtfully.

'If you're sure…?'

Brianna nodded vigorously, mouth set firm against his incisive perusal, before he disappeared, thankfully, down the ladder.

Giseux watched as first one boot, then the other, were thrown down from the platform to the ground below, one narrowly missing his head. One boot ended up with its toe stuck into the cold fire pit, releasing a puff of grey ash into the air. Brianna crawled forwards, eyes rooted with determination on the top rung of the rickety ladder. Turning around, she reached down as far as she could with her good foot, toes skimming the rung. Gritting her teeth, she swung her other leg down. Pain chewed through her, burning, lacerating, as she forced her left foot down on to the next rung, sweat slicking her palms as she gripped the sides of the ladder. Her gown was riding up, catching against the rough wooden rungs, revealing her legs.

'Stop watching me, will you? Wait outside, or something!' she hissed, tipped her head down to him. Her face was flushed, a light sheen of sweat covering her skin. He folded his arms across his big chest, the black wool of his surcoat rumpling with the movement.

'I'll stay,' he replied, infuriatingly. He eyed the shapely indent of her knees, the elusive gleam of her lower thighs before they disappeared into her rucked-up, bunching skirts.

Catching the flash of interest in his eyes, Brianna jumped backwards, a rash decision. Her feet hit the ground, hard, both feet taking the full impact of her body weight. Throbbing pain shot through her damaged foot, sending raw fingers of agony clutching through her heel and her calf; she yelped, staggering backwards, falling, landing in a heap of skirts.

'Hell's teeth!' she cursed, banging the flats of her

hands against the hard-packed ground. 'You put me off, unnerved me. I could have done it!' Tears of frustration stung her lashes; they shone like tiny black feathers beneath the fine arch of her brows.

He ignored her, crouching down to glance at the bottom of her foot. 'Stay there while I fetch some water.'

He returned, moments later, carrying a shallow, earthenware bowl slopping with freezing liquid, leaving the door ajar. A rush of fresh morning air stirred the dead ashes in the stone-circled fire pit. He flicked her hem up swiftly; the lilac material riffled across her pale calves as he surveyed her injured foot with a critical eye.

'I like to do things for myself.' Breath bundled in her chest as she tried to explain her stubbornness, to try to lighten the blossoming tension. The tendons strained as his fingers supported her heel, lashes fanning down over his gimlet eyes as he proceeded to clean the wounds, dark spots speckling the dry earth from the wet, sopping cloth.

'You don't need to remind me,' he replied drily. Cupped in his big hands, her foot was small, the bones delicate, pink skin contrasting sharply with his tanned fingers. The translucent colour of her nails reminded him of the pearly insides of seashells.

'In the last few years, while Hugh has been away…' she paused, searching for the right words '…I have felt free.'

He laughed. 'What, with Count John's men on your back?'

She frowned. 'Nay, you don't understand. Nobody was telling me what to do. I could run the manor, run the farm exactly how I liked. I loved it, making my own decisions every day. Especially after…' Her voice trailed away.

'After…?' he nudged. His heart contracted as the high arch of her instep tensed against his grip.

'After my marriage,' she whispered. 'Walter, my… my husband, made every decision for me, what I wore, what I ate, what I would do. And if I failed to carry out his orders…'

Giseux's hands stilled, droplets of water raining down from the cloth back into the bowl.

'…then he would beat me.'

Rage sliced through him, sharp, piercing, tapered fingers twisting savagely into the cloth. It was not unusual for a husband to treat his wife in such a manner, but for it to have happened to her, this beautiful, delicate maid, with her indomitable spirit, her feisty ways, made his heart split with anger, with disgust.

'No man should treat a woman thus.' One big thumb smoothed against her satiny cheek, trying to erase the frozen hurt from her expression.

Brianna shrugged her shoulders, resisting the urge to turn her face into the warm cup of his palm. 'It was over in six months. Some women have to endure such marriages for a lifetime. I was fortunate.'

His laughter was abrasive, ragged. 'Only you, Brianna, only you could look back on such a situation and say that you were lucky.'

'I have to think about it like that, otherwise…' Otherwise the memories came crowding in, black and fast, overwhelming.

His storm-cloud eyes skewered her, sensing her hesitation in telling him the full truth of her marriage.

'Why did you marry him?'

'I think my parents had given up hope of my ever finding a husband. Walter was their last chance to see me settled, happy.' Her voice trembled. 'And then they died, within weeks of each other, so I could never tell them how…' Her eyes rounded in the dim interior of the cottage, pools of cerulean light. 'They thought he would be good for me.'

Giseux's eyes blackened. So that was it. Her parents had arranged the marriage to Walter in order to beat the spirit from her, to fall into line, to conform to the expected standards in society. He was glad they hadn't succeeded.

'I'm surprised you agreed to the marriage,' he muttered. Glossy, hazelnut-brown locks fell over his tanned forehead as he smeared her skin with a thick, pungent salve, wrapping the whole foot in a linen bandage, tying the ends tightly over the top of her foot with practised efficiency.

She drew in a sharp breath, forlorn. 'Daughters of noblemen have little choice in these matters, Giseux. Surely you know that? We do what our parents tell us to do. I had resisted marriage for so long, I think they were beginning to despair of me. I had to marry…for their sake.'

His nod was curt, brisk, fingers curling at his sides as he stood. Why hadn't she held out for longer, resisted further? At least then she would have been spared such a harrowing experience. In a rush of realisation he wished he could have been there, could have done something to prevent it from happening. But what? He had been a knight since the age of twelve, committed to fighting for his country, embroiled in battle after battle, in a place where women held little significance other than for fleshly gratification. He would have looked on and done nothing. So what had changed?

'You can't go back there, Brianna. You can't go back to Walter.'

She looked up, stunned, hitching herself on to her knees so she could clamber to her feet. The bandage felt hot, bulky around her foot. 'But I must go, I promised Hugh.'

'Break the promise.' He caught her elbow, helped her to her feet as she staggered slightly. 'I can fetch Matilda and the boy.' His brilliant eyes spiked her with steely precision.

'You'd do that?' Her heart trembled at his unexpected kindness.

'I've told you, Walter wants you back. You are the trade-off.'

'Nay! Not this again!' She staggered away from him. 'Why will you not believe that Hugh doesn't hold my best interests at heart?'

'Because he told me, Brianna. He told me what he planned to do. You're riding straight into a trap.'

She clutched her arms about her chest, moving back slowly towards the door, limping slightly. 'It doesn't make sense, Giseux. You don't make sense.'

'And you're a fool if you persist in this stubbornness. Why would I make something like this up?'

'I'm going, Giseux, whether you like it or not. I can stand up to Walter.' Blood boiling in her ears, she pulled at the simple wooden lever, wrenching open the door. The cool air smacked into her flushed face; she sagged a little, a tiny voice in her brain telling her she had been stupid, so stupid. With every word, she pushed Giseux away, yet every fibre of her being wanted him to stay, to come with her.

'Are you coming?' Her voice was small, muted, her fingers playing furtively with a rough snag of wood on the latch. A little knot of sorrow hardened around her heart. Why must she be so outspoken?

'After the way you talk to me?' He caught the flash of vulnerability in her eyes, swiftly suppressed.

'I'm sorry,' she whispered, a huge sense of loss beginning to coagulate around her heart, 'it's just that…'

He waved her apology away, packing up the spare bandages into his leather saddlebags, pushing the cork stopper back into the jar of salve. 'Forget it…I've told you, I will go with you.' He drank in the beauty of her cerulean eyes, the coiled amber strands of her hair, the seductive tilt of her curves in the clinging velvet gown. If he were a wise man, he would leave now, before he became too embroiled, too snarled up in the whole domestic tragedy of Brianna's life. But something about this woman entranced him, lured him, made his heart sing when he was at her side; there was no way he could leave her now, especially with Hugh's words of betrayal ringing constantly in his ears. He would make sure she was safe, safe and protected, and then he would go, leave to carry on with his own life, whatever that was.

Chapter Ten

Northwards from Thornslait, the countryside opened up, smoothing out into a series of high, rounded chalk plateaux. Down in the valleys, deciduous trees clustered, bare branches skeletal against the scrubby hillside, studded with the untidy nests of crows, messy baubles against the lucid blue sky. Rooks rose sporadically in the air, black wings like flashing knifeblades, wheeling and circling in the weak sunlight. Higher up, on the rougher moorland blasted continuously by a keen, penetrating wind, the trees were few: small sessile oaks and stunted hawthorns clutching on to the tussocky ground with roots exposed.

Giseux, the hem of his surcoat flapping out at the sides, galloped up ahead, the muscled rump of his horse shining with sweat, lumps of sticky white earth flying up from beneath the hooves. He kicked his animal on, urging it to move faster, more rapidly, over the easy ground. With her bandaged foot held gingerly within the stirrup, Brianna found it difficult to keep up with his relentless pace. Despite great effort, she was dropping back, the distance between them growing further, wider. Hunger gnawed at her stomach; Thornslait had been barely stirring when they had clattered out of the village at first light, no fires lit, no prospect of food in sight. She eased back on the reins, slowing to a walk. The wind cut in around the back of her neck and she raised the voluminous hood of her cloak to cover her bright head.

His horse covering the ground in great, long strides, Giseux's head whipped around. Sawing roughly on the reins, he wheeled the animal about, charged back to her. 'Why have you slowed down?' he roared at her over the sifting wind, massive shoulders silhouetted against the washed-out blue of the sky. 'We need to keep going.'

'Giseux,' she replied patiently, her cheeks ruddy from the smarting wind, 'I'm hungry and thirsty; we've been riding for *hours*.'

His silvered glance followed the line of her hem as it curved from the palfrey's neck to its rump. 'Have you changed your mind?' he murmured. Every sinew in his body clamoured for her to turn around now, to avert the danger which she was placing herself, but reason told him that she would never trust him until she realised the truth of her brother's betrayal for herself. He could only stay by her side and protect her.

Brianna angled forwards, patted her horse on the side of its neck. The short-cropped grey coat was sleek, a velvet nap beneath her fingers. 'Nay, of course not.'

Her voice hitched. The closer they travelled to Matilda's home, *Walter*'s home, the bigger the sunken pit of anxiety grew within her. 'I *am* hungry, really hungry. I'm not one of your soldiers who can march for hours and hours on an empty stomach.'

His mouth levered into a half-smile, gaze running over her slender curves. 'No, you're not,' he admitted. 'We can stop at Whitton, it's further up, at the end of this ridge.'

They were in luck; it was market day in the small town. Crowds of people thronged the square, pushing and jostling against each other as they fought to buy, to sell, to barter. The cries of the vendors rang out, clashing with the noisy shouts and laughter emerging from the ale houses bordering the square. Each merchant had tried to outdo the next in attracting customers: bright, rippling silks sat next to floury rounds of bread, piled high in teetering, yeasty mounds. Wheels of cheese balanced on top of each other, next to a stack of candles; a vat of salted ham. The smell of roasting meat filled the air, coupled with the honeyed scent of mead and the acrid smell of animal dung.

People dropped back when they saw Giseux, broad and impressive on his glossy destrier, eyeing his shining armour covertly, respectfully, as he walked his own horse, and led Brianna on her palfrey to a wooden bar where he could secure the bridles.

'Do you want to stay here?' He eyed the white gleam of her bandaged foot.

Brianna scanned the colourful, chaotic mass of the

market, the smell and noise entrancing her. It had been a long time since she'd had the pleasure of wandering through a street market; normally she was the one trying to sell her wares. 'Can I come?' she asked tentatively.

'You don't normally ask permission,' Giseux commented drily, extracting her scuffed leather boot from the saddlebag resting on the rump of her horse. A jolt of exhilaration shot up her calf as he gripped her heel, sliding her foot carefully into the loose-fitting leather. 'How does that feel?'

'Much better.' She swung her leg over the rump of her horse, aiming to dismount, but he caught her waist, lowered her down gently.

'Take it easy; there were some deep cuts that will take a bit of time to heal.'

Brianna laughed, rummaging for her money pouch. She had a few pennies, enough to buy a bread roll that would fill her stomach. 'Fear not, Giseux. I'm not about to go running about just yet.'

Her laughter was like music, rippling, magical, the sheer beauty of the sound spiking deep into his chest. The pale, beautiful oval of her face lifted with her smile. He couldn't remember when he'd seen anything so wonderful.

'I think that's the first time I've seen you laugh,' he said, sticking his arm out at a right angle, indicating that she should take it, and, with a lifting heart, she curled her arm around the crook of his elbow.

'It's because I feel so…' Happy, she had been about

to say. Happy that he was with her, happy that he had stayed, despite her not believing his words about Hugh.

'You feel so…?' His voice nudged her for an answer.

'So…much better. My foot, I mean,' she ended lamely.

Her heart danced as they walked as a couple through the market, on that cold, jewel-bright winter day. She knew he only held on to her to prevent her falling flat on her face, but even so, she could enjoy the sensation of his muscled upper arm pressed into her shoulder, bolstering her. They wandered across the rutted, uneven mud of the main square, negotiating the rank, open drains and empty barrels tipped over outside an inn, to a row of stalls, some only trestle tables, decorated with colourful flags, or fluttering awnings strung from one side of the stall to the other.

'Is that all you want?' Giseux asked, as Brianna handed over her few pennies for a couple of bread rolls. 'I thought you said you were hungry.'

'This will fill me up,' she replied firmly. It was enough that he was escorting her; she couldn't start borrowing money from him as well. She hadn't thought to ask Hugh for any coin before she had left for the trip.

The wizened old crone behind the stall parcelled up the warm bread into a cloth bag. 'I bet you're glad your husband is home…alive.' The woman nodded in the direction of Giseux, his attention distracted by a squabble to his left between two stallholders. Her watery eyes studied the sleek chainmail, the sparkling hilt of his sword.

'Oh, but he's not my…' Brianna's words faltered on

her lips, cheeks ripening with faint colour. She glanced covertly at Giseux, but he was watching the argument; he hadn't heard, thank God. Was it really possible that they had been mistaken for man and wife? Heat suffused her bones, heart sparkling with the thought: is this how it would feel, married to Giseux? As quickly as the image arose, she quashed it, smartly; it could never be. But for this moment in time, she could enjoy the comfortable pressure of his arm in hers, the support of his powerful, long-limbed body against her side, and treasure the memory for ever.

At Giseux's suggestion they rode to a quieter spot outside the town, to a glade of silver birch, their nude branches swaying like tendrils of hair in the breeze. Down in this valley, the wind was less fierce and the climbing sun pierced through the branches, casting a dappled shade that reminded her of spring. From the back of his horse, Giseux produced a blanket, which he spread over the thin, spindly grass growing beneath the trees.

He flung himself down on to the tight woollen weave, propping his back against the slim trunk of the birch. Ripping open his saddlebag, he spread his purchases before him: cheese, roast meat, bread and fruit, and began to eat with appreciation. Dismounting carefully, Brianna's mouth watered; she wanted to hide the small cloth bag containing her own meagre fare.

Giseux glanced up as she sat down, folding her knees to one side beneath her as she perched on the edge of the blanket. 'Please, share some of mine.' He threw her a wide, unexpected smile. 'I bought too much.

I've spent so long chewing my way through charred, unidentifiable meat—when I saw what was on offer at that market, well, I couldn't resist.'

Nibbling on her bread roll, Brianna eyed the food laid out before him. 'Maybe a bit of cheese?'

'Take it.' He pushed a round of cheese towards her, throwing his silver eating knife after it, so she could cut a slice. He leaned his head back against the trunk, closing his eyes. 'God, this food tastes good. You were right to make me stop.'

She wished she could stay, here, in this place for ever. Like the sound of the sea against shingle, the wind shivered through the branches above, moving spots of shadow over Giseux's face; he was so still, his face upturned to the sun, that she wondered whether he slept. Both his knees were drawn up, the skirt of his tunic falling back against his thighs to reveal the tight, bunched muscle of his legs beneath his close-fitting armour.

'We've not much further to go, Brianna, till Walter's castle. Are you still insisting on doing this?'

Brianna placed her half-eaten roll carefully back into her bag. 'I must, Giseux, I must face Walter.' *Otherwise he will haunt my whole life, colour my behaviour for ever.* 'I must face my demons,' she said, finally.

'This trip isn't about Hugh at all, is it?' One huge hand appeared across the rug, lifting her cold fingers, encircling them, lightly. 'You've never recovered from what happened to you, have you?'

Hot tears sprung to her eyes. 'I…' Words deserted her—his understanding was so surprising.

'It's fortunate there were no children,' he murmured, studying her closed, pinched expression. 'Otherwise you would never have been able to leave.'

'No, no children,' she whispered. The pulse in his corded wrist beat against her slender white hand. 'The marriage was annulled after six months.' Her knife-belt had slipped and she twisted it around, so that the weapon lay flat against the side of her hip. She threw him a wan, shy smile, trying to appear braver than she felt.

'The marriage was annulled?' He appeared incredulous, slanting his upper body towards her, seeking clarification. The light granite of his eyes deepened to obsidian.

'Yes, what of it?' Brianna eyed him suspiciously, shifting uncomfortably at the change in his tone. Through her gown, the loose weave of the blanket prickled her limbs.

'The marriage was annulled…after six months?'

'Yes.'

'But a marriage has to be unconsummated for an annulment to take place.'

Face reddening, she began to pack his food back into the saddlebags, intent on busying herself, anything to avoid that searching gaze. She recalled those long, dreadful nights, afeard that Walter would come to her, would try to make love to her, and fail. Then he would hit her, bellowing accusation after accusation at her, telling her it was all her fault. She was too thin, too unattractive. But even as those blows rained down, her heart had sung with relief. Throughout it all, she had remained innocent.

'Was it consummated?' Giseux asked again. For some inexplicable reason, his heart began to lift, to soar with the knowledge that the maid before him had known no man.

Damp sweat slicked her palms. 'I can't believe you're asking me such things!' Her whole body vibrated, hot flames of embarrassment searing through her as she began to brush the crumbs from the rug, busy, industrious.

'Was it?' The low baritone of his voice resonated through the hushed glade, a velvet command.

She lurched back on her heels, smoothing her hands down the front of her skirts. 'No, never.' As she traced the individual threads that formed the bright warp of the blanket with a frowning intensity, her flush deepened.

'It's not something to be ashamed of.'

Her eyes flicked up, sparking anger. 'Ashamed? I am not ashamed, Giseux. I find it embarrassing to talk about such things with you, but ashamed—' she shook her head defiantly '—nay, far from it.' The pitch of her voice rose, husky, shaky with emotion. 'I'm glad if you must know, relieved that he could never manage to have his filthy way with me…despite everything, despite all he did to me, I am still a virgin… Oh!' She clapped one hand over her mouth, her ears ringing with the word; her tongue had blurted out her inner thoughts, speech tumbling forth in her anger, her rage—she had never meant to say such things to him.

'I'm glad to hear it,' he drawled. Was he smiling at her?

'I've said too much.' She scooped up her leather bag. The fine heather-coloured wool of his mother's gown emphasised the slimness of her arms as she reached forwards. Her hood had fallen back, loose gathers around her pale and slender neck.

'It doesn't always have to be that way.' Giseux rose, seizing the edge of the blanket to shake it out.

'What doesn't?' Brianna responded irritably, rattled by her own admission in front of this formidable man. She had never spoken to anyone, anyone, about what had happened with Walter.

His eyes devoured her. 'Love. Marriage. Don't judge either of those things on the basis of your past experience.'

'Oh,' she snorted, her small frame bristling from her unwitting exposure before this man. 'And you would know, would you?' Yanking the blanket from his arms, she started folding it in short, brief jerks. The full meaning of her words slapped into her, and she gasped, pressing her palm to her mouth, remembering Nadia, his whispered words. 'I'm sorry...I didn't mean...'

He read the sorrow in her jewel-bright eyes, but he hadn't even been thinking about Nadia. Only her whispered apology had jogged his memory. Aye, he knew about love, he had loved. A wistfulness wrapped around his heart, but it was muted, subdued, somehow. He had loved and lost, an experience he never, ever wished to repeat. The thought cleaved his chest as his gaze roved over Brianna's neat figure, the flushed curve of her cheek. It was enough that he could protect her from Walter. He prayed it would be enough…for both their sakes.

Rain slewed down, swilling across the cobbles, churning down the ornate lead guttering as Giseux and Brianna clattered into the inner bailey of Walter's castle. Steam rose from their horses' flanks as grooms, heads ducked against the squalls of raindrops, sped out from the stables to clutch at the reins, to hold the animals steady. Leaden clouds pressed down atop the high curtain walls, trapping Brianna, closing her in; she felt like a prisoner once more. How many times had she stood at those narrow slit windows, staring out to the open countryside, beyond the walls, tracking the soaring flight of a buzzard, or the quick darts of a swallow? How she had longed to be with them, carried away on the warm rising air, far away from Walter, to freedom, to independence.

'Brianna?' Giseux had dismounted, was waiting to help her. His hair was flattened to his skull by the heavy rain, giving him a sleek, leonine appearance, emphasising the taut cut of his jaw, the tanned slash of his cheek. She took a gulp of air, a deep, steadying breath.

'I'm ready.' She accepted his hands on her waist as he swung her from the saddle, set her on the ground. Her dress and cloak stuck uncomfortably to her skin; she was much wetter than she thought. Giseux made to move towards the stone steps that led to the main door, but she checked him, placing one hand on his arm. 'Giseux, I am not certain why you are here, but I, for one, am very glad that you are.'

His head whipped back in surprise at her solemn, unexpected words, face splitting into a grin. 'So you finally accept that men might have their uses after all?'

Her mouth was tight-lipped, features stern. Within the alabaster purity of her face, her eyes glowed like limpid sapphires. 'Not all men. Just you,' she replied, her voice reserved, guarded. Head held high, she swept past him, damp hem dragging in the mire of the cobbles, and climbed the steps, slick with raindrops. As she neared the top, the door cracked open and a wan, pallid face peered out.

'Matilda!' Brianna called out in greeting as she recognised the younger woman. Despite the travesty of her marriage, she had been close in age to Walter's daughter; the two had been good friends. Matilda held both hands out to Brianna, smiled tentatively in greeting. Her glossy dark hair, like the pelt of a cat, was half-covered by a thick linen scarf, the ends crossed at the throat and then tied at the back of her neck.

Matilda gasped. 'Brianna! It is you! I thought I would never see you again.'

'As I you, Matilda. But Hugh…'

'What about Hugh?' Matilda's voice appeared forced, unnatural.

Brianna frowned, a delicate line crinkling her forehead. 'Hugh has returned from the crusade, Matilda. He's been very ill, but he's alive. He sent me to fetch you!'

Matilda teetered on the threshold, held a shaking hand up to her cheek. 'Why…why would he do that?'

'Because he wants to marry you, Matilda, he wants to do right by you and the child!'

Matilda staggered back into the dim hallway, almost as if punched by some invisible hand, her voice drifting back into the shadows. 'It's not possible...'

'She's had a shock.' Giseux elbowed his way past Brianna, sweeping up the half-fainting girl to deposit her on a narrow wooden chair in the hall. He pushed her head down briskly between her knees. 'She'll feel better in a moment,' he explained briskly, his expression unconcerned.

'I don't understand.' Brianna moved into the hallway. A sharp breeze from outside chased against her skirts, a burst of rain sprinkling her neck; she hefted the huge door closed behind her. 'Surely she knew that Hugh would come back for her?' She knelt down on the hard, uneven flagstones, chafing Matilda's cold hands.

'How long has it been? Three or four years at least since she last saw him,' Giseux said. 'Maybe she thought he hadn't survived.'

Matilda's head lolled upwards, brown eyes hazy with confusion. She attempted to focus on Brianna's concerned face. 'Please forgive me,' she whispered. 'My father...Walter, said that he was still alive, that he had received messages from him recently, but I never believed it.'

At the mention of Walter's name, Brianna sprang to her feet, casting a furtive glance along the dim corridor, heart beginning to race. 'Is he here?' she demanded, voice raised a notch in agitation. 'Walter? Is he here?'

Matilda shook her head, a strand of glossy, black hair escaping from the confines of the headscarf. 'Nay, he's further north, inspecting his lands. He's due back tomorrow.' The cage around Brianna's heart shifted, eased a little; the news came as a reprieve.

Matilda placed her hand on the oak table beside her, levering herself upwards. 'Look, I am sorry. You caught me unawares—what a surprise!' She threw a pinched smile to Giseux, then back to Brianna, trying to regain some composure, some equilibrium. Her fingers reached out to cup Brianna's shoulder, as if noticing for the first time how wet Brianna's clothes were; how the fabric of cloak and gown clung to her frame, how her brilliant amber hair had darkened with rain. 'You're soaked through!' Matilda gasped. 'Come, let me show you to a chamber...you'll stay?'

Brianna nodded. 'Aye, we will have to wait for Walter. Hugh has sent me to ask your father's permission for him to marry you. He wants me to bring you and the child back to him in Sambourne; he's desperate to see you.'

Matilda's head drooped, large brown eyes fixed on the floor. 'I see.' Brianna frowned at the girl's muted response—surely she should be glad, overjoyed that Hugh was alive and wanted to marry her?

'Do you think Walter will have a problem with this?'

Matilda's hands moved up to her heart-shaped face, fluttered around her mouth: a nervous gesture. 'Nay,' she replied, choosing her words carefully, 'I don't think my father will have a problem.' She pulled her back up straighter, her initial vulnerability being quickly replaced by that of an efficient, practical hostess. 'Come, you tarry too long in these wet clothes. We will talk later. Let me show you both to the guest chamber.'

'Guest *chambers*,' Brianna corrected. 'We need more than one room.'

'Oh, forgive me, I thought…' Matilda's speech drifted off, as she glanced from Giseux, his wet tunic plastered across his broad chest, to Brianna, her cheeks beginning to adopt a rosy hue.

'We're not *married*,' Brianna hissed. 'Giseux is…' Her sentence trailed off as she stared at the tall, forbidding figure, backlit by candlelight from a floor-standing candelabra. Who was he? How could she explain the presence of this man, this immutable force who had ridden at her side, protected her, kissed her? She clasped her hands together, trying to find the right words, but all she could conjure up was the firm line of his lips, his mouth.

'I brought Hugh back from the crusade,' Giseux cut across the silence, gruffly.

At the mention of Hugh's name, Matilda's lips gripped into an unforgiving, rigid line. 'I see,' she responded tersely. 'Two chambers, then. Follow me.'

A damp, musty smell clagged Brianna's nostrils as she preceded Matilda into the chamber. It was the smell of unaired linen; of old, sagging straw in the mattress, of dust gathering in corners. Giseux had already left them, shown into a similar room by Matilda, further along the corridor. Despite the smell, the room was light, with an impressive rectangular window set with thick hand-blown glass, looking out on to the countryside beyond. White woven linen, bordered with an uneven blue stripe, hung from the top of the four-poster bed, sweeping down to the dull wooden floorboards. Anxiety clutched at Brianna's heart; she wondered whether she would be able to sleep here, here in the castle that had caused her so much misery.

'I will have one of the maidservants light the fire,' Matilda said, tawny eyes darting evasively, furtively, around the oak-panelled walls, fixing on the cold, dead grate. She seemed unable to meet Brianna's eyes. 'The room is chilly, I'm sorry.'

'Don't be sorry,' Brianna tried to reassure her. 'You had no idea we were coming.'

'The servants have been told to bring the hot water up.' Matilda nodded briskly at the wooden tub in the corner. Her words tripped over each other, stumbling.

'Matilda, what is the matter?' Brianna reached out, clasped her hand. 'You seem so agitated, so nervous. What is it?' The sopping-wet material of her sleeve clung uncomfortably to her skin with the movement.

Matilda quailed beneath Brianna's bright blue gaze. 'I'm surprised you came back, that's all. I'm surprised to see you.' Eyes wretched, Matilda tried to keep her voice light. 'After the way my father treated you.'

'I was fortunate he decided to end the marriage. Otherwise I might have been imprisoned in it for ever.'

'Annulment was your only way out,' Matilda agreed,

plumping down on the edge of the bed. The embroidered linen coverlet dimpled beneath her slight weight. She hitched one knee up to rest it on the top of the bed, her skirts shifting to reveal a pink satin slipper peeking out from beneath her flowing hemline. 'If you had tried to run away, to flee, he would have hunted you down like a dog.' She stared at Brianna with hopeless eyes, her olive complexion smooth, tightly drawn over high cheekbones.

Brianna nodded. 'He would never have been able to deal with the humiliation—he would have never let me go after that.' A shudder ricocheted down her spine. She had played her hand carefully, all those years ago; it had paid off. If she had made one tiny mistake, put one foot in the wrong direction, then her fate would have been so different.

'I did miss you, Brianna. I missed having another woman to talk to, I missed my friend, my confidante.' Matilda's face creased in consternation, her finger tracing a looping swirl of crimson chain stitch on the bedcover.

'I'm sorry, Matilda.' Brianna squeezed in beside the girl, hitching one hip against the solid carved bedpost. 'But I'm here now…talk to me. You seem so worried about something. Am I right?'

Matilda's hands flew upwards, covering her face. 'Oh, Brianna,' she moaned through tapered fingers, 'I've fallen in love with another man.' Eyes red-rimmed, watering with unshed tears, she snatched at Brianna's hands. 'Please, please don't tell my father! I can trust you, can't I?'

'But…I don't understand…' Brianna clung to Matilda's fingers as a great hollowness caved out her chest. 'I thought you loved Hugh. You were betrothed. You had a child together.'

'I know…I know.' Matilda was openly crying now, great gasping sobs choking at her throat, tearing at her breath. 'We were childhood sweethearts…we did love each other. But he's been away too long, Brianna.'

'What about your child? Shouldn't he know his father?'

Matilda nodded jerkily, but her eyes remained cast down, unsure. 'Our son died soon after he was born, Brianna. I sent messages to Hugh, but from your words it seems he never received them.'

'I'm so very sorry,' Brianna breathed. She moved forwards, clasping Matilda's rigid shoulders, hugging her tightly. 'Your baby…it must have been devastating. I am so sorry.' She could only begin to imagine how brutal it would be to lose a child.

'It was a long time ago.' Matilda's voice shook into Brianna's shoulder before she pulled away. 'Father kept telling me that Hugh was alive, that he would come back for me, and I chose to ignore him. I didn't believe him.'

'Hugh will be so sad at the news,' Brianna said. 'How am I going to tell him?'

Matilda hung her head, picking frantically at an errant thread on the coverlet. The smooth wings of her ebony hair, emerging from the headscarf, curved around the bottom of her ears like black silk, glossy, undulating. 'Please don't let this change things between us,' she mumbled to the floor. 'Stay here tonight, then you can leave on the morrow before my father returns.'

Brianna jumped off the bed. 'I will speak to Giseux. He will know what to do.'

Chapter Eleven

A fathomless groan of appreciation emerged from Giseux's lips as he lowered his big frame into the tub of hot, steaming water. The servants in Walter's castle had worked hard, bringing up bucket upon bucket from the kitchens, sloshing it liberally into the generous, circular tub. By propping his neck against the edge, and closing his eyes, he could blot out the drab, unadorned walls of the guest chamber, the bare wooden floors, the empty grate. Hot water was obviously the only luxury to be had in this castle; the chamber was serviceable, but that was all.

What had Brianna's life been like in this place? He couldn't imagine her living here, in this cold, bare castle, devoid, empty of all trappings. His hands balled into fists beneath the water-line, jaw rigid at the injustice of her marriage, the sheer utter waste of her character on a husband who failed to appreciate her. He pictured her surrounded by beauty, the rich colours of intricate tapestries framing her slender form, her flawless skin illuminated by millions of candles, cared for by a man who loved her. He pictured her in Provence, in Queen Eleanor's castle, where he had trained as a knight, walking through the serried rows of lavender, the heavy scent filling the air at the end of a long, hot summer's day. A beautiful place for a beautiful person. The luminous oval of her face swam into his mind: her soft voice, dulled, hollow, telling him of the travesty of her marriage, the hectic flush of her face when she blurted out her innocence. A lightning bolt of desire lanced through him; he seized the flannel from the side of the tub and began to scrub furiously at his chest, his shoulders.

A light tap at the door. 'Come,' he murmured, half-heartedly, resenting the intrusion into his thoughts.

'Giseux.'

His head whipped around, astonished, droplets flying out from the ends of his wet hair. Brianna? Water clung to the broad muscle at the back of his shoulders, the fading light from the window casting a metallic sheen across his skin.

Her breath caught, clung, words deserting her, swept away on a sudden whirlwind of exhilarating, pulsing desire. An invisible fist squeezed her heart, then released, suddenly, a rush of blood hurtling through her arteries, her veins. Inside her boots, her toes curled, undecided—should she stay, or should she go? Giseux's naked back, a mass of honed muscle, taunted her: it was a test. Fighting to keep her balance, fighting to keep her senses steady, she wondered if she would pass. The solid muscles flexed beneath his skin, the carved, shadowed line of his spine disappearing beneath the hewn edge of the tub.

'What is it?' His eyes roamed over her, predatory. The water dripped like strings of silver chain from his massive arms.

'Er…' Her mind scrabbled for the answer to his question: What had she come to tell him? Her breath, once trapped, now emerged, quick, uneven. 'I… Excuse me, I'm sorry, I'll come back.' Her hands fluttered up to her face, as if to ward off, to hide the incredible sight before her, and she twisted away, the curve of her hem whisking, sibilant, against the dusty floorboards.

'I'm almost finished here,' Giseux replied. He wanted her to stay, to keep her there.

The door hazed before her vision, the planks shimmering, a blur. Her fingers stretched out in panic, fumbling for the iron ring, the handle to freedom. A delicious throb began to beat in the pit of her stomach, and for one horrible, insane moment she wondered whether her legs would support her.

'Hold a moment. Brianna, wait. What's the matter?'

She heard the splosh of water, the distinctive sound of someone standing up, rivulets sliding down naked limbs. A dryness scraped at her mouth. If she just told him, then she could go, run for her life. 'Matilda doesn't want to marry Hugh any more…' the words staggered from her '…she's in love with another man.'

'So we've come all this way for nothing.'

Quick, hot temper, an anger fed by desire, by unravelling feelings over which she had little control, rose at his scathing words. 'I'm sorry if I've wasted your time!' She spun round, forgetting.

Too late.

Giseux stood in the tub, a white linen towel bunched between his hands. Water sluiced over his magnificent form, emphasising the bulging plates of his chest, the flat, horizontal lines of muscle across his stomach, his narrow hips, his manhood. Framed against the dark oak panelling behind the bath, his tanned silhouette faded to a warm, honeyed hue all over.

Brianna's eyes slid over him, drinking rapidly, greedily, before they slipped away, aghast at her open perusal. She forced herself to study the grain of the wood in the door, resisting the temptation to press her forehead against those cool planks. Desire pulsed through her, dangerous, incandescent, seizing her with a wild trembling that she fought to control. She pressed shaking fingers to her cheeks, appalled at her reaction to his nakedness.

'I shouldn't be here,' she mumbled weakly, blindly reaching for the iron circle to lift the door latch. Her arms moved like wet rope, sapped of energy.

'Stay, Brianna, talk to me.' His powerful voice stalled her, commanded her.

'I cannot.' Her feet toed the edge of an unknown abyss.

'Why not?'

'Giseux, you're naked!' Her voice pitched upwards, a burst of flustered panic.

'Not any more.'

She edged her gaze around, cautiously. The linen towel was secured around his waist, the snug fit of the material emphasising the leanness of his hips, the muscular outline of his thighs. In the chill of the room, goose-bumps had appeared on the rounded muscles of his upper arms.

'What did Matilda say?' Giseux prompted.

Brianna stood by the door like a startled colt, round-eyed, breathless. With her lips slightly apart, he glimpsed a row of neat, even teeth, the slick sparkle of her tongue; his loins throbbed with treacherous waves of desire. The lilac-hued gown stuck to her in damp folds, clinging lovingly to her bosom, tracing the slender curves of her waist. And that heavy knife-belt, always the knife-belt, the thick leather strap, the hilt hanging diagonally over her hip incongruous against the fluid wool flaring out below her waist. But whereas before he had wanted to throw it away, lose it for ever, now he realised, understood why she carried that gleaming blade of protection, always.

Palms braced flat against the door behind her lent Brianna a sense of security. It would take only a moment to flee, to duck out into the darkened corridor. She battled to recall the problem, the reason that had brought her to Giseux's chamber in the first place. 'I told you—' the words left her mouth in a hectic rush '—Matilda loves another man.' Her eyes, moving distractedly over the ridged muscle of Giseux's torso, riveted suddenly upon his face. It was safer to look at his face. 'How on earth am I going to tell him?'

Stepping out of the tub, the linen towel straining

tight around his haunches, Giseux moved over to his clothes, bundled on a carved oak coffer at the foot of the bed.

'Why are you asking me?'

A sheen of water gleamed from his collarbone, highlighting the strong rope of muscle that ran down the sides of his neck. He had obviously dipped his head in the water and scrubbed away the dirt and mud of the journey; now each strand lay flat, thick and sleek against his head. A droplet of water trickled down the honed plane of his cheek; he brushed it away as it tickled his chin.

'Brianna?' He studied her so intently, she wondered if he could hear the pounding of her heart, the flex of her lungs as her breath punched out. She wrenched her eyes away, hammered her gaze resolutely to the floor. Why would he not dress? Swallowing hurriedly, she forced herself to concentrate, ignoring his question. 'Hugh, he'll take the news badly; it was his dream to marry her, to set up home at Sefanoc—my God, it will destroy him.'

Giseux tilted his head to one side, massive arms crossed over his chest. 'No, Brianna, it will not,' he replied firmly, his tone authoritative, reasoning. 'It will not destroy him.'

'Hugh is nothing like you,' she flashed back. 'You might have fought in the same battles, ridden the same campaigns, but he's sensitive, emotional. He—' She stopped, recalling her brother's wild behaviour at Sambourne. 'He's fragile at the moment.'

He wanted to laugh out loud and strangle her at the

same time. How could she be such a poor judge of character? Sensitive? Emotional? From the small amount of time he had spent with Hugh of Sefanoc, he knew he was nothing of the sort.

'Hugh is no different from me, Brianna,' he replied evenly, his bare feet covering the boards to stand before her. His lashes were wet, black spikes radiating out from pewter depths. 'He's a soldier, a fighter. You're overreacting—aye, he will be sad, but he will recover from this setback.'

'Like you have?' The words were out before Brianna could prevent them slipping from her lips. He was close now, toes grazing the long hem of her skirts, the honed sculpture of his chest on a level with her eyes. The skin on her neck flushed a betraying red, strung with a peculiar tension, responding traitorously to his presence. Her heart skipped, then plummeted, headlong, into a rush of awareness.

'What do you mean?' The dangerous timbre of his voice kissed her neck; she shivered with…aye, with excitement.

'What happened to you in Jerusalem,' she blurted out. 'You can't forget it. The memory of it affects you every day. You think of it all the time.'

'Look at me, Brianna.' The huskiness of his voice rolled over her, embraced her. Slowly, in trepidation, she lifted her eyes. His torso was an expanse of bare, gleaming flesh, so close that she could smell the freshness of the water on his skin, mingled with a sensual muskiness. Her senses flared, off balance.

'I'm not thinking of it now.' His eyes prowled over her, irises flecked with savage desire.

She took a step back, heels jagging against the door. Every blood vessel, every nerve ending in her body quivered, vibrated with his nearness, his big body looming over her. Her breath hitched, jittery. Intending to push him away, she placed two hands on his shoulders; her wrists buckled as he moved nearer, bracing her lissom frame up against the wood panelling with his substantial weight.

Time caught, suspended in the thick air.

'Nay,' Brianna whispered huskily as his mouth descended, but her heart disagreed, pounding deceitfully. She had the briefest impression of silver eyes darkening before his leonine head dipped down. His mouth ground into hers, fierce, demanding; she whimpered beneath his onslaught.

Arms swept around her neat waist as he slanted against her, melding the lean, long hardness of his bigger body against her own delicate curves. The ridges around each door panel pressed into her spine, but she didn't notice. A rough craving flamed in her belly, a hunger, an aching…for what? As the firm curve of his mouth grazed hers, softer now, she yearned to yell, to scream with joy at the exquisite sensation. All she wanted was him, his mouth, and the sweet movement of his lips. She was incapable of resisting, flesh dissolving into a burning pool of liquid at his touch. The heady smell of him enveloped her, plucking at her senses, promising more, much more.

She arched into him as he deepened the kiss,

demanding, insisting. He moaned, a feral passionate sound, as she opened her lips to him, clawing at his shoulders. Yoked together in ravenous, desperate embrace, reality receded, to be replaced by a shining bubble of blistering, hot-blooded temptation. Her hands fluttered over his shoulders, crept up into the feathery strands of his hair at the nape of his neck, pulling him down, ever closer. His hands smoothed up her flanks, cupping the warm, heavy roundness of her breasts, his heart rapping strongly against her own. She had never known it could be like this, two people locked together with such passion, such feeling; her head swam with the implication. If Walter had never released her, then she would never, ever have known.

He tore his mouth away, suddenly, leaving her bereft, lips burning in the aftermath of the kiss. Stunned at the abundance of passion in her small frame, aware that he had only flirted with the edges of her desire, his eyes flooded with a stormy, turbulent light, grey ringed with iridescent blue. He strode to the middle of the chamber, a safe distance away, yanking a long shirt down over his naked shoulders. Suddenly he didn't trust himself around her any more.

'Brianna, if you value your self-preservation, I suggest you leave, right now.'

Strength sapped, she sagged, barely holding herself upright against the panelled door, wisps of copper locks curling around her forehead, across one cheek. Her breathing emerged erratically; she touched one finger to her bruised lips.

He stared at her, hard, flint-edged, before whisking

the damp towel away, powerful gaze openly challenging her, wanting to push her away, to leave. The shirt fell to mid-thigh, hem skimming the light brown hairs sprinkled over his thighs. She kept her eyes resolutely pinned to his face.

'You should leave,' he repeated, harshly. 'There's no telling what I might do next.'

'I am not afraid.'

Did she realise what she was saying? His head jerked up at her simple admission, his heart flowering, melting, beneath the import of her words. She wanted him, desired him; he saw it in her eyes, read it in every slender line of her body. The impulse to gather up her fragile beauty in his arms, to throw her on the bed and make sweet, passionate love to her, hazed across his vision.

'You should be,' he croaked. His whole body vibrated, hummed from the feel of her soft body folded into his, her lips moving across his own. He should never, ever have started, never touched his lips to hers, not now, not ever. She drew him, again and again, like a moth to a flame, bewitching, delightful, irresistible. He burned for her.

Dove-grey fingers of light seeped through the thick, bubbled glass of the windows as Brianna's eyes cracked open the next morning. For a moment, her befuddled mind scrambled to decipher her surroundings: the grubby velvet bed canopy above her head, the lumpy mattress prickly with old straw. A sense of relief flooded over her; it seemed she might avoid meeting Walter altogether, the meeting that she had dreaded throughout the journey. Matilda had asked her to stay the night, and she had fulfilled that promise, but today she had to return, travel back to Sambourne and break the news to Hugh.

Head supported by a half-filled feather pillow, she touched a finger to her lips, relished the flick of sensation in her chest, the curious gathering, building in her loins. She ran one hand restlessly over the coverlet, the bumps and whorls of embroidery rustling against her palm. The top of the linen sheet was folded back, over the coverlet: a soft material, yet cloying against her skin, suggesting the sheets had lain on the bed in the damp, chill room for too long.

What would Giseux do now? she wondered. Her heart tripped crazily at the thought of his name, stacking her mind with images of the tanned angles of his face, his demanding, savage kiss. He had been kind, escorting her this far, but now he had no reason to stay by her side. He had helped her so much, and what had she done for him? She had been foul and prickly on their first few encounters, so determined to be independent, self-contained. But now, now all she wanted to do was…aye, that was it, she wanted to love him. She loved him.

She twisted restlessly across the mattress, frowning up at the drooping linen above her. A spider's web, fragile grey netting, stretched over one corner. Her nightgown had bunched up around her waist as she wrenched it down beneath the covers. Love. Did she even know the meaning of the word? Her experiences with Walter had warped her mind; this unfamiliar, cleaving feeling—was it love that she felt for Giseux? Less that a week ago, her course had been set, determined to remain single, coupled to no man, in a world where marriage was the only option for the majority of women. Now, the faint hope of an alternative future stuttered to life in her heart. She quashed such a thought quickly, doubting he held the same sentiment. After every kiss, he pushed her away, visibly shutting down before her, face closed, sealed like an armour-plated door, immediately regretting his actions. She could only hold the sensation of his touch, the fiery savagery of his kiss, tucked close to her heart, to keep them for ever, after he was gone.

But there was no denying that her body sang, even now, with the memory of his mouth moving over hers, tiny thrills of expectation, of excitement, dancing along her veins. Was this how it should be between a man and a woman? Something deep within her lurched, changed; she felt altered, newborn. His sparkling eyes had held raw passion as he tore away from her, breath tearing at his sinewy chest, a twist of vulnerability in the set of his mouth. Maybe this was how he was with every woman he kissed…and maybe not.

'Brianna! Are you dressed? Come and have breakfast with me.' Matilda's lilting tones at the door hauled her from her thoughts—had she lain awake, thinking, for that long? She bounced out of bed, slipping out of her nightgown and stuffing it back into the saddlebag that lay slumped over the wooden floorboards. She had to start moving, have something to eat, then start the long journey south once more. Pulling on her chemise, followed by the velvet gown, she tightened up the crossing leather laces at the front of dress swiftly, securing them in a bow at the low, rounded neckline.

'Matilda!' she greeted the younger girl, stepping out from the chamber, touching her hair self-consciously; she had forgotten to comb it, to do anything with it! Even the plaits that she had gone to bed with seemed to have loosened during the night! The glorious bundle of amber locks tumbled down her back, sweeping the curve of her hips.

Matilda giggled as she pressed her hand against her mouth. 'Oh, Brianna, you don't change. Let me do your hair for you. You're not even wearing a veil!'

Reluctantly, Brianna moved back into the room and sat down on a small stool, conscious that time, precious time, was ticking away. She had no wish to stay in this place longer than was necessary.

'I used to do your hair for you before, do you remember?' Matilda commented as she pulled a small, ivory comb from the embroidered pouch hanging from her girdle. She began to pull the fine teeth through the shining length of Brianna's hair, working her way through the occasional knot with her tongue caught between her teeth.

'Aye, I remember.' Walter had always insisted that her head was completely covered with a thick linen scarf, losing his temper if he spotted a hair shining through.

'It's so beautiful,' the younger girl murmured. 'Where is your veil?'

'I lost it…on the journey here.' She recalled burying the flimsy silk in the damp earth, hands trembling with fear that those soldiers would find her.

'I'll lend you one of mine and a circlet as well; I'll fetch it after breakfast,' Matilda promised, securing the end of each braid with a leather lace, before coiling each one around itself to form a tidy bun at the nape of Brianna's neck.

'There!' Matilda said proudly, pushing the last gold hairpin in against Brianna's scalp, standing back to survey her handiwork. 'You look perfect.'

'Thank you.' Brianna rose from the stool, surveying the younger girl. Her skin looked white, pasty, lines of exhaustion etching her face. Blueish shadows smudged beneath her eyes. 'Did you sleep at all last night?'

Matilda chewed at her lips, tears welling, threatening to spill. 'I couldn't stop thinking about Hugh, about what I'm doing to him.' She hung her head.

'I'm sure he will understand,' Brianna replied faintly, wondering whether he would. His insistence that Brianna was to fetch Matilda had almost bordered on desperation.

'Maybe he will…but I'm sure my father will not. He wants me to marry Hugh now…curious, as he was so against it in the past. I'm so frightened he will force me into something I don't want to do.' A pleading look moved into her pale eyes. 'Take me with you, Brianna. I must leave, go away from here, before my father returns. Once I've married Thurstan, my father can do nothing.'

'Are you certain about that?' Brianna had no intention of worrying Matilda, but she was sure that a father had to agree to his daughter's marriage. If there was no agreement, then he was perfectly within his rights to drag her back home again and suffer the consequences.

Matilda hunched her shoulders, turning her comb, again and again, between her fingers. The ivory tines gleamed like milk. 'If he cannot find me, then he will not be able to being me back.' She opened the gathered neck of the silk pouch, pushed the comb back inside, decisively. 'I have to try, Brianna, I have to have a go at living a normal, married life. I don't want to spend the rest of my days here, rotting under the unpredictable will of my father. I want to have a husband, to kiss him in the morning, to lie with him at night, to care for him and any children that we might have. Is it so wrong to want that?'

'Nay,' breathed Brianna. 'You're right, so right.' As Matilda spoke, Brianna's heart had filled with a sensation of such longing that she realised that she wanted the same things as Matilda. A husband to care for, to have and to hold. Even if she never saw Giseux again, at least he had given her back one important thing: hope.

Brianna followed Matilda down the curving, spiral staircase, lit by the thin light streaming through the narrow arrow slits. Giseux's door had stood open as they had passed, the bed empty, the covers in disarray. Had he left already? Her heart plummeted, sadness pooling across her chest. Once downstairs, Matilda drew aside the heavy curtain that separated the great hall from the stairwell, preceding Brianna into the high-ceilinged chamber, hung with a veil of smoke from the newly lit fire. A solitary figure sat in the middle of the top table.

It was Walter.

Chapter Twelve

Brianna's innards quailed. Her step faltered on the threshold, legs rickety. The compulsion to howl, to place her hands childishly across her eyes and bawl out at the unfairness of life swept over her, a violent, formidable wave. But instead, nails digging into her palms, she clamped her hands to her sides and stuck her chin in the air, willing herself to move forwards, to confront this man. Her fingers touched the hilt of her knife, relieved that she had armed herself on leaving the bedchamber.

'He wasn't due back until this evening!' wailed Matilda, casting a horrified look back to Brianna. Her nut-brown eyes filled with utter desperation, as her hand clutched frantically at the curtain edge for support.

'Ladies! An unexpected pleasure. Do come and join me!' Across the bluish haze of smoke, Walter raised his pewter goblet and drank deep, smacking his loose, flabby lips.

'What are we going to do?' Matilda hesitated, balancing on her toes, a startled deer about to bolt.

Brianna glanced at the two soldiers, clad from top to toe in chainmail, flanking the door behind them. Although they stared straight ahead, faces impassive in their hoods of silver links, she suspected that the slightest sign from Walter would result in their lances being crossed before the door, preventing herself and Matilda from leaving the hall.

'We will stay and talk to him,' announced Brianna decisively. There was nothing this man could do to her now; their marriage had been annulled, he had no claim on her. She had the protection of her brother… and possibly, from Giseux? She began to walk towards the high dais, catching Matilda's hand and pulling her along, past the handful of servants quietly setting out the lines of pewter plates along the trestle tables for the rest of the household to break their fast. It was still early. A thick fog outside the high windows filled the cavernous hall with a leaden, grey light as Walter's tiny, deep-set eyes, black dots in the florid expanse of his face, marked their progress.

'I must say, I'm extremely surprised to see you,' he remarked, peering at Brianna as they each took a seat to one side of him, Matilda deliberately leaving the space of two chairs between herself and her father. A greasiness slicked his grizzled locks, grey tendrils of hair straggling out from a balding pate and, as he reached up a hand to push his hair from his eyes, Brianna noticed that his hand, ridged with pronounced veins, trembled.

'Aye, well, it seems my journey was unnecessary after all,' Brianna explained brightly. Matilda kicked her under the table—was that to stop her telling Walter that Hugh had returned home, alive?

Walter hunched forwards, brown eyes opaque, flat. His gnarled face studied her closely. 'And I am most surprised that you agreed to your brother's proposition.' He cackled out loud, the wheezing laughter finished by a fit of prolonged coughing. 'But, knowing Hugh, I suppose he didn't leave you with any chance to protest.'

Brianna's heart lurched. Her brother's proposition? What was he talking about? Giseux's calm, reasoning voice echoed in her brain, telling her, warning her. Beneath the table, her hands crept to her knife, resting quietly in its sheath on her lap.

'I'm not sure I understand you,' she pronounced carefully.

Walter used one dirty fingernail to try to dislodge a piece of meat stuck between two greyish teeth. 'Then let me explain,' he replied, his tone smug, placid. 'Hugh has agreed to give you in marriage, again, to me, in exchange for the hand of my lovely daughter here.' He swept one hand theatrically towards Matilda, who shrank in her seat. The gathered fold of Walter's sleeve caught the lip of the pewter goblet, full of mead, tipping the contents out. The amber liquid spread, soaking into the grubby, stained tablecloth.

'Hugh would never do such a thing,' Brianna replied,

slowly, carefully. Doubt chewed at her innards. 'He knows how much I hated my marriage to you in the first place.'

Walter slowly folded a slice of ham between his spindly fingers, before wedging it into his mouth. 'Then you obviously have no idea of how much he wants to marry my daughter.'

'Nay, you're lying!' Her voice wavered with uncertainty; she shook her head, not wanting to believe. Giseux had warned her, told her exactly the same thing.

'Face it, Brianna. Your brother made this decision for you and you'll abide by it. You will never leave this castle again. You have no choice.'

'I think she does.'

Three heads turned in surprise as Giseux bounded up on to the high dais. Through the haze of smoke billowing fitfully from the fireplace, he appeared like a Greek god, bronze and vital, his muscular physique a complete contrast to the hunched, dried-up form of Walter.

Walter staggered to his feet, wiping his fat-slicked mouth with a used napkin. 'And who might you be?' he demanded, pointing a querulous finger at Giseux.

'I came with Brianna.' His metallic gaze poured down over her, his arm nudging into her side. 'Are you all right?' Lit against the gloom, the tallow candles, suspended above the high table in the heavy circle of an iron chandelier, cast shadows down on the taut angles of his face.

She nodded shakily. 'I…' The need to explain, to clarify her reasons for not believing him, for not trusting his word, bubbled near the surface of her consciousness. Her fingers crept over to his sleeve, rubbed at the fine wool of his tunic. His hand covered hers.

'Answer my question, sir!' Walter ground out, irritably, thumping the tablecloth. Matilda jumped like a startled deer, clutched at her throat.

'I am Giseux de St-Loup, son of Lord Jocelin of Sambourne, and I am here to take Brianna home.' His eyes fixed on Matilda, gleaming strands of hair falling across his forehead. 'And anyone else who wishes to leave this place,' he added meaningfully.

Walter slumped back in his chair; the name of Giseux de St-Loup was well known—as a nephew of Queen Eleanor and trained alongside King Richard, he was a powerful man in his own right. Walter would have to be careful.

'You said…' Brianna stuttered out, touching one hand to her forehead. 'You told me…and I refused to listen.' The sapphire of her eyes radiated despair.

'It matters not…I am here.'

'I'm so sorry, I'm so sorry…' His fingers curled around hers.

'Now, look here,' Walter blustered, interrupting her whispered apology, 'your brother and I talked about this, on the crusade. It was a simple swap. Matilda for Brianna—Hugh was in full agreement; he knew what he wanted.'

A raft of dizziness threatened to topple her. She clutched more firmly at Giseux's sleeve, bracing herself against the steadying buttress of his body. 'Giseux, he truly did this! How could he? How could he do such a thing?' She swayed, her eyes seeking his face, the firm curve of his mouth, the spiky black lashes. 'You warned me and I wouldn't listen!' Her voice rose on a half-sob. 'What kind of fool was I, not to trust you?'

'Why would you believe the words of a stranger over your own brother, someone you had known for years? No one else would have done any different.'

'What am I going to do? Hugh is my guardian—there's no way out!'

Walter smiled, slowly, like a spider waiting at the edge of his web. At his side, Matilda perched on the edge of her seat, completely still, a stupefied look in her eyes. Even the servants, moving about their chores in the main part of the hall, seemed to work more slowly, throwing covert glances up to Walter as they watched the drama unfold at the high table.

'Hush.' Giseux's arm came around her slender back, balanced her. 'There is a way out, but you have to trust me—will you do that?'

Perplexed, she stared at him, trying to decipher his thoughts, trying to read the intention in his granite eyes. Within those elusive depths, she had seen the pain, the despair he carried, but she had also seen a kindness and concern. He had come after her, insisted on travelling with her, even when she had refused to believe him, to accept this awful truth about Hugh. This man was no stranger to her now. She knew him, she cared for him.

'Yes, I will,' she murmured.

'Then let's go.' He smiled. Turning her within the circle of his arms, he glanced at Matilda, cowering back into the ornately carved chair. 'Come and bid us farewell, Matilda.'

'Wait! No! You cannot do this, you cannot take her!' Bits of half-chewed meat spilled from Walter's mouth when he realised what was happening. 'She is mine!' He choked as a big piece of chicken jammed in his throat and seized his goblet, drinking quickly to release the constriction. His eyes darted nervously towards the guards, standing in front of the only exit from the great hall, before alighting on the curtained doorway itself. His countenance brightened. 'Now,' he pronounced, 'here is someone who can tell you.' His broad grin revealed a jagged row of rotting teeth, pegs of yellowing charcoal in his loose-lipped mouth.

Framed by the floor-length curtain, his frame slumping a little, stood Hugh. Matilda gasped, half-rose, listlessly, before collapsing back into her chair. Her brown eyes, the colour of polished elm, searched for Brianna's in desperation. 'I am lost!' she murmured.

'Nay!' Brianna replied firmly. 'Never that!' She glanced up at Giseux, brilliant aquamarines meeting sparkling flint, reading the unspoken warning in his chiselled features. 'Let me talk to him, at least. He cannot have been in his right mind when he agreed to this.'

'We will both talk to him,' Giseux replied as she brushed past him. Chewing her lip, she descended the wooden steps from the high dais, holding her gown high, the dullness in her heart presaging doom. She knew already what Hugh would say, but she had to hear it for herself. She had to hear the truth from her brother's lips: that he had sold her to the man she hated most in the world.

Features washed white, Hugh teetered on the threshold, the veins in his forehead standing out, blue, rigid. His clothes hung off his skeletal frame; his illness had shaved any excess weight from his tall body.

'Hugh, what are you doing here?' Brianna rushed up to him, thinking he would fall. She grasped at his hands, led him to the nearest bench, urging him to sit. He sank down, holding on to her; his hands looked like an old man's, frail and knotted.

'I…had to…make sure,' he answered, his breathing laboured, uneven. 'I had to make sure you were here. When Walter failed to send a message that you had arrived, I began to worry.' He touched a fluttering hand to his sweating forehead.

'I…encountered some difficulties on the journey,' she explained hurriedly. 'But luckily Giseux came to my rescue, brought me here.'

'So I see,' Hugh remarked sourly, throwing Giseux a cursory glance. 'I asked him to escort you here, you know, and he refused.' His features cleared suddenly. 'You told her, didn't you! You told her of my plans for her. I knew it!'

'She deserved the truth, at least,' Giseux replied. 'But out of loyalty to you, her brother, she refused to believe me.'

'Tell me, Hugh, tell me that you didn't do this, please!' Brianna placed one hand on his shoulder, the bones beneath his tunic pinching into her palm.

'Brianna, you should learn to trust me.' His bright

blue gaze narrowed upon her face. 'Walter is a good man, much changed since his time on the crusade. The marriage will be much better this time, you'll see.' His eyes fastened on the slim, dark-haired girl at the top table, distracted. 'Why does Matilda not come and greet me?' he whined. 'What's amiss with her?'

Brianna's hand sprung away from her brother's shoulder, hovered in the space to the side of his head. Reality crashed around her, broken to smithereens. Bewildered, suddenly bereft of care for her sibling, the urge to hit him boiled within her, to spring at him like a snarling cat and scratch at his face. Breath punching from her lungs, she gripped her fingers together, making a fist.

'Easy.'

Giseux.

Brianna took a vast, shuddering breath, drawing strength from the muscular warmth behind her, the reassuring baritone of his voice. Through the blur of hot, angry tears, she couldn't see him, but she could feel him. And it was enough to give her energy, to give her the power to control her emotions, to stand up to her brother.

'I cannot believe what you have done.' Finally she found some words, her speech emerging as a low, shaking whisper. 'How could you betray me like this? After everything I told you about that man!'

'Oh, stop being so melodramatic,' Hugh admonished her sternly. Colour had begun to return to his cheeks. 'This way, Matilda is mine and you are looked after for the rest of your life. We haven't any money, Brianna, it all went to fund the crusade.' His eyes tracked back to the high table, his expression fretful. 'Why does she not come over?' His voice adopted a petulant thread. 'Can't she see that I'm ill? Brianna, go and fetch her, will you?'

It was as if she hadn't spoken.

'Hugh, listen to me, will you?' Brianna snapped, injecting more power into her voice. She wanted to hurt, to fight back. Maybe if she told him the truth it would shake him out of this odd complacency about both of their futures. 'Matilda doesn't love you any more; she wants to marry another.'

'Hah! Listen, I know you're angry about the decision with Walter, but there's no point in telling me lies to try to hurt me.'

'It's the truth, Hugh.' Matilda's hesitant voice floated up from beside Brianna. At the top table, Walter craned his neck, trying to catch the conversation—was he really going to have to shift from his seat in order to hear anything?

The Adam's apple in Hugh's throat bobbed up and down several times as he scrutinised the olive features of the girl standing next to his sister. His face turned white, then red; a greyness pawed at his mouth. His mouth opened and closed a few times, flapping uselessly. 'Nay, you're wrong, Matilda,' he replied, his voice wavering around an unusual note. 'Remember all those promises we made to each other before we left; remember the child!'

Matilda's eyes reddened. 'Our child died, Hugh, he

died of a sickness a few months after you left. I tried to send you word…'

'Walter…?' His voice stumbled. Brianna wondered if he were going to cry. 'Walter could have told me, when I met him in Jerusalem.'

Matilda shook her head, the tied ends of her linen veil brushing stiffly against her shoulders. 'My father never knew about the child… He would have killed me if he had known—the child was born in secret.'

'Our secret,' Hugh whispered. His eyes glazed slightly, as he remembered. Without warning, he lurched up out of his seat, staggering. 'Nay, this is not happening!' he yelled, clutching out at Matilda who backed away rapidly. He stumbled forwards into the empty space where she had once stood, reeling, his arms scrabbling comically into air. 'I will marry you!' He punched his arm out in Matilda's direction. 'And you…' he turned wide, condemning eyes upon Brianna '…and you will marry Walter. That is what was going to happen and that is what will happen.' The skin on his face was florid, enraged; his blue eyes were crazed beyond recognition. Brianna stared at him in horror—what was happening to him? He seemed truly crazed, sent mad with the turn of events. Where had her brother gone?

Giseux stood close to Brianna, his upper arm grazing her shoulder, watching her distraught face, stark with disbelief. 'What do you want to do?' he murmured, his voice so low that only she was aware that he had spoken.

'Please, talk to him.' Her periwinkle-blue eyes shifted to his. 'I don't know him any more.'

Giseux nodded, placing one hand on Hugh's shoulder in order to lead him away, out of the great hall. 'Make yourself scarce,' he muttered grimly, 'until I come back. And I will come back.'

The cheerless shadows of the corridor, dim after the relative brightness of the great hall, enveloped Giseux as he propelled Hugh forwards to what he hoped was a vacant room.

'Let go of me!' hissed Hugh, rolling his shoulder to dislodge Giseux's grip. 'You're supposed to be on my side!' It was he who pushed through a door into an empty chamber, a dingy room furnished only with an unpolished table, a chair by the lifeless grate. Cold seeped up from the damp flagstones on the floor, claggy, penetrating, and into the air the breath of both men emerged: white puffs of exhalation.

'It will do no good, Giseux, you talking to me!' Hugh rounded on him, blue eyes wide with annoyance. 'My mind is made up!' He stumbled over to the window, twisting around to prop his gaunt frame against thick-cut stone that formed the window surround. Greyness ringed his mouth.

'Then maybe you should change your mind,' Giseux replied evenly, settling his sizeable frame into the high-backed elm chair, ornate legs mottled with a bluish mould. Lifting one foot, he rested it casually on his opposite knee, sprawling elegantly.

'I have no intention of changing my mind!' Hugh stabbed the air with one finger, agitated. He frowned, an entrenched furrow appeared between his sparse brows. 'In fact, I cannot see that it is any of your business—why are you so interested?' His voice adopted a tone of suspicious probing. 'A couple of days ago you refused to escort my sister here—what's changed?'

Long, black lashes framing an exquisite pair of cerulean eyes danced into Giseux's mind, swiftly pursued by the hesitant embrace of a silken mouth, the press of rounded curves against his own. Her pale, angry face as she remonstrated with him about Almeric of Salis, her courage, her scent, everything. His fingers tightened around the claw-fashioned end of the chair arm. 'I have no wish to see Brianna married to Walter…again.'

'Why? I don't understand why?' Hugh screwed his eyes up, searching Giseux's impassive features for some clue, for some reason as to his interest. Shaking his head with mirth, he clapped one hand against his mouth. 'Giseux, are you in love with my sister?'

Love? Was that the term for the way he felt towards Brianna? The fragile bonds that had strung between them over the past few days, shackles that at first had been constructed from protest and argument, had now strengthened, flourishing from shimmering lengths of spider's silk, to thick, unbreakable ropes, binding them. Emotion speared his heart; it shifted, lightened.

Breathing heavily, Hugh staggered over to the table, supporting himself on both arms, white fingers bony against the rough, drab wood. 'Who'd have thought it? Giseux, the great warrior, falling for my useless scrap of a sister!' His tone mocked, taunted. 'I thought you had sworn never to have another relationship with a woman again, never to marry, after what happened with Nadia…after what you did.' His voice took on a deadly poignancy. 'Oh, yes, everyone knew, Giseux. Everyone knew about the siege of Narsuf. I heard you were a broken man, devastated, incapable of love.'

'I thought so too,' Giseux murmured. *Until I met Brianna.* Joy leapt in his chest, for Hugh's comments left him strangely unaffected. He could insult him all he liked; his words made no difference; they did not apply to him, not any more. A week ago, maybe, but so much had changed since then. Every time he was with Brianna, he became whole once more, the iron case around his heart melting, just a little, slipping away by degrees.

Hugh absorbed his words. 'Oh, please, you're making me feel quite ill.' A dangerous light filled his eyes; he brought one clenched fist crashing down upon the tabletop. 'You have no part in this, so I advise you to keep out, to walk away now. Brianna is mine, I am her guardian, and I'm free to do with her what I want. And I want her to marry Walter, otherwise I will not have Matilda.'

'You cannot force her,' Giseux murmured.

'Aye, I can,' Hugh vowed, straightening up, mouth warped into a sneer. 'And you will not stop me.'

Giseux sprang from his seat. One stride brought him to the table, facing Hugh. 'I will stop you.'

Hugh held his hands up, feigning surrender. 'My, my, such passion. I never knew you had it in you, Giseux. Aye, Brianna whinged on about things not being quite right in the marriage when she came crawling back the first time.' He shrugged his shoulders. 'I didn't pay much attention.'

'My God, you're her *brother*.' Giseux tried to breathe deeply, evenly, keeping a rein on his temper. His tanned face moved close to Hugh's, fingers itching to strangle this man, this fellow Crusader, this man whose life he had saved. 'You're supposed to protect her.' A muscle jumped along the line of one high, defined cheekbone. 'That man nearly destroyed her,' he spoke quietly, voice edged with steel. 'And I am not about to let it happen again.' He wheeled away, abruptly.

Hugh blinked as the door closed behind Giseux, the iron latch rattling back into place. With one shaking hand, he wiped away the beads of sweat sprinkling his brow, smoothed down the short strands of his gold-red hair. Damn, damn, damn! Why Giseux, of all people? Why did he have to be involved?

His mind tilted crazily, sliding away from reason, from good sense, and plunged into an abyss of egocentricity, of self-absorption. Self-pity cloaked him; he hunched his shoulders against the invisible garment, throat constricting. Giseux was planning to stop him, to stop him gaining everything he had prayed and hoped and yearned for. All those nights on that senseless crusade, sleeping under the desert stars, clinging to the one thing that pushed him through those dry, hot days: the dream of coming home to marry Matilda, to see his son inherit Sefanoc. Sadness gripped his chest; already his baby son was dead, and with Giseux's words, his marriage to Matilda threatened to topple, to break into splinters at his feet. But it would happen; he would make it happen. No matter that Matilda loved another; she had loved *him* before and she would love him again. He couldn't allow this man to interfere, there was too much at stake. Giseux would have to go.

Chapter Thirteen

'Mother of Mary! How long does Walter intend to incarcerate us up here?' Brianna paced across the woman's solar, stopping once again to kneel up onto the stone window ledge to peer out of the casement. But she already knew her efforts were fruitless; the solar was too high, at least three floors above the muddy-looking moat: too far to jump, too dangerous to climb. She had watched the watery sun move across the sky, from before noon, when a soldier had been tasked by Walter to lock both women in this chamber, to now, when the ball of liquid fire was about to drop below the horizon. Not a soul, not even a servant with some food, had visited them all afternoon. Not even Giseux.

'Brianna, please sit down, you make me nervous with all this striding about.' Matilda perched on a stool, wedged up against a table in the centre of the room, restlessly turning a piece of embroidery in her hands.

Loose white threads from the unfinished hem on the linen dragged across her dark sleeves.

'Sorry. I wish I knew what was happening.' Brianna approached the table, then slid into a seat opposite Matilda.

'Do you think Lord—er…Giseux will be able to talk some sense into Hugh?'

Brianna stretched her hands out across the table, clasping her fingers around Matilda's frozen digits, crushing the needlework. 'I hope so. He might be able to change his mind.' She wrinkled her nose—what had Giseux meant, when he asked her to trust him, when he said there was a way out?

'It seems to be taking quite some time,' Matilda whispered, her milk-white skin glowing in the low light of the chamber.

'Aye, well, as you know, my brother can be stubborn.' She refused to voice her fears that Giseux had failed in his attempt. Slapping her hands against the table, she levered herself to her feet. 'This is ridiculous; we can hardly see in here. Do they intend to make us sit in the dark?' Brianna whisked over to the door, wrestling with the latch, although she knew it was locked from the outside. 'We need some light in here, now!' she ordered, thumping on the planks with the flat of her hand. To her surprise, the door swung inwards and she had to jump away to avoid being hit by the cross-braces, the black metal of the latch.

'Not thinking of leaving us, Brianna?' Hugh swaggered into the chamber, a self-important bluster to his demeanour. His eyes sought Matilda, feasting avidly on the polished gloss of her ebony hair, her willowy figure, and she shrank back into her seat at his blatant scrutiny, trying to fold herself smaller.

'No such luck!' Brianna retorted smartly. She surveyed her brother warily; there was an unsettling, volatile look in his eyes, a look she had never seen before. His movements were jerky, agitated; he seemed excited, his cheeks florid, unusually red.

'That's good, good!' He clapped his hands together. 'I wouldn't want you flying the nest, especially when we have a double wedding to prepare!'

'Wh-what?' Deflated, Brianna plopped down on the stool next to Matilda. She had been so sure, so sure, that Giseux would succeed. What, in Heaven's name, had happened?

'I said, 'we have a double wedding to prepare'.' Hugh smiled nastily. 'Why did you think Giseux would manage to talk me around? Think again, sister.'

'Hugh, you cannot do this. Why make both of us unhappy? Matilda loves another and I…I…' Her speech floundered. She had been about to say that she never wanted to marry again, but the vivid image of a rippling torso stormed her brain, catching her unawares, depriving her of words.

'You want to marry Giseux,' Hugh finished for her, brushing at an imaginary fleck on his sleeve. Brianna half-rose from her seat, a subconscious gesture of protest, but Hugh held his hand up, silencing any argument. 'Please, spare me the maidenly outrage. It's perfectly obvious for everyone to see.' He scoffed at her, a dry brittle laugh emerging from his cracked lips.

'Your pathetic simperings, your flirting, the mawkish way you look at him—truly, sister, it's quite revolting.' Despite his command of the situation, Hugh's illness had left him with sickly cast, a yellowish-grey pallor that suffused the hollow pits beneath his eyes.

'It's not true,' Brianna croaked. How dare her brother rip apart something she held so dear? It was if he trampled on her heart.

'But it is, my poor, misguided fool. Do you believe a man like that would ever marry?' A snarl pulled at his mouth, full of contempt. 'Giseux is incapable of forming any sort of relationship again; he is a shell, empty of feeling.'

Brianna shook her head, her fingers touching his sleeve, rustling against the cloth. 'Hugh, is this really you?'

'Of course it's me,' he snapped, but the vacant, glazed look in his eyes told her otherwise.

'Where is he? Where is Giseux?' she whispered.

'How sweet.' Hugh threw her a secretive misshapen smile. The expression clawed into her, coiling ripples of fear in her belly. 'Did I not say?'

'Where is he?' she whispered.

'Gone. Left. He claimed he had other business to attend to. In truth, Brianna, I think he was relieved to be rid of you. The poor man couldn't wait to leave.'

The cruel words hacked into her, gouging her already fragile spirit. Giseux had asked her to trust him and she had. She had been certain that he would stay here for her, fight for her—could she had been mistaken?

'I don't believe you,' she whispered. Giseux had

gone nowhere and in the tight and secure place around her heart, she knew it.

The smug, set smile plastered on Hugh's face slipped; for a moment, he appeared completely lost. He wore a pale blue tunic, the slash at the neck decorated with a band of gold braid…and something else. Her gaze honed in on the tiny marks covering the fabric over Hugh's chest, no bigger than a pinhead. He began to talk again, recovering his equilibrium, aiming to plough through her doubt, to pummel her into submission with words. And yet, as he burbled onwards, arms spread open, gesticulating demonstratively, his voice rising to a hysterical squeak in an attempt to gain her attention, Brianna's heart flipped, skipped a beat. The flecks covering Hugh's tunic were red: minuscule spots of blood.

Something had happened to Giseux.

Brianna paid little attention to Hugh as he continued to talk, although she was careful to keep her expression neutral, to avoid raising her brother's suspicions that she had guessed anything. But beneath her blank features, her mind worked feverishly. All that she wanted was for Hugh to leave, to leave them in peace so she could think. Despite the icy temperature in the chamber, a heat spread through her body, a wild frustration at the unfairness of the situation, at her imprisonment. Giseux needed her help, of that she was certain, and her toes jiggled within her leather boots, eager to bolt past Hugh and sprint down the corridor as she called out Giseux's name. But such a hurried, desperate action would be curbed before she even started, with a burly soldier standing sentry outside the door. Nay, she needed to think and plan. At last, after what seemed like ages, Hugh spluttered to a halt, muttering something about speaking with Walter.

Brianna waited a few moments after the door closed behind her brother, listening intently as the sound of his footsteps gradually faded along the corridor. Spinning around, she snared Matilda's brown-velvet gaze, her own features stricken. A weight pressed down on her chest, staunching her breath, constricting her throat with a rabid dryness.

'I know,' Matilda announced miserably, pushing her thumbnail into a crack, warped with age, on the tabletop. 'It seems we must go through with these marriages. There is no other option.'

'It's not that,' Brianna replied in a tremulous voice, her whole body vibrating with trepidation, a sense of apprehension. 'It's Giseux.'

Matilda smiled weakly. 'Not quite the knight in shining armour, after all, methinks.'

'He wouldn't leave me,' Brianna stated with conviction. 'Something's happened to him…there were specks of blood on the front of Hugh's tunic; Giseux is hurt… or worse!' A hysterical sob threatened to break from her throat; she quelled it swiftly. To lose her head now would not help Giseux.

Matilda rose to her feet, the movement graceful, precise. 'Brianna, I know you care for the man, that is plain for all to see, but truly, those marks on the front of Hugh's tunic could be *anything*. What makes you so sure?'

The colour in Brianna's eyes deepened to midnight blue. 'He's in danger, Matilda. I know it. And I feel it, here.' She thrust a fist against her chest, against her heart, tears springing to the corners of her eyes. 'He asked me to trust him and I did. I still do. I have to find him.'

'How?' Matilda swung her arms out, a gesture of futility. 'Hugh will no doubt keep us locked up until we are marched forcibly into the chapel.'

'You need to help me.' Brianna's gaze lit on the small stool vacated recently by Matilda. 'Move that stool near to the grate while I fetch the guard. I think it's time he helped us light the fire.'

The thickset soldier positioned outside the women's solar was only too pleased to be asked to help the ladies within. He had witnessed the scenes in the great hall earlier, and, despite being in Lord Walter's employ, had a certain amount of sympathy for the two maids. After listening to their request, he locked the door again before trotting off eagerly to fetch one of the burning brands slung into iron brackets to illuminate the corridor. Tapping at the door, he listened politely for their acquiescence, before letting himself in, locking the door and hooking the key back on to his belt. Both Brianna and Matilda stood together, beside the fireplace, smiling demurely. The flaring brightness from the brand highlighted the liquid quality of their skin, enhancing its beauty. The soldier returned their smiles, his whole day lifting with the sight of such bewitching company. He crouched down at the fireplace, the bones in his knees cracking as he knelt on the cold hearth-stone and shoved the flaming brand into the mess of brittle sticks, stacked like a bird's nest over a bundle of dry, wispy grass. Pain slammed into the back of his head; his mouth jolted open, gaping with shock, before he pitched sideways, crumpling to an unconscious heap on the floorboards.

'Hurry, Matilda! He might not be out for that long!' Brianna promptly detached the key from the soldier's belt, checking him anxiously for any signs of consciousness. But his eyes were firmly closed, his short, stubby arms and hefty legs sprawled in ungainly fashion across the floor. She hoped she hadn't hit him too hard with the stool; it hadn't appeared heavy until she had hefted it up by one leg. Still, it had made an effective cosh, and would hopefully give them enough time to both escape the castle.

'Matilda, you must go, leave this place now and find your man!' Brianna spoke rapidly, her voice muted, as she locked the soldier into the chamber that had been their prison. 'Do you think you can leave without being seen?'

Matilda nodded, throwing her arms around Brianna, eyes glittering in the semi-darkness. 'Thank you, so much, for all that you have done, Brianna. I hope we meet again, in better circumstances.'

'I'm so sorry about Hugh,' Brianna admitted. 'I had no idea he was capable of such behaviour. It's as if... as if he's gone mad.' A dull, cold sensation pitted her chest. She should have known, could have predicted this outcome; his behaviour at Sambourne had been unusual, but she had attributed his wild look, his jerky mannerisms to the illness and not to anything more deep-seated.

'Stop apologising and go.'

For a moment, Brianna followed Matilda's tripping gait along the corridor until she vanished in a flap of pale cloth. Gladness bundled in her heart, a surge of pleasure at the prospect of the girl's happiness. But the image of Giseux lying injured barged violently back into her mind, dislodging all other thoughts. Whirling about, she headed for the spiral staircase that twisted its way down one of the corner turrets. She had no time to visit Giseux's chamber; her better option was to go to the stables to see if his destrier was still there. Cautiously, she made her way down, the folds of her dress lapping the rough wall, her leather soles quiet on the damp stone. She moved like a ghost, treading on the outer edges of her feet, as her brother had taught her in the forests of their childhood. A peculiar pain gripped at her: the pain of betrayal, of disbelief that her own brother could behave in such a way towards her.

Relief seeped through her as her hand touched the hard metal ring of the outside door; she plunged outside, grateful for the freezing air against her skin. The cold gave her clarity, focused her thoughts after the chaotic events of the day; the ice in the air touched against her tongue, clean-tasting, robbing her of breath. Over to the west, above the regimented silhouette of the high curtain walls, the sky held the last vestiges of sun: streaks of reddish gold painted across the dark-blue velvet. The faint light was enough to see her way.

Flicking her gaze hurriedly across the inner bailey, making certain nobody was about, she scampered across the cobbles, heading for the stables, praying that no one had spied her from the upstairs windows of the castle. Who knew how long her brother would sit in conversation with Walter, who knew how long it would be before the guard became conscious and would start to yell in outrage at his own imprisonment? Her time was short; she only hoped that the stables would yield some clue, some hint, as to Giseux's whereabouts.

The smell of horses pervaded the stables, pungent, acrid. Ducking neatly inside the double-width open doorway, making sure she was hidden from view, Brianna hesitated, one hand supporting herself against one of the square-cut oak pillars that supported the lintel. Doubt scissored up her spine. What if she were mistaken about Giseux? What if, after having no success in talking to Hugh, he had simply taken his leave? Brianna shook her head, the flaming silk of her hair shining in the darkness, endeavouring to divest herself of such unwelcome thoughts. Hold on to that silver promise in his eyes, she told herself, that glittering look as he had led Hugh from the great hall. It was all she had, but it was enough.

'My lady?' Her fingers flew upwards, knotting around her throat, clutching in shock at the little voice, while her eyes raked the shadows for the source of the sound. Her leg muscles faltered, skewering her to the spot; she had been so certain that the stables were empty!

She sighed with relief as a boy emerged from one of the vacant stalls, blinking, the whites of his eyes glistening in the strange half-light. A stable boy, by the looks of him, dressed in ragged braies, a torn tunic. His feet were bare, shins smeared with dirt; his hair stuck up at odd angles, as if he'd been sleeping.

'Don't be frightened,' Brianna stretched out her hand towards him. 'I'm sorry if I woke you. I'm looking for something…someone.'

'Mayhap I could help?' the boy offered, a spark of excitement in his eyes. His grin was impish.

Brianna moved forwards, her boots sinking into the piles of straw that spilled over the cobbled walkway from each stall. 'I'm looking for a man, a…a friend. I think something bad may have happened to him.' Her eyes swept along the stable, searching for the black, shining rump of Giseux's destrier.

The boy tracked her worried gaze. 'His horse isn't here. They loaded him onto it, led him out.'

Her head whipped round and she grabbed at the boy's shoulders. 'What happened?' she rapped out, her voice deepened with urgency. 'What did you see?'

The boy smirked. 'They didn't know I was here,' he stated proudly. 'I saw everything. He came in with two of Lord Walter's soldiers; they told him something was wrong with his horse's hind leg. When he bent down to have a look…well, they bashed him.'

Brianna's stomach plunged with fright, with a dreadful loss. 'Tall, light brown hair, black tunic?' In her panic, she fought to remember the details.

'Aye, that's him! This was left behind.' Fear gripped Brianna's heart as the boy retrieved a spill of cloth hanging over one of the stalls. A cloak. Giseux's cloak.

'I have to find him. Which way did they go?'

'North, I think. The soldiers were talking about the forest, which lies in that direction. I can show you, if you like.' The boy's expression was eager.

'Nay, thank you. But there is one way you could help me.' She assessed the boy; they were the same height, roughly the same size.

The boy nodded. 'What is it?'

'You can lend me your clothes. I'm too conspicuous like this.' She swept a disparaging hand over the voluminous fabric of her gown. 'And too hampered.'

Consternation crossed his face. 'But…my lady…' he flushed with embarrassment '…I only have another tunic that is clean, some ragged braies and a short cloak.'

'That's ideal,' Brianna reassured him. 'Go, go now and fetch them for me.'

His face brightened; he scampered over to a wooden ladder, leading up through a dark, square hole in the planked ceiling. 'I sleep up here, normally,' he explained as he climbed upwards. His upper body disappeared for a moment, before reappearing, his hands clutching a bundle of clothes. 'But tonight it was just too cold.'

'Thank you.' Brianna tore the bundle from his hands.

'I'll change at the back here. You keep watch for me, let me know if you see anyone.'

In the deep recesses of the stall, Brianna ripped off her gown and her chemise, hiding both garments under a heap of straw in the corner. She had to remove her boots in order to haul on the braies, but they fitted well, if a little snug about the hips. She flexed her toes, mindful of her healing foot, before pulling her boots back on. The tunic was wide-necked, a rectangular shape that simply dropped over her head and fell to mid-thigh. Her knife-belt gathered the fabric in, the knife in its scabbard resting on her thigh. The boy had thoughtfully supplied a hat, wide-brimmed, felted, which she jammed on her head to cover her hair. Swinging the short cloak about her, her fingers fumbled and slipped on the leather laces; she stopped, filling her lungs with air. *Mindless panic will not help you*, she admonished herself. *Keep calm, think logically. Only that way will you be able to find him.*

'My lady,' the boy whispered. He was bent over, holding on to the collar of a dog, a huge bloodhound, darker patches of black mottling its tan fur. 'This dog will help you find him. Let him smell the man's cloak, he'll find him for certain. The dog is trained to stay with the horse, you don't need to worry about him.'

'Clever boy,' Brianna replied in hushed tones. Even as she presented the bundle to the dog's excited nose, she could hear, through the sifting night air, the sounds of doors slamming, of shouts and running feet.

'They know,' she murmured.

'How will you get through the gatehouse? The guards will be on alert now.'

'We'll ride double,' she explained. 'Hopefully they will think we're just two boys, larking about. Fetch me a horse, a fast one.'

'I'll saddle one for you.'

'No saddle. No time.'

'At least take my water bottle—it may be a long ride.' Holding the leather flagon, the boy boosted her onto the back of the mare that he insisted she should take, then sprang up behind her, perched gingerly. The hound was excited, tail constantly wagging, damp nose moving almost continuously a spare half-inch across the ground.

'You'll have to hold on to me,' Brianna told him. 'This is going to be fast.'

Bunching the flowing mane between both hands, the heavy weight of Giseux's cloak bundled against her stomach like a talisman, she pressed her knees into the horse's flanks, urging the animal into a trot, then a canter. By the time they reached the gatehouse, the animal was moving at a respectable speed, the dog gambolling easily at its side. The lad played his part admirably, raising a hand to the guards standing sentry, grinning broadly. The soldiers smiled back, remembering their own youthful exuberance, as the horse clattered through the gates and over the drawbridge. Brianna rode hurriedly away from the castle, the boy clinging to her waist, nimbly keeping his seat behind her, and headed for a small copse of trees. Under cover of the branches, she slowed up to let the boy slip off.

'Not too far to walk,' she whispered down to him. 'I cannot thank you enough for all that you've done.'

The boy eyed the dog, sniffing about in the undergrowth. 'The dog is a good one, mistress, well-trained. He'll pick up the trail soon enough. You must trust his instinct.' He squinted up at her, raising a hand in farewell. 'I hope you find your man.'

'So do I.'

Chapter Fourteen

Giseux groaned, a deep-throated, grumbling protest, then cracked open one eye. A lacerating pain seared from the base of his skull, flaring upwards towards his left ear. His vision blurring, he tried to make sense of his surroundings: rough, wooden walls, a square-cut hole for a window, the lintel buckled and warped, no glass, the uneven outline of a door. What in the devil's name had happened to him? His back was pressed against an earthen floor, dank, musty; the sweetly rotten scent of cut wood filled the air. He could hear the sound of trees, branches jostling wildly in a rising wind; perhaps he was in some kind of forester's hut, used for wood storage? Outside, thick sleety rain pattered on leaves, spurting into vicious squalls with each blast of wind.

He made to lift his hand, to run his fingers along the back of his head, to check his injury, but his hands jerked uselessly, futile, tied fast with a thick, greasy rope across his stomach. His ankles had been bound as well. Rage flooded through him, a livid, incandescent anger that powered him upwards into a seated position, one shoulder buttressing the wall to support his body. He was dizzy with throbbing pain and his head swam; he hitched backwards until the breadth of his shoulders wedged into the corner of the hut. Hugh, he thought ruefully. Hugh had happened to him. After their unsuccessful conversation, Giseux had searched for Walter, who had conveniently disappeared. On his way from the great hall to the women's solar, a groom, eyes nervous and flickering, had waylaid him, muttering something about an injury to Giseux's horse. Like a fool, he had suspected nothing, following the boy to the stables. The lad had appeared genuinely concerned. It was only later, as he bent down to inspect his destrier's foreleg, in that rushing instant of awareness before the heavy object smashed down on the back of his head, that he realised he had been duped.

Lifting bound hands to his lips, he began to tear at the foul-tasting rope with his teeth. He had to escape, had to reach Brianna before the marriage took place! Hugh seemed to have taken leave of his senses, but he would still have the wits to hold the ceremony as soon as possible, aware that it would only be a matter of time before Giseux would return. No doubt Hugh aimed to keep him out of the way just long enough for a priest to rattle his way through the wedding vows, to destroy the lives of two beautiful women in a moment.

Mouth smarting from the abrasive fibres in the rope,

he rested the side of his head on the wall, long black lashes shuttering down over his eyes. Hopelessness washed over him. He had asked Brianna to trust him, believing he could help by persuading Hugh to change his plans, when, in truth, he had been no help at all. He hoped she wouldn't judge him too harshly.

His eyes snapped open, slivers of polished iron.

Outside the hut, a noise—through the incessant background hiss of the rain, a rapid, methodical scurrying increasing in volume. Then an urgent whisper, a distinct command carrying through the dark. His ears burned, honing in on the sound. Propelling himself upright, wincing at the swirling pain in his head, he jumped, two great springing bounds to the entrance, positioning himself so that when the door opened, he would be hidden behind it. An odd panting, snuffling sound worked a path along the bottom of the door, followed by a furious barking. It was a dog, he thought, a dog had been set to find him! He hoped it was friend rather than foe.

The door creaked back, hesitant on rusty hinges.

She was there. Brianna.

The lambent glow of her hair percolated through the darkness: a smooth, rippling braid snaking down her back as she edged into the hut. Did she even know that he was there, barely holding his tall frame upright, behind her? Too exhausted even to speak her name, he teetered on the edge of consciousness. Slipping down the wall, tunic catching on the splintered wood at his back, he sat, knees drawn up, on the damp earth.

Brianna's head whipped round, spangles of rain

flying out from her hair, twinkling in the half-light from the open doorway. Shining eyes alighted on his crumpled figure, the sickly pallor of his face. 'What have they done to you?' She crouched down beside him, her hands cupping his cheeks, fingers tangled in his hair. She had found him! Relief shot through her, palpable, a cloak of comfort, falling heavily. Her arms came about him, furling around his shoulders, drawing him into her soft frame, the tantalising curve of her neck. Tears coursed down her limpid cheeks, dropping into the buff-coloured springiness of his hair.

His head tipped forwards, forehead resting in the crook of her neck, warm, fragrant, her skin silky; her damp body emitted a faint lavender smell, reminding him of long, hot summers in Provence. Her slim arms held him tight, pressed against his back, and, despite his aching head, desire surged through him, desire coupled with an intense gratitude.

'Giseux...what did they do to you?' Brianna's voice sounded muffled, somewhere above him.

He concentrated on the steady beat of her heart, clung to it, shoved away the dark fingers of unconsciousness threatening to take him down. 'It's nothing,' he croaked.

'I thought...' She managed to choke the words out. 'I thought they had killed you.'

A squall of rain flung angrily through the open doorway, spattering the dry earth floor with dark spots. Brianna drew away from him carefully, supporting him with one hand braced against a shoulder, drawing out her knife to cut the ties at his wrists, his ankles. The rope fell in bits, pale worms littering the wool of his braies, the ground. She watched the blood return to his white fingers, veins pulsing, sensation returning to his hands.

'It's not nothing,' she chided him, biting her lip in concern as she studied his sagging form.

He lifted his chin, eye sockets blotched with pain, flexing his fingers to relieve the stiffness in them. 'They hit me on the back of my head,' he explained. 'It's only a scratch. I should have known better.' He smiled ruefully.

Hitched around to the back of him, Brianna bade him shuffle forwards, so she could part his hair and gain a closer look at the damage inflicted on her brother's orders. The gash in his white scalp was nasty, oozing, a dark, purplish bruise surrounding the impact site. Lines of concentration appeared on her forehead, she needed to clean the wound, somehow.

'Will I live?'

She smiled in the darkness at his half-hearted jest. 'I need to clean it up…I'll fetch my water bottle.'

The horse stood by a small hawthorn tree, waiting patiently; Brianna hoped the animal would remain, having no means to secure it. The dog, lying exactly where she had commanded it to stay, lifted its sleek brown head from its paws and whined when she emerged from the cottage.

'Good boy,' she whispered, bending down to pat the animal's head. The dog's skin wrinkled in loose folds around his eyes, giving him a permanently sad appearance. 'You found him for me, you found him.'

Happiness bubbled up in her heart; Giseux was alive—injured, but alive. Her instincts had been correct.

'How on earth did you find me?' Giseux's silvered eyes snared hers as she walked back inside. She knelt behind him and began to separate his hair gently, revealing the injury. His big shoulders tensed as she began to clean the wound, using the edge of his cloak soaked in water. 'I'm sorry, this might hurt,' she said.

'How did you find me?' He repeated himself, ignoring her worried words.

'The stable lad suggested I bring a dog, one of the hunting dogs. Their sense of smell is incredible. Your cloak was in the stables. The hound followed your scent easily.' She tipped her leather bottle, drenching the blood-soaked cloth once more, dabbing carefully at the wound.

He turned around so that her hand fell from his scalp, the wet cloth dropping into her lap. 'They loaded me on to my horse and brought me out here, hoping to keep me out of the way until the marriages had taken place.' His eyes sparkled over her. 'And it might have worked. But Hugh hadn't reckoned on you, had he? His reckless, unconventional sister.'

Brianna blushed, unnerved by his close attention. 'Hugh told me you had left, that you were fed up, bored with the domestic shenanigans at Walter's castle.' In the curious, shadowy light, her delicate skin glowed like pale marble.

'And you chose not to believe him.'

Brianna chewed on her bottom lip, attempting to temper her concern. The square-necked tunic that she wore, a size too big for her, gaped dangerously to one side, disclosing the graceful line of her collar bone. Something deep in Giseux's belly knotted, tense with anticipation.

'I knew something wasn't right,' she whispered, her voice hesitant, unsure how much she could reveal of her concern for him. 'You told me to trust you…and then you…' her breath snagged, recalling the utter horror she had felt on seeing her brother's blood splattered tunic '…and then you disappeared.'

'You trusted me?' He echoed her words with disbelief. He gave a short bark of laughter, then winced as pain lanced through his skull. 'You, Brianna of Sefanoc, who dares to trust no one, not one living soul, placed her trust in me?'

Brianna wriggled uncomfortably, her toes beginning to prickle in the awkward kneeling position. She threw him an awkward smile. 'Don't tease me.'

'Nay, I'm flattered.' His big hand curved around the side of her face and she resisted the urge to turn her cheek into his palm's caress. 'I thank you for it,' he murmured. The low, velvet tones of his voice wrapped around her, tantalising, soporific. 'Your courage never ceases to astound me. Who would have thought it, so much power, so much bravery in such a little thing as you?'

She laughed softly, tucking a loose, curling strand of hair behind her ear. 'It was more like desperation; the thought of being a virtual prisoner in marriage again, with that man, drove me on.' As the words tripped from her tongue she knew she avoided the truth: she had made no attempt to escape before realising that Giseux had been in danger. It had been he, he who drove her on. Her sapphire gaze trawled the lean angles of his high cheekbones, the generous curve of his mouth.

'So you dressed in boy's clothes and made your escape.' Giseux's smiling glance absorbed the finer details of her attire: the tight-fitting braies enhancing her shapely calves, the vast folds of tunic that only served to make her appear more dainty, vulnerable.

'Helped by one of the stable boys,' she explained. 'And an alert, keen dog. I couldn't have done it alone.'

'However you did it, Brianna, I am grateful. Thank you.' The mesmerising fluidity of his voice sent shivers of exhilaration chasing up her spine. She fought to maintain reason—Giseux had been hurt, he needed to lie down, to rest. His chiselled features loomed close, so close that she could see the glint of bristly stubble on his square-cut jaw. His hand still cupped her cheek; her small fingers rose, as if of their own volition, skimming the ridged sinews on the back of his hand, the rounded outcrop of wrist bone. The touch of her cool fingers knocked at Giseux's self-control, the slow burn of desire kindling in the pit of his stomach. His breath sucked in, sharp; he fought to concentrate on her words.

'I was so worried for you,' she admitted. Her speech emerged, a tremulous rush. 'I thought they had killed you.' She was shaking her head now, clinging on to his fingers, tears forming silvery trails down her cheeks.

Giseux clasped her other cheek, heated fingers moving across the sensitive lobe of her ear. 'You mustn't cry over me,' he murmured shakily. 'I'm not worth it.'

Her eyes blazed over him, over the steely flint of his eyes, the shock of tawny hair falling over his forehead. *You are*, she thought, *you are worth it. You are worth every scrap of emotion that I have in my possession. I would give you it all, if you asked it of me*. The beauty of her jewelled gaze told him everything he needed to know: she wanted him, she needed him. Restraint fractured, split the air, brimming with expectancy. Stark desire clamoured at him, forced out all reason, all sense of right or wrong.

He was lost.

Powerful fingers tangled in her hair, palms cupping her face, hard, pulling her nearer, nearer to his lean, chiselled features. He was out of control and he knew it; his mouth slewed down over hers, rough, unsparing, wild. She gasped out loud at the onslaught and his lips sank closer, cleaving, demanding entrance.

Her insides melted, liquid desire. She knew what was about to happen and welcomed it.

It would only take one kiss. One kiss to quash the infernal desire that ravaged his frame, that tore through his loins like wind-whipped fire. But even as the thought sprung into his mind, he knew he lied to himself. It would take much more than that. Much more. His hands dropped from her face, seizing her waist, clamping her fiercely in a tight embrace, questing fingers ripping at the leather lace securing her hair, releasing the magnificent burnished bundle. Lips raging against hers, he brought her in one swift movement on to his lap, one arm supporting her back, the other wrapped up in the scented mass of her hair, until his fingers trailed downwards.

She mewled in delight as his hand touched the rounded push of her bosom, her mouth opening beneath his. His tongue plunged inwards, filling her mouth, sparking incandescent showers of exhilaration. Within the tight circle of his arms, she shook, her slight frame on the teetering verge of being unable to cope. Blood hurtled at breakneck speed through her veins, a delicious sensation building, building deep within the very core of her being. With every increasing beat of her heart, with every new surge of sensation, she felt her body fight, strive for something, she knew not what. A hot flush suffused her skin; she clung to his wide shoulders, a solid raft in a storm-tossed, turbulent sea. As his mouth tore into hers, her crushed breath emerged in short, rapid pants, a gigantic flood of need ravaging through her, unstoppable. *Please, please don't push me away now,* she begged him silently. *Let me have this one time with you.* The past, the future, all vanished beneath her fierce desire, the need to be with this man, together.

Breathing hard, Giseux wrenched his lips away, silver eyes cutting into her flushed face. 'You have to stop me.' Raw desire chipped at his voice. 'For I cannot stop myself.'

Her slender fingers grazed the stubby bristle on his chin. 'I don't want to.' Her heart bumped recklessly.

'Brianna, you know what will happen.' His charcoal eyes searched hers.

She nodded.

A guttural moan sprang from his throat as his lips crushed against hers, seeking, finding. His hands moved into her tumbled hair, delighting in the soft silken tresses. She tore her lips from his, laughing, kissing his cheeks, kissing the soft fronds of hair that curled over his forehead, feeling the scrape of his beard against her skin. His hands moved downwards, lifting the hem of her tunic, tugging it over her head; the cool air from the doorway chased up her spine.

'Mother of God,' Giseux breathed, eyes darkening as he absorbed the alabaster perfection of her high-rounded bosom, the flatness of her stomach. She flushed, shy beneath his blatant perusal, and crossed her arms self-consciously across her chest. 'Nay,' he breathed, seizing her hands, pulling them down. 'Don't cover yourself. You are beautiful.'

She lost all sense of time then, from the moment when he stood, sleek and muscular before her, to the moment when she lay naked alongside him, her creamy curves milk-pale against his strong, tanned limbs. Outside, the icy rain had turned to snow, white flurries spinning inwards, scurrying across the uneven floor.

Her hand smoothed over the rounded gleam of his biceps and trailed forwards over his chest: a shelf of solid muscle. A deep groove ran down the centre of his chest, from the hollow of his throat to fade out in the flat, rippling muscles of his stomach. Her fingers moved down his sternum, across his stomach, curious, questing.

His sharp intake of breath stilled her fingers.

'Giseux…?' she murmured. Her heart fluttered, the barest hint of panic as his hot thigh nudged her hip. She swallowed hastily, mouth suddenly dry.

'Hush, don't be afeard. I will take care of you.' He told himself to go slow, to take time to savour this beautiful maid. But at every hesitant touch of her fingers, every press of her sweet body, her rosebud lips, his body danced, nerve endings sparking with anticipation, desire coiling tighter and tighter in his belly. He couldn't hold out for much longer.

He wrapped her in his arms, the hot crush of her slim frame against his own, dipping his head to scorch a fiery trail along the rigid line of her collarbone, to plunder the scented hollow of her throat. She gasped, and in the moment, at the sound of her escalating desire, he knew he would not, could not stop. His lips found her mouth as he gathered her into him, urging her back on to the earthen floor. Her diaphragm contracted, then flexed with a delicious awareness, exhilaration flooding within her. She thought she would explode beneath his touch, the accelerating whirlpool of need, amassing powerfully within her.

'Giseux…I…'

Twisting his hands into the coppery ropes of her hair, he lifted his mouth; his eyes glittered down over her, diamond chips of unquenched passion. 'Hush now… trust me,' he whispered, elongating his brawny strength beside her; her body flamed at the nearness of his naked flesh, the hard evidence of his desire scorching her thigh.

And then he was moving over her; her body pulled

taut, every muscle ending stretched, strained as he pushed carefully into her, easing his way through tender folds. She gripped the sides of his face, watching, trusting the dynamic brilliance of his eyes, as she relished the wild, churning maelstrom the invaded her heart, her blood, her belly. Her fingers clawed at his shoulders, urging him closer, nearer to her, before running up and down the rigid rope of his spine.

He surged into her then, overtaken by a rush of desire. Brianna gasped, stunned, as the fragile membrane of her virginity tore away in an instant. The careful consideration, Giseux's own admonitions to move slowly, all cleared from his brain in an instant, extinguished by the need to possess, to claim her for his own. He pushed into her, filling her completely, utterly.

Muscles straining, he shifted within her, beginning to increase his pace, every movement suffusing her body, her mind, with the building promise of shuddering ecstasy. The mild pain she had experienced on losing her virginity was swiftly replaced by a swelling, churning fullness that slowly intensified; she rocked beneath him, skin, breath, body quivering with anticipation, keen to discover the unknown place to which he carried her. She opened herself to him, willing, unafraid, dancing to his rhythm, matching his escalating powerful thrusts with an excited eagerness of her own. The tightening, spiralling desire forming at the deepest nub of her womanhood skewed to a point where it could go no further; a chaotic darkness began to engulf her, shoving away all logical thought. Her eyes closed; her body went loose, breath punching out in short, laboured gasps as he drove her higher and higher, faster and faster until the last ramshackle barrier between them, the pulsating, gossamer skin, brimming with unspoken delight, burst open with a terrifying violence. She clung to his heaving shoulders as a thousand trembling stars of desire exploded, cascading through her, pulverising her; white-hot needles of light arched through her brain. She mewled out loud at the overpowering sensations bombarding her body, a shout of utter joy, of climax, and Giseux cried out simultaneously, throwing his head back as he shuddered within her.

'Sweet Brianna,' he murmured, collapsing on top of her, his body replete, satiated and completely possessed.

Chapter Fifteen

One arm bracing his head, Giseux stared upwards, his expression bleak, ravaged, tracing the looping whorls in the low, planked ceiling. He had woken early, the throbbing pain at the base of his skull dragging him relentlessly from deep, languorous sleep. That, and the slobbery tongue of the dog washing his face as it had slunk its way inside out of the cold; he had pushed the animal away, and now it lay, head resting across its paws with one eye open, regarding him balefully. The odd, haunting whiteness of the light within the hut, the curious muffling of sound, had confused him momentarily, until he spotted the shallow drift of white blown in at the doorway. It had snowed in the night; now, the morning sun bounced off the crisp white flakes, sending a shaft of scintillating light through the open door, the pallid warmth touching his bare feet.

Beneath his thick woollen cloak, drawn over their

cooling, naked bodies in the hushed, stunned aftermath of their lovemaking, Brianna lay, tucked into his side, the slope of her breast crushed into his chest, her creamy, polished flank to his stomach. Silky calves wrapped around his rough, hairy legs; her thighs were soft and smooth. One shining coppery tendril of her beautiful hair snaked over his ribs. He wanted to stay there for eternity, listening to the steady beat of her heart against his own, tasting the sweetness of her breath, luxuriating in the tethered heat of their flesh. She snuggled against him; the fractional movement catapulting desire through his body, unbidden, and he gritted his teeth, attempting to dampen the sensation.

Desolation churned in his gut. How, in Heaven's name, could he have done such a thing? He had behaved like a brute, coercing her into coupling with him, breaching her virginity without mercy, without any thought or consideration for her naïvety, her innocence. Blind, foolish passion had gripped him by the scruff of his neck, driving him on with relentless force, the shackles of self-control dropping away without trace. It was if he had been a callow youth, in the first awakening throes of manhood. He had wanted to help Brianna, protect her, but now he had violated the very trust he had asked her to place in him. This was the thanks she received for finding him, for tending to his wound, for the tears she had wept over him: an assault on her womanhood. He was no better than all the rest of them, no better than Walter, or her brother.

Brianna snuffled against him, her bottom lip relaxed, pouting slightly in sleep. He cringed at the rawness around her mouth, the red scrapes left by the short stubble of his beard, gripped by a dawning revelation. His relationship with Nadia had been comfortable, enjoyable, a place of solace, of sensual release, in that hard, desolate land, but it had not been love. This time with Brianna had shown him that much: never before had he experienced such a sense of completeness, such wholeness; never before had he reached a point where he had forgotten himself, utterly. It scared him, but even as he acknowledged the flick of fear, the wild craving in his body screamed out for more. Self-loathing smacked him in the face; his black heart didn't deserve her, didn't deserve her care, or her beauty…or her love. The thick weight of leaden guilt that pulled down on his heart would be with him for ever. He would drag her down with him, sullying her spirit, her vivacity, corroding her goodness.

Mumbling softly in her sleep, Brianna's fingers splayed out across his chest, scuffing the mat of light hair that hazed over his burnished skin. The simple caress jolted shudders of delight direct to his heart; his body, already inflamed by her nearness, threatened to tip him down the same disastrous route as before. Very, very carefully, he extracted his arm from behind her, the silken curtain of her hair slipping over his shoulder, as he rested her head on the bundle of her tunic. Her eyelids flickered, long dark lashes quivering on her flushed cheeks, but she did not wake.

Jamming his legs into his discarded braies, his feet into his leather boots, he yanked his chemise, then his tunic, over his head. Hitching on his sword belt, fingers unusually clumsy as he fastened the buckle, he dived outside, gulping in the fresh, chilly air. His boots sank into the snow, a deadened, squeaking sound as the ice crystals compressed under his substantial frame. A layer of white coated everything, thickly, as if every dark, bare branch had been adorned with a trim of white fluffy ermine in the night, delineating every angle of the knotted ash, the silvery birch. Snow had blasted against the ribbed trunks, a net of sparkling white splattered across the brown, soaked bark. And beneath the trees, a disgruntled horse, whinnying gently as Giseux approached. The animal had escaped the worst of the weather by sheltering beneath the dense pack of trees; now, it blew warm draughts of air from widened nostrils over Giseux's hands, as he reached forwards to stroke his neck.

The squirrel fur on the inside of Giseux's cloak tickling her chin, Brianna rose, deliciously, gently, back to consciousness. She stretched out her legs, wiggling her toes to release a slight cramp, delighting at the sensual, replete sensation suffusing her flesh. How could she have known? How could she have known how completely wonderful, how precious, such lovemaking could be? She would cherish it for ever, the precious memory wedged close to her heart, fine details etched in vivid definition. Every muscle, every nerve ending in her body thrummed with the memory of his feverish touch, the heated imprint of his honed masculinity moulding to her curves, the scorch of his mouth on her mouth. Desire flared anew and she twisted her head on the makeshift pillow. The hut was empty.

Gathering the voluminous cloak around her, she staggered clumsily to her feet, bare feet tingling as they encountered the errant snow dusting the threshold. The big, molten eyes of the dog followed her movements, leaping to its feet and pushing a cold, wet nose into her palm. Brianna jumped, startled; she had forgotten about the dog, but now she smiled down at it, patting its square-shaped head. Scanning her surroundings, she narrowed her eyes against the low-lying morning sun, a huge flaming ball out to the east, shafting a blaze of light through the thin, pinkish trunks of the silver birch.

'Put some clothes on. It's freezing.' Giseux's husky voice, brusque and clipped, broke from the shadow of the trees. Raising her hand, she shielded her face, gradually discerning the dark outline of his broad shoulders, his tall frame, as he moved out to stand in the open.

'It's so beautiful!' Brianna smiled around at the sparkling snow, the cold spreading a rosy glow across her cheeks; she hopped up and down on the threshold to keep her toes from turning into ice blocks. The snow reflected the brilliance of her eyes, transforming them to jewelled chips of pale aquamarine. Her mouth tilted up to him, shyly, that single, heart-stopping glance holding all the secrets of their night together.

Giseux's heart flipped at her expression, the promise within her gaze reminding him only of his selfish, hedonistic self-gratification. He strode forwards, his mouth set in a rigid line, unsmiling. 'I said, "put some clothes on".' Flakes of snow melted on his tunic, dampened his springy hair.

Uncertainty began to spiral, slowly, deep in her belly. The pressure of joy in her heart lessened, sank. *Please don't do this*, she wanted to shout at him, *please don't spoil what we had together, destroy such a precious memory.* She spun on her heel, hot tears threatening as she barged back into the dim sanctuary of the hut, dragging on the stable boy's chausses, the chemise and the tunic. Her boots had been flung in the corner, chucked back in the shadows, dragged by Giseux from her shapely ankles, his gaze hungry and wild, desiring her, wanting her. Judging by his mood this morning, he obviously believed he had made a huge mistake. She wanted to crawl into the corner and hide, flashes of her behaviour from the night before, once so exciting, so sensual, returning to humiliate her. Dressed, she stood hesitating, self-confidence shrivelled, unwilling to go out and face his contempt, his indisputable distaste towards what had happened. He had found her lacking, disappointing. Obviously she was no match for Nadia, the woman who haunted his mind.

Suddenly, he filled the doorway, arms braced upwards against the sagging wooden lintel. Ice crystals spangled the tousled fronds of his hair. 'What are you doing in here? Walter and your brother will send out a search party before long. We need to go.'

She turned wide, limpid eyes up towards him, needled by his bullying tone. 'Why are you being like this?'

His eyes narrowed, piercing gimlets. 'We tarry too

long here. It makes us vulnerable.' The hardness of his voice bit into her, unforgiving.

'Why do you not speak of what happened?' she whispered. 'Was it so terrible?' Timid beneath the glare of his pewter gaze, her voice faltered, but she had to know. How would it be between them now?

'Terrible?' he scowled, dropping his arms to fold them across his chest. 'Nay, never that. But what I did—it was unforgivable.'

She sucked in her breath, heart flowering. 'There is nothing to forgive, Giseux. It was the most beautiful thing I have ever known.' Reaching down to sweep the short cloak from the uneven floor, she drew herself up to her full height, head tilted to one side.

His eyes widened, amazed at her simple declaration; his arms itched to wrap her to him, to enfold her, but he kept them firmly crossed, resistant, shaking his head. 'Brianna, you don't know what you are saying. I was selfish, greedy, took something that was not mine to take—'

'I wanted you to,' she blurted out. *I wanted you to have my innocence*, she thought, *no one else*. There would be no one else.

'You should have stopped me.' His bright eyes appraised her, silver bonds reaching out to her, tangling her senses. 'I've ruined you.'

'For whom?' she retorted. 'I've told you before, I never want to marry again.'

Not even to me? The question fired through his brain, unexpected, shocking. Within the tight fold of his arms, his hands trembled. 'Marriage would bring you protection,' he stated, carefully, the pieces of an insane idea slotting rapidly into place in his mind.

'I—'

He held up one hand, stopping her words. 'Spare me the speech about being able to protect yourself. Under the laws of this land, your brother has complete control over you. He is your guardian.'

'I don't want to marry. I want to be free.'

He gripped her shoulders. 'Don't you understand? With your brother around, you will never be free. And if he dies, then your guardianship will revert to King Richard, and he or his statesmen will decide whom you will marry.'

'I could hide myself away.' But even she heard the doubt stringing her words.

'And live your life in fear, hoping they will never catch up with you? What a waste.' Giseux's fingers skimmed her cheek, then jerked away. He took a deep breath. 'Brianna, I have a suggestion.'

Her eyes clung to his.

'Marry me.'

Shock, a huge boot planted firmly in her solar plexus, forced her stumbling backwards. Her hands fluttered upwards, grasping at air, trying to find solidity within his bewildering words.

At the horrified look on her face, he laughed, a dry, withering bark. 'It would be a purely practical arrangement. We are the same, Brianna, you and I, two people battling the demons of the past. You must realise that I can offer you nothing else but the protection of my name, a place to live, security. Nothing else.'

His curt words rained down over her, icy hailstones gouging her heart. Nothing else—no love, no kisses, no shared pleasures. But he had pointed out her options with a stark finality: this was the only course of action open to her if she wanted to be safe from her brother. And even if she didn't have his love, she would be close to him. It was a choice she was prepared to take.

'Are you telling me you have no idea where my nephew is?' Queen Eleanor demanded, elevating one finely arched eyebrow. Wrinkles formed across the thin, parchment-like skin of her forehead. Perched in the carved oak armchair opposite Lady Mary, every vertebra in her spine stretched rigidly upwards, she plucked unnecessarily, fractiously, at the gold embroidery on her skirts. Her hair, faded auburn streaked with silver, was exquisitely arranged beneath a diaphanous silk veil, a fashionable silver circlet studded with twinkling gems holding the material in place atop her head. At seventy winters, the Queen was still a beauty, Mary thought, even if her high-handed, imperious manner rankled with some. But, to be fair, the older woman had much to deal with at the moment; with her son, Richard, a prisoner, the affairs of state had fallen back to Eleanor, drawing her out of a quiet retirement in southern France.

'That is precisely what I am saying, my lady,' Mary replied, respectfully, hoping that Jocelin would appear at the door of the women's solar very soon and take his agitated older sister away. 'Giseux is old enough to look after himself.'

'Sending Robert de Lacey in his stead to Germany, when I specifically asked for Giseux! Fortunately for him, Robert seems to be making some progress, although the ransom demanded by the German Emperor is extreme.' With gnarled fingers, Eleanor untied, then re-tied, the knot in her girdle. The trailing ends were finished with silver tags; the heavy metal swung against her voluminous skirts, bumping gently.

'I have no idea about any change to Giseux's plans,' Mary explained patiently. 'We watched him leave here and I assumed he was headed for the coast.'

'It appears that he never reached Southay. Why have we heard nothing?' Eleanor's voice notched upwards, a plaintive whine. She levered herself out of her seat, a dignified figure, sweeping elegantly towards the window. Despite the frigid air of winter outside, at this time of day, the solar grew warm, absorbing every scrap of noonday sun. 'That boy had a direct order from me—from me, the Queen!' She scratched her nails absentmindedly across the planed wood of the windowsill.

Mary twisted around in her chair, studying the svelte form of her sister-in-law silhouetted in the streaming light through the glass. She prayed that Giseux had not been taken prisoner himself, but the thought was fleeting; her youngest son was renowned for extricating himself from the most problematic of situations.

Scrubbing at the misted window pane, her enormous sapphire ring clicking against the glass, Eleanor peered out at the pattern of small fields beyond the castle walls. Snow dusted the ground, white over muddy green, each section of pasture land bounded by scruffy hawthorn hedges. She shivered—what a God-forsaken country! Why Jocelin wanted to live here was beyond her. Despite being her illegitimate half-brother, she had a good relationship with him, felt a certain responsibility towards him. He wasn't to blame for their father's waywardness. She had given him the choice of two estates, Sambourne, or a smaller one nearer to her, in Poitiers. But when the cool beauty of Lady Mary drew him again and again to the English shore, she knew which estate he would choose.

A grittiness scraped the inside of her eyelids; she blinked, then rubbed at her eyes, trying to relieve the soreness. She hadn't slept well, the damp leaching from the thick stone walls of her bedchamber, seeping into her old bones, making her stiff, unyielding. Compared with her luxurious château in France, this place seemed dark, inhospitable. The food—*quel horreur*—the food was leaden, too much pastry for her liking, sitting heavily in her stomach. And this morning, porridge again! Great vats of it, steaming lumpily, a grey mess, in the wooden bowls. Hopefully she wouldn't be here for too long, but the need to raise the ransom to secure Richard's release had forced her hand.

She rubbed at the glass again, a slick of condensation obscuring her vision. Something…nay, someone, moved across the field: a horse and rider, a stark outline, picking their way across a white field. She peered closer, eyes watering as she tried to focus; nay, she was mistaken, she could see two figures on the back of the horse, a man and a young boy sitting before him.

Mary joined her at the window, her willowy figure

matching Eleanor's tall, slim build. 'Giseux would have followed Richard straight to Germany, if it hadn't been for Hugh of Sefanoc.' Mary felt the need to explain her son's behaviour. 'The knight was so sick, Giseux brought him back to England. It delayed him.'

'An errand of mercy.' Eleanor frowned. 'Such a noble act after—' She stopped suddenly, her face set in apologetic lines.

'You mean...after what happened in Narsuf?' Mary broached the subject that Eleanor failed to speak. 'He is still capable of caring for people, you know.' Her words ended in a flick of anger. Why should everyone make such damning judgements about her son?

'Please, don't upset yourself. I haven't seen the boy, since it happened, and you have. I only base my judgements on what I have heard.'

'Then wait until you see him again, please. He doesn't deserve your harsh words.' But Mary's heart wilted. She knew her son had changed; she has seen it in his face on that first morning back at Sambourne, his wish to have died with his men, that it was all his fault.

'Who *is* that?' Eleanor's attention had been diverted, once again, by the two riders.

Mary leaned up to the glass, squinting out. She fastened on the flare of gilded light-brown hair, the familiar broad-shouldered figure and her mouth slackened, aghast, hands clapping up to her cheeks. 'Eleanor, it's him, it's Giseux!'

Approaching Sambourne from the north, across a countryside sparkling with snow, Brianna, wrapped in Giseux's firm embrace, glanced up at the towering walls of the castle with trepidation. The doubt that had plagued her mind for most of the journey, a doubt exacerbated by Giseux's aloof, detached manner, clawed at her brain. Who could advise her if this marriage was a huge mistake? She had no one to tell, no one with whom to share such information. After leaving Walter, she had vowed, promised herself, that she would never marry again, but that promise had been made with the assumption that her brother would be in full support of her decision. And, as Giseux had pointed out to her, unless she married, she would never be free of Hugh's guardianship. Loneliness sliced through her; despite the warmth of the man pressed against her back, she felt utterly, totally alone.

Brianna glanced down, acutely conscious of her legs encased in the rough chausses of a stable lad, the messy ropes of hair trailing across the tunic, pooling in her lap. 'Giseux, stop a moment!' She clutched at his forearm. His arms tensed around her as he eased back on the horse's mane, stopping in the lee of a high blackthorn hedge, out of sight of the castle windows. The horse's hooves drummed against the frozen muddy ruts, a makeshift path along the side of the field. A blackbird, rustling industriously in the hedge, flew off with an indignant squawking, ebony wings glossy against the snow-covered mud. The dog, tongue hanging out after the exertion of keeping pace with the horse, snapped playfully as the bird flew past, before slumping down and eyeing them with mournful accusation.

'Why stop now?' Giseux demanded. 'We're almost

there.' His hot breath tickled the sensitive lobe of her ear.

Swivelling precariously without the support of a saddle, her hip dug into his inner thigh; she flushed, trying to ignore it. The lean angles of his face were ruddy, whipped by the bitter east wind; his wide, uptilted mouth, the mouth that had roamed her flesh the night before, that had made her gasp aloud in pleasure, was very, very close: a hair's breadth from her lips. Her breath hitched—would she ever reach a point where loving him would not be so painful? He held no love for her, he had said as much, stating that he could give her nothing other than his name. This marriage would be a simple business transaction; she prayed her heart would survive.

'Brianna?' His eyes glinted down at her. 'Why have we stopped?'

Mind jumbled chaotically by his devastating proximity, she scrabbled for her reason. 'I can't go in there looking like this! Your parents would have a fit!'

He glanced down at her slim form. His fingers curled unconsciously around the mane. Restless, the horse sidled beneath them.

'They won't mind. They probably won't even see you.' His voice was chilly, dispassionate. The man she had made love to last night had all but disappeared. 'Wear my cloak around you until you reach a chamber, then I'll fetch you something.'

She nodded and he began to undo his cloak, his thoughts racing ahead. He had offered her marriage as an escape, to take his name, and his name only, as protection. But did he truly believe that was how it was going to be? In name only? He had said that in order to persuade her to agree, for, after her previous experience, any hint of a normal marriage would have her fleeing like a hare. Loving her last night had devoured his mind; she was like a magic potion, an elixir, and he would have to draw on every reserve of self-control to avoid touching her again.

Chapter Sixteen

Using his thigh muscles gripped tight against the horse's flank to maintain their joint balance, Giseux swung the heavy cloak from his shoulders, a swirl of cloth in the pellucid morning air. He leaned back in the saddle, chest moving away from Brianna's neat shoulder blades, creating a space between their two bodies, settling the cloak around her slender frame. The light blue wool formed a striking contrast to the brilliant gleam of her hair, tumbling in loose coils around her shoulders. Desire punched him in the gut, low, unexpected: a vivid image of Brianna lying beneath him, hair rippling out in riotous beauty from her pale face to puncture his threadbare self-control.

He jumped down, irritated, annoyed with his lack of self-restraint, moving towards the horse's head. 'I'll lead us in from here,' he announced.

'My hair,' she moaned, edging back into the dip of

the animal's back, missing the strength of his body behind her. 'I have nothing with which to secure my braid.' She had pulled most of the errant strands into a plait on one side of her head. 'Have you anything?' she asked, hopefully.

'Nothing.' His gimlet eyes trawled her face. 'Tuck your hair beneath the collar of the cloak and stop worrying. You look fine.'

He started forwards, his leonine head on a level with the horse, his tunic straining across the heavy, bunched muscles in his shoulders. The dog, immediately alert at the slightest movement, unfolded its smooth, tan-pelted body and trotted after them, occasionally drifting to the base of the hedge to follow an exciting smell.

As Brianna studied the back of Giseux's head, hair matted with dried blood, an acute sense of foreboding built up within her. They were so formal with each other, the conversation so stilted, that she felt exhausted with the very effort. Was this how it was going to be between them? For ever?

'Giseux?' Her breath floated out in white drifts on the icy air. The sunlight, so full of promise earlier in the day, nudged behind a shadowed straggle of cloud. She shivered.

He turned, expression guarded. 'What is it now? I told you, you look fine. Enough to smuggle you in without alarming anyone, anyhow.'

'You don't have to do this, you know.'

'What? Marry you, you mean? No, I don't.' A few flakes of snow, carried on the stiff breeze, settled on the dark wool of his shoulder, sparkling.

'Then why are you?'

He shrugged his shoulders. 'Why not? I have nothing to lose.'

'But you do. You're sacrificing so much. For me.'

His eyes pierced into her, molten granite. 'And what, precisely, do you think I'm sacrificing?'

She hated his formal, distant tone, wanted to shake him, to jar him into some kind of emotion; she wanted to see the man she had witnessed last night. Clutching the flapping sides of his cloak, she yanked it sharply around her.

'A wife to love you.'

'I told you before,' he replied tonelessly, 'I'm a soldier, not a family man.'

Unbidden, a vision of their children sprang to life in his mind's eye, *her* children: a little girl, hair a fiery brand, with his grey eyes. A blue-eyed boy standing tall beside his mother. A shiver of delight, of sheer, unbridled joy, flooded through him; he quashed it smartly.

'You might feel differently in a few years.'

'I doubt it.'

'People can change.'

'Not me.' But even as he answered her, his voice cautious, wary, he knew he lied. He had changed; Brianna had changed him. She had made him turn back from his duty to King Richard, she had kept him in this country when his first instinct was always to run, to find some mindless battle somewhere with which to engage. The massive stone of guilt that had shackled his heart, dragged at his conscience ever since Narsuf, had reduced, little by little in the time that he had known her. But after what had happened, could he dare to hope to love another?

'I realise it's difficult to see me as some form of salvation, as a way out, but believe me, I am your only solution. Even now, your brother might be chasing at our heels,' he reminded her. 'You have no choice.'

'Aye, but you do, Giseux. You do have a choice. Please, think carefully.'

He shrugged his shoulders, dismissing her concerns in an instant. It was the only way he could keep her by his side, protect her, cherish her. He had no wish to let her go, to see her deal with the unpredictable nature of her brother. He told himself it was purely an altruistic gesture, but in truth he knew it was because he cared.

They moved through the last few fields, climbing a short, steep bank to reach the stone-strewn road that led to Sambourne. Brianna gave a start; the castle was closer than she thought, white limestone walls rising up in a jumbled succession of turrets and crenellations. Rooks wheeled and circled above one of the towers, their incessant cawing the only sound across the muffled, snow-bound countryside. The gatehouse was hushed, empty, the clattering sound of the horse's hooves echoing in the cramped space.

'You see,' Giseux declared as he led the horse into the deserted inner bailey, lifting his head up triumphantly, 'I told you, no one about.' The dog, seeing a pack of his own loitering near the stables, bounded off happily, tail wagging.

But Brianna's eyes were fixed on a point above his head. 'Then *who* is that?' she whispered.

Giseux followed her dismayed expression, spotting two women poised on the top step of the main entrance. An impressive stone arch, receding in graduated layers above them, framed their colourful figures. 'Ah, well, maybe not quite deserted.' His tone held a scant note of apology.

'I recognise your mother,' Brianna said, studying the slender lines of Lady Mary, a gown of rose velvet clinging to her elegant frame, 'but who is the other lady?'

Giseux grimaced. 'My father's sister. My aunt. Queen Eleanor of Aquitaine.'

Immediately Brianna hunched down in the saddle, cringing, trying to hide herself away. 'Hell's teeth, Giseux, she's the King's mother…royalty!'

'They must have seen us from the windows,' Giseux announced, unperturbed, throwing a brief, terse smile at her cursing.

'I can't, I can't meet her like this, dressed as a stable lad! You have to do something!'

Laughter rumbled in his chest; he slid two hands beneath her shoulders to lift her from the horse. One thumb strayed inadvertently over the rounded softness of her breast as he lowered her to the ground; at his errant touch a leap of passion scythed through her. 'Act as if we care for each other, love each other,' he ordered her sternly. 'I don't want my mother to think there is anything unusual about this marriage when we tell her.'

I can do that, easily, she thought. *I don't have to act.* An overwhelming crushing sensation burst through her chest; she wanted to weep. Her mouth wobbled with emotion; she took a deep breath, steadied herself.

'Come on.' Giseux tugged at her hand, oblivious to the brimming wetness of Brianna's eyes. 'My aunt will understand.' He led her across the cobbled courtyard, fingers laced with hers in a fast-paced walk. Brianna clutched frantically at the sides of the cloak, trying to hide her peculiar attire.

'Giseux, what is the meaning of this?' Eleanor's voice boomed down as they reached the bottom of the steps and started to climb. Giseux's fingers tightened on Brianna's—a gesture of reassurance, of support? 'I gave you a direct order to go to Germany and you dare to disobey me? Fortunately for you, Robert de Lacey has conducted himself admirably in your stead!' One critical eye scoured the girl at his side, a pathetic figure wrapped in a cloak several sizes too big for her. Keeping her eyes trained on the maid, she wrenched her mouth to the side, hissing at Mary, 'Who is that chit? And what has she done to her hair? It doesn't look right.'

Mary struggled to keep the elation out of her voice, and the curiosity—her son was still here, in this country, and with Brianna! Undiluted happiness fluttered through her heart; she yearned to know the details, but for now, with Eleanor's tense, demanding demeanour at her side, she chose to answer her sister-in-law's question. 'The girl is the sister of a fellow Crusader, Hugh of Sefanoc. And she hasn't done anything to her hair—that is the problem.' She flashed a warning look at her son, who appeared to be dragging the poor girl reluctantly up the steps.

'My Lady Eleanor, Mother, at your service.' Drawing level with the two women, Giseux greeted them formally, bowing low. Clamped to his side, Brianna had no choice but to bow as well. One long red-gold strand slipped out from beneath the cloak's fur collar.

'Hardly at my service, young man.' Eleanor sucked in her breath, studying the girl's dishevelled appearance with disapproval. 'There had better be a good explanation for this.' But even as the words issued from her lips, a smile twitched her face. Giseux had always been her favourite nephew.

'Oh, believe me, there is,' he replied. 'We need a priest, and fast.'

Eleanor's eyes rounded, pupils dilating rapidly in the faded grey of her eyes, plucking haphazardly at Mary's sleeve. Lady Mary took a step back, almost knocking into the wide-planked door behind her. A gust of wind seized the hem of her gown, blowing it sideways, rose-coloured fabric rippling against the silvered oak of the door.

'I beg your pardon?' Eleanor asked, her voice rising querulously. She shook her head, fractionally, as if she hadn't heard him aright.

'I said, 'we need a priest,'' Giseux repeated calmly. 'To marry us.'

Eleanor's gaze narrowed suspiciously at the portion of Giseux's cloak covering Brianna's stomach, lips curling in irascible distaste. 'And why do you need a priest so quickly?' she demanded.

A piercing draught of wind cut around the back of Brianna's neck, chafing her frozen face; she shivered. Balanced on that top step, she wondered whether she clung to a dream. Maybe she would have been better slinking away, away from all this when she had had the chance. Lady Mary caught her slight movement, acknowledged the cold, pinched lines of Brianna's face and pitched her a look of sympathy.

'Mayhap we should continue this conversation inside, where it's warmer,' Giseux's mother suggested, resting her hand on Eleanor's slim arm, clad in a tight-fitting sleeve of green silk. Eleanor nodded briskly, tossing her head around to march inside, close to Mary. Even following at a distance, Brianna could hear her strident mutterings… 'What does he think he is doing? Who is that girl?' She failed to decipher the low tone of Mary's calm responses.

'She's taking it well,' murmured Giseux as they moved along the shadowed corridor in the wake of the two ladies.

'You think so?' Brianna whispered, incredulous. 'I would hate to see her when she objects to something.'

'Believe me, this is mild by comparison,' Giseux remarked. 'We'll be married by the end of the day.'

Her heart plummeted, then leapt in one crazy, jagged sensation. She paused, a shaft of light pooling from a high window lighting her face. Her skin was translucent, glowing with a pearl-like lustre. 'This doesn't feel right, Giseux.' Her words jolted out.

His expression was like stone, inscrutable. The limpid light shining into the corridor highlighted the sculptured angles of his face, lending him a devilish air. 'I'm not like Walter, if that's what you're worried about. Marriage to me means freedom for you, more freedom than if you remained unmarried.'

'You'd do that…for me?' Her eyes traced the two definite points on his upper lip, the generous fullness of his mouth.

'I've no wish to curb your ways, your spirit, Brianna. Surely you knew that? You will be able to do exactly as you wish in this marriage, hang on to that independence that you value so highly. I'll not bother you.'

Her heart folded in upon itself, packing down tight, smaller and smaller. Other than giving her his name, he wanted nothing more to do with her. Would they even live together?

As Giseux pushed aside the thick curtain that screened the entrance to the great hall, allowing Brianna to precede him, Eleanor and Mary had already reached the top table, where Jocelin sat, his head bent, body hunched over a stack of papers. He glanced up, disconcerted, as Eleanor launched into a high-pitched tirade, her beaded gown sparkling in all directions as she gesticulated with a thrusting arc of her arm towards Giseux and Brianna.

'You had better tell me everything, Giseux,' Jocelin urged, his grey eyes moving with studied interest over Brianna's slight form. 'Come, sit beside me, both of you.' He indicated the two empty seats on his right-hand side, before stacking the loose parchment into a pile, pushing it away from him.

Giseux sat next to his father, raking one hand through his hair, pulling Brianna into the seat beside him. 'There's no time, Father. We want to marry and

Hugh's against it. He's probably on his way here now.' The husky rumble from his chest reverberated through Brianna's slight figure; her spine tingled.

Jocelin's attention turned to Brianna. 'And you, my dear, I assume you're the bride-to-be?'

Brianna nodded, mouth suddenly dry. This was it; this was the moment when she would have to start living the lie.

'You wish to marry my son?'

'I do,' she whispered. That, at least, was not a lie. She clamped her lips together, reluctant to enter into the finer details, sure that in her befuddled state she would let some vital snippet of information slip, information that would not tally with their story and give them away, reveal the falsehood of their situation.

'And your brother is your guardian? I understand both your parents are dead?'

'That is correct, my lord.' Brianna folded her trembling hands in her lap, adjusting her position so that the unfastened sides of Giseux's cloak would not fall open to reveal her boy's garments.

'As your guardian, he has the right to decide whom you marry.'

Giseux sprung to his feet, impatient, eyes firing darts of pure silver. 'Hell's teeth, Father, we know all this! But once she is married to me, he will be unable to do anything about it! That is why we need a priest, now!'

'Eleanor can give you the permission you need,' Lady Mary's quiet voice chimed in, wondering at the passion in her son, wondering at the lightness in his eyes. He was different, different because of…this maid, Brianna, who sat quietly at his side. She leaned forwards, smiling, snaring her son's brilliant eyes. 'She is the Queen of England, after all.'

'This is preposterous, Mary, if you think I'm going to do a thing like that…such unseemly haste…' Eleanor stared resolutely ahead, jewelled fingers tapping in irritation on the wooden table, the hanging pearls in her filigreed silver circlet winking with each dissatisfied jolt of her body.

'Eleanor, stop treating Giseux like one of your subjects!' Jocelin flared back at his older half-sister. 'The boy is your nephew, he's family!'

Eleanor glared at him, then her fixed, rigid expression softened; she laughed. 'I had forgotten.' she expelled her breath slowly. 'Only you, only you, Jocelin, would dare to speak to me in such a way!'

'Will you do it?'

'Fetch the priest.'

Brianna wriggled her hips down into the hot, silky water. The linen cloth draped over the inside of the wooden tub to prevent splinters rumpled beneath her thighs. The water spread with delicious heat over her legs, swilled over her stomach, a rippling sound. She was grateful for the solitude. The panelled timber of the walls glowed in the light from the charcoal brazier, burning coals shifting, coalescing, in the iron basket in the corner. Outside, the gathering low cloud signalled more snow, but inside the warm cocoon of the chamber, she felt safe, comfortable. Resting her head on the back of the bath, her eyelids shuttered. The heat suffused her limbs, driving out aches from muscles, the tension that frayed her nerves. It was done; Queen Eleanor had agreed to give permission to the marriage, although without her presence, Brianna was certain Giseux would have ploughed ahead with the wedding anyway and damn the consequences.

There was a tap at the door. Brianna shifted her head, opening her eyes to see who entered. Lady Mary walked in, a sheath of shining blue silk laid carefully across her outstretched forearms. She moved over to the window, laying the gown reverentially across the carved oak dresser. Beneath the gown, she was carrying a pair of blue silk slippers, each toe encrusted with pearls, set in the shape of a flower. A maidservant followed Mary, carrying a gossamer veil, spun silk, and a jewelled circlet. She stood respectfully in the shadows, head bowed, as Mary moved forwards to speak to Brianna.

'This was my wedding dress.' Mary looked down at Brianna, a tender expression on her face. She clutched her hands together, as if searching for the right words. 'I am so happy for you and Giseux… I could see how you felt about each other, when you were here with your brother.'

'Truly?' Brianna frowned. From what she could remember, she and Giseux had argued continually.

'Giseux seems happy, too,' Mary continued. 'I never… We never…' Her voice trailed off, unable to verbalise her true fears for her son when he had returned from the Orient.

Brianna snatched at the washcloth, folded in a neat rectangle over the side of the tub, pushed the cream folds deep into the water. Shame washed over her, shame at the fallacy that would be this marriage, humiliated that Lady Mary was so happy because of it. She itched to confide in the older lady, to tell her none of it was true, that Giseux was merely helping her out of an impossible situation, but one look at Mary's shining eyes, her flushed, excited face, and she knew she could not.

'Eleanor is insisting that she escorts you into the church,' Mary continued on a practical note. 'I hope you don't mind; she has these peculiar ways. I think it all comes from being in charge for too long.'

'I don't mind at all,' said Brianna. It would make it easier with the irascible Queen at her side.

'And I have brought my maid, Magdelena, to help you dress.' Mary indicated the raven-haired girl standing in the shadows.

'Thank you,' Brianna said. 'I feel quite overwhelmed. You have done so much for me.'

'Not as much as you have done for my son, Brianna. You have given him…' she paused '…his life back. No one could do more than that.'

A pang of humiliation swept over Brianna as the door clicked behind Giseux's mother. A knot of doubt began to grow in her stomach; she screwed the water from the sopping washcloth and smoothed it flat, over the side of the tub, looking around for a towel.

'Here, my lady.' The sibilant tones of the maidservant emerged from the corner of the chamber, followed by the girl herself, carrying a large white towel. 'Do you wish to dry yourself?'

'Thank you,' she murmured. Gripping the sides of the bath, she stood upright, runnels of water streaming over her pearly skin. Long, curling tresses, darkened to ancient rust by the water, plastered over her back, rippling over her high bosom. Plucking the towel from the girl's fingers, she dried off the excess water before stepping out on to a thick, woven mat, which absorbed the water from her feet. Once dry, she wrapped the towel around her like a cloak and moved over to the pile of shining clothes laid carefully along a low bench near the window.

Brianna pulled on the undergarments, the weightless silk whispering against her skin. Her fingers trailed hesitantly across the rippling blue fabric of the wedding dress: Lady Mary's wedding dress! She had no right to it, did not deserve it!

'Shall I dress your hair, my lady?' The serving girl's question interrupted her roiling thoughts.

'Please.' Brianna's voice seemed squeezed, stunted, surfacing on a tightly held breath. In her borrowed undergarments, she perched on a three-legged stool near the brazier, the heat from the glowing coals flaring against her face. The maid towelled her hair with deft, brisk movements, before combing through the tangled locks. The ambient heat from the brazier flowed around Brianna; her hair dried quickly. Once the maid had combed out all the knots, she twisted Brianna's hair into two plaits, before winding them together into a glossy bundle at the nape of Brianna's neck, skewering the whole gleaming mass with long, pearl-studded hairpins.

'And now for the dress.'

Brianna's face appeared from the scooped neckline, decorated along its curve with a spangle of pearls. She pushed her slim arms into the tight-fitting sleeves, the material of the bodice hugging her waist before flaring out into wide skirts. The front of the dress was split, opening to reveal a panel of blue samite, interwoven with silver thread. Brianna smoothed her hands down over her hips, the maid securing the girdle twice about her waist, leaving the two tasselled ends to swing free. Her heart felt leaden.

The door burst open. Queen Eleanor stood on the threshold, her expression one of haughty irritation, eyebrows raised high into a forehead of wrinkles. 'How long does it take you to prepare yourself, Lady Brianna? I thought you, at least, would have a notion of speed in this whole affair if only to avoid any ugly business with your brother!'

'I am ready, my lady.' Brianna curtsied.

Eleanor swept a critical glance over Brianna. 'Aye, you'll do, my dear. But I have something else for you.' She raised imperious fingers in the air, clicked them rapidly. Two guards staggered in, puffing heavily, a vast leather trunk carried between them.

'Set it down here,' Eleanor ordered, pinpointing a precise spot in the middle of the chamber, 'and leave us.' She threw a thin smile in Brianna's direction. 'I only arrived yesterday, practically in the middle of the night. Not all of my bags were brought to my chamber.

Truly, I don't know how Jocelin copes with the sloppiness of his servants.' Her sharp eye spotted Magdalena, hovering in the corner by the brazier. 'You! Come over here and open this.'

The maid scuttled forwards, sinking to her knees in front of the trunk. Three golden lions, the symbol of the King, decorated the surface of the lid, gold leaf stamped into the stiff leather. The girl's slight fingers fumbled with the heavy straps, the unwieldy buckles holding the lid tight shut.

'Come on! Come on, girl!' Eleanor paced behind her.

At last the lid was pushed back, revealing the shadowed interior. Frowning, Eleanor peered in, scanning the contents. 'For goodness' sake! Those complete imbeciles have brought up the wrong trunk. This one belongs to Giseux! He left it in Poitiers the last time he was there. I am simply going to have to go down myself!'

She cast an apologetic glance in Brianna's direction. 'I mean for you to have my silver circlet, child. It will sit well upon you.'

Brianna nodded jerkily as Eleanor disappeared, exchanged a rueful smile with the maid. 'You had better go with her, Magdelena, before she turns the whole castle upside-down looking for this thing!' The maid nodded, slipping out of the chamber in pursuit of the formidable Queen.

Brianna's eyes drifted across to the open trunk. Giseux's trunk, lying open before her, the shadowed confines tantalising, offering a fragile link to his previous life. Mindful of the delicate silk of the wedding dress, she knelt with trepidation on the floorboards, peering into the spicy depths for some clue, some hint to the man she was about to marry. The silver-blue gown flowed out from her hips, the material settling in the circle around her slender figure. A smile lifted her mouth when she spotted the books stacked up on either side; no wonder the guards had looked like they were about to expire! She picked up one of the leather-bound volumes, riffled through the stiff parchment, the laboriously inked words. Latin. She had never learned the language of Rome, never had the chance. Being a knight had given Giseux the privilege of education. In the middle of the books, clothes, a bundle of tunics and braies—there was nothing here of any significance. She looked again. A bright corner of gold peeked out from beneath the pile of blues and greens, snaring her gaze. Her questing fingers dug, deep into the pile of material, pulling at the fabric, drawing it out into the light.

Tiny gold circles, hanging in bunched clusters from a heavily embroidered bodice, tinkled against one another. Sweat slicked her palms, as her nerveless fingers cradled the rift of heavy material, sparkling. A low, curved neckline, designed to display a perfect bosom; the waistband curtailed so a flat, toned midriff could be revealed. She had never seen such an item before, but she had listened to tales, heard the stories of these revealing outfits from the Orient. An exotic perfume rose in the heat of the chamber, sensual, exotic, taunting her.

Her heart fractured into a thousand pieces.

She shoved the material back into the trunk and slapped the lid down. Despair sloshed over her, icy, froze the very marrow of her bones. What was she doing? All this time, he had kept a piece of Nadia's clothing, buried deep in the recesses of his trunk, a physical reminder of the woman he had loved. Who he would always love. She couldn't fight this. Why had she even hoped, dared, that he would love her instead?

Chapter Seventeen

In the dimly lit confines of the vestry, concealed from the main body of the church by a billowing velvet curtain, the priest rubbed the back of his big, fleshy hand across his sweating forehead. His hand closed around the neck of an earthenware flagon, lifting the vessel to his lips, drinking deep. He didn't normally imbibe, but, by God, surely the circumstances demanded it? A wedding, no less, and no time to prepare! He hated to be rushed, but already his lord and lady, together with members of the household retinue, sat on simple wooden chairs in front of the altar. No doubt Lord Jocelin was already tapping his fingertips impatiently on his knee; the man couldn't abide waiting for anything.

The curtain snapped open. One of the fraying leather laces that secured the curtain to the pole across the doorway spun down to the flagstones with the sharp movement.

'Are you ready?' Giseux's handsome face pushed into the gloom, steely eyes glowing with vitality, cheeks kissed with ruddy streaks from the cold.

Cowering back against the hard stone wall, the priest nodded, smoothing his hand nervously down his brown habit, his stubby fingers searching for the comforting presence of his crucifix, his rosary that hung from his girdle.

'Come on, then.' Giseux reached into the vestry, seizing the man's shoulder in a friendly grip. 'We haven't got all day.'

'Aye, my lord, let me just lift this.' The priest hefted the heavy leather-bound Bible between his arms, following Giseux out into the church. Outside, the snow had ceased falling, the heat of the sun clearing the sky to a bright, periwinkle blue. The light shafted through the tall Gothic arches of the stone-framed windows, pooling onto the large rectangular flagstones, warming the assembled crowd chattering excitedly to each other. Conscious of Jocelin's fierce regard, the priest positioned the book carefully on the high carved stand, turning the thick parchment with fastidious slowness to find the appropriate place. Lord Giseux occupied one of the chairs in the front row, a tunic of green samite hugging his formidable frame.

At the southern end of the church, the iron latch rattled upwards, the door swinging slowly inwards on creaking hinges. Heads turned, the crowd rising to their feet, hushed gasps of amazement, of wonder, echoing up into the cavernous vaulted ceiling.

'Lord in Heaven, she is a true beauty!' Mary whispered to her husband, hot tears flooding to her eyes, blurring her vision. She clutched at Jocelin's arm, trying to suppress the sound of pure joy that rose in her throat. Giseux sprung from his seat, dazzling granite gaze rippling over his bride, his expression proud, hungry.

With Queen Eleanor behind her, Brianna stood poised on the threshold, framed by the carved stone arch. In the time that she had been preparing for the wedding, Lady Mary had raced around the gardens, pursued by various servants, scouring the snow-covered borders for suitable greenery with which to decorate the church. She had succeeded. Huge, trailing swards of ivy garlanded the grey stone, black berries studding the green mass like shiny beads, winking in the sunlight. Bunches of holly were tied to each chair that lined the aisle, forming a pathway of green, the red holly berries gleaming out like rubies. Encased in the silken gown of blue, Brianna appeared as an angel, the pale luminosity of her face hinting at some magical distant land, a place of light and joy.

Giseux sucked in his breath, hands rigid at sides, trying to restrain the urge to bound down the aisle and sweep her into his arms, to kiss away the anxious furrows on her brow. He studied the floor, the slightest crawl of shame darting up his spine. He had pushed her, forced her into this marriage, with the promise that she would gain more freedom. But now, he seriously wondered whether he could keep such a promise. More than ever now, he wanted her at his side, for ever. But one look at Brianna's terse, hesitant expression told him the importance of treading carefully.

'Come on, girl, come on, I'm freezing out here!' Several people in the congregation smirked as Queen Eleanor's hectoring tones echoed around the church. Brianna jolted forwards, the pearls in her borrowed silver circlet swinging in unison, as she began to move down towards Giseux, the breath of veil lifting from her shoulders. Mary glanced down at the posy of quivering snowdrops in her own hands, suddenly remembering to whom they belonged. As Brianna drew level with her, Mary pressed the delicate flowers into her chilly hands.

'May God go with you, child,' Mary blessed her.

Brianna threw her a wan smile, then glanced up towards Giseux, her blue eyes large, serious. A ray of brilliant sunshine punched a diagonal shaft through the window nearest to the altar, highlighting his tall, commanding figure, his tousled hair shining, gilded, the silver threads in his samite tunic sparkling like ice crystals. A hollow pit of doubt puckered her stomach at his unreadable expression. Would he come to regret his decision in time?

She moved to stand beside him, heart closing up with sadness. At least she had the memory of these last few days together, the memory of their night together. At least that belonged to her, even if his heart did not. The touch of Nadia's bodice still rasped against her fingers.

'Brianna?' Giseux's low rumble broke into her jittery stream of thought.

The priest was asking her something. 'Do you consent to this marriage?' His voice droned out into the church, a monotonous, nasal drawl. Eleanor shifted restlessly on the narrow wooden chair: she was as impatient as her brother.

'Aye, I do,' Brianna replied, her voice quiet, subdued.

'Are you sure?' The priest's voice held a tint of suspicion as he eyed the bride's wan face. He rustled the pages of the Bible in important fashion, raising his shaggy eyebrows significantly.

Brianna glanced up, frowned. Giseux loved another woman, the evidence was undeniable—could her own love for him be strong enough to contend with such an immutable force? The woman had died; it was if his love had died with her.

'Oh, for goodness' sake!' snapped Jocelin, bouncing out of his seat. 'She said so, didn't she? Are you completely deaf?' Lady Mary dragged at his sleeve, an anguished look on her face, trying to pull her husband back down, to restrain him.

The priest turned another page, the thick, handmade paper crackling under his fingers.

'And who gives this maid in marriage?' he intoned laboriously.

'I do!' Queen Eleanor boomed out from Brianna's left-hand side.

The priest peered at the older woman. 'And you are?'

Jocelin, who had sat down, leaped up again. 'Are you a complete and utter fool, man? She—' he pointed to Eleanor '—is your Queen, the Queen of England and France, so watch your step or you'll be seeking new employ.'

The priest sunk his face closer to the print on the page, trying to hide his portly frame behind the lectern, mumbling his apologies. As if to make amends for his mistake, he began to speak more quickly, rattling through the marriage vows at breakneck speed. Brianna watched his fleshy lips churn out the words with a feeling of dread, her body, her legs, wooden and stiff, her shoulders rigid. She jumped, started forwards with panic, as the crowd roared with delight when the priest finally pronounced them man and wife. Giseux's head dipped, his cool lips grazing her own, a scant, perfunctory kiss.

They proceeded down the aisle in a whirl of dried rose petals, carefully preserved from the summer and now thrown high by the eager, admiring crowd, Brianna's hand tucked delicately into Giseux's crooked arm. Watching their progress, Lady Mary sobbed openly beside her smiling husband, and even Queen Eleanor dabbed covertly at one eye with a tiny white handkerchief. All around the couple, as they made their way along the path that led to the castle's inner bailey, people shook Giseux's hand, curtsied to Brianna, shouting their congratulations. The rosy hues of dusk streaked the sky overhead, the silver crescent of a new moon rising above the crenellated silhouette of the castle turrets. It should have been a perfect day. But when Brianna glanced up to meet Giseux's narrowed regard, a hollowness gripped her and her heart swelled with grief. He seemed so distant, so withdrawn. It was if by marrying him, she had lost him.

The glass in the windows of the great hall reflected

the last rays of the winter sun, beckoning them. Flanked by three soldiers, a man stood at the bottom of the steps leading up to the main door, a nobleman dressed in a sweeping green cloak, black braies, coppery-red hair.

'My God! Giseux, it's Hugh!' Brianna gasped, her head jolting up to Giseux. The diaphanous silk of her veil floated out behind her, revealing the glossy beauty of her hair, the unfathomable blue of her eyes.

'So I see,' Giseux replied grimly, observing her stricken expression. 'Brianna, he can do nothing now we are married. He has no power over you now.' His hold tightened; she leaned into him as they walked, drawing on his muscular strength.

'Stay close,' he murmured gently as they approached Hugh. Her heart flared at the possessive tone in his voice.

'Please tell me this isn't what I think it is!' Hugh spluttered, a peculiar light darting through his blue eyes. Tiny flecks of spittle landed on his chin, winking in the evening half-light. He moved forwards, unexpectedly, grabbing Brianna's shoulder, then released her just as quickly when Giseux placed one big palm in the middle of his chest, pushed him roughly back.

'Brianna is now my wife.'

'How dare you? How dare you marry my sister without my consent? I'll have you for this… I'll have you!' Hugh jabbed the air with one stumpy finger, a purplish colour suffusing his cheeks.

Giseux shook his head, eyeing Brianna's brother with pity. 'I should lay you flat for what you've done to your sister, but somehow you're not worth the effort.

I suggest you take your paid thugs—' he indicated with a nod the three soldiers standing alongside Hugh '—and leave.'

Hugh's eyes narrowed with fury. 'I should have killed you when I had the chance. A knock on the head was too good for you.'

'You need to accept that you have lost, Hugh,' Giseux replied evenly. 'Matilda—'

'Has disappeared, no thanks to you.' Hugh fixed his sister with a baleful stare. 'And Walter is fed up with the whole affair; he practically threw me out of the castle this morning when I couldn't find you. I have nothing left.' His gaze switched to Brianna, his tone more wheedling. 'Why have you done this to me, sister, why have you betrayed me so?'

Brianna's tongue cleaved to the roof of her mouth; she could barely swallow, let alone answer. Sadness rippled through her: the brother she had once held dear had become a stranger to her.

'You've forced her into this; Brianna would never have agreed to marry again so readily,' Hugh continued, sweeping back a greasy lock that had fallen over his forehead. Straightening his spine, collecting himself, he drew himself up to his full height. 'I shall seek an immediate annulment.'

'Too late,' murmured Giseux. Brianna's cheeks flushed; she averted her eyes to the ground, suddenly taking an intense interest in the velvety pillows of moss growing in the crease between the steps.

Her brother's eyes, prominent and bloodshot, bulged with rage; the skin around his mouth turned white.

'Come here!' he roared, lunging at Brianna, drawing his sword at the same time in order to fend off Giseux. But Brianna was too quick for him, too light on her feet, and she danced away from his haphazard, uncoordinated assault. The burgeoning emotion that had built steadily during the wedding ceremony threatened to consume her, pushed on by the memory of that golden bodice, cool and treacherous within her fingers. It was as if she tiptoed along the edge of a yawning whirlpool, feet continually slipping on the loose rubble edge. She was about to fall.

'Nay, she belongs to me!' Giseux roared at Hugh, hefting the hilt of his sword.

'If you stay with this man, Brianna, you'll never see me again, do you hear?' Hugh harangued her over Giseux's broad shoulder. 'I shall go abroad; I cannot bear to stay here and watch you make a mess of things again!'

'Go!' ordered Giseux. 'I shall see that you are personally escorted to the coast.'

'Stop it!' Brianna yelled at them. 'Stop it, both of you!' The tears, threatening to bubble up for most of the day, spilled chaotically down her cheeks. 'I belong to no one. No one. This marriage…this marriage…' Her eye caught the worried observation of Lady Mary, who stood at the forefront of a circle of concerned onlookers, and the words died on her lips. Through the haze of tears, her gaze switched to Giseux.

'I need to talk to you,' she stuttered out between the gulping sobs, 'I need to talk to you…now.'

Giseux sheathed his sword immediately; one glance

towards his father told him that Jocelin would deal with Hugh. Taking Brianna's arm, he bounded up the steps with her, away, away from the crowds of well-wishers, down the long, shadowy corridor to a small ground-floor chamber, lit by the last few rays of the setting sun.

'Now,' Giseux murmured gently, smoothing a wayward strand of auburn hair away from her cheek, 'what's all this about?'

Brianna folded her arms about herself, trying to stop the incessant shaking that threatened to engulf her body. She stepped back from his devastating nearness. 'I cannot do this,' she gasped out, sobbing, shaking her head. 'I cannot be married to you. It would be too painful.'

He frowned. 'But I told you, Brianna, I will leave you alone. You will have the freedom you so desperately crave. A freedom within the safety of marriage.' His pupils darkened, velvet stone threaded with seams of silver.

Her fingers reached out, grazed his sleeve. 'Oh, Giseux, I thought I could do this, I thought I was strong enough.' Her voice trembled, the breath of silken veil drifting forwards over one shoulder. 'But I cannot. I am so sorry. I love you too much.'

'What did you say?' His jaw dropped, revealing his white, even teeth, staring at her, openly stunned.

Caught in her own churning thoughts, she failed to hear the question. 'I found Nadia's bodice,' she sobbed. 'I'm so sorry. Queen Eleanor brought your trunk up to my chamber by mistake… I looked in and I found it.' Her hand slid down his sleeve, fell away.

'Nadia's bodice?' He frowned, trying to remember.

Brianna lifted her limpid, tear-washed eyes to his, her sobs easing as she spoke. 'Your heart will always be with her. I couldn't bear it.'

'Nay, you have it wrong, Brianna,' he said softly, remembering. 'The bodice was…is intended for my mother. The amazing needlework from the East—she would love it. It never belonged to Nadia. Why would you think that?'

'Because you still love her? Because you think about her every day?' Brianna whispered, her heart splitting, anguished. 'I thought I could live with the knowledge, even had the notion that I would persuade you to love me—how ridiculous is that?' She spluttered to a halt, colour rising in her cheeks.

'It's not ridiculous at all.' He smiled, brushing her cheek with tapered fingers. 'Brianna, I did love Nadia, but she is part of my past. With you I have found a new future.'

'You have?' She threw him a shaky smile, touched her veil, her circlet, with an awkward, self-conscious gesture.

'And I think you have too.' His arms wrapped around her waist, heavy, possessive.

'Giseux…what are you saying?' Newborn joy fluttered around her heart.

'Brianna, when I came back from the Crusades, I was angry, devastated…I was a broken man. But I was so fortunate…I met you.'

Brianna's eyes shone with happiness. The rigid knot of sorrow binding her heart unravelled, furiously, the shackles of anxiety releasing their grip. The fiery rays of the evening sun glowed through the uneven glass of the window, illuminating the lustrous oval of her face, the generous rosebud curve of her mouth.

'I love you, Brianna. I think I loved you from the first moment I saw you.'

She swayed beneath the solemn import of his words, pure delight flooding through her limbs, driving out the doubt, the sadness that there would be nothing for them beyond this moment. 'What, knocked unconscious by Count John's thugs?' She laughed, lightness frothing in her chest.

He smiled. 'Even then. I loved you from that day, but you, and only you, were the one to show me how.' Sable strands, touched with gold, fell forwards across his forehead. 'Your kindness, your care…your love—' his pupils dilated, black pools against silver grey '—your love has driven the darkness from my soul and healed my spirit.'

'Oh, Giseux!' Brianna flung her arms about his neck, pulling his head down to hers, her whole body suffused with joy. 'I never thought it could be…I wished it, I yearned for it, but I never thought it could be!' Giseux laughed, a low rumble of pleasure, before tilting his head and slanting his mouth over hers in a kiss to seal her to him, for ever.

* * * * *

A sneaky peek at next month...

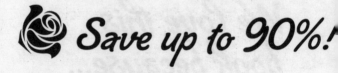